Praise for RITA® Award-winning author

EVELYN VAUGHN

"Evelyn Vaughn's excellent love triangle,
complex characters and believable heroine
leave readers wanting more."
—*Romantic Times BOOKclub* on *A.K.A. Goddess*

"I just read *A.K.A. Goddess* by Evelyn Vaughn.
What a fabulous book! I fell in love with the sexy
hero, Lex Stuart. Every time he came into a scene,
my heart constricted wonderfully."
—Gena Showalter, author of *The Pleasure Slave*

"It's funny. It's romantic. It's unexpected.
It's everything I would want in a great read.
Finally, the Bombshell line lives up to its promise.
This book rocks."
—*www.allaboutromance.com* on *A.K.A. Goddess*

"The author's characters continue to be
particularly well written, making *Her Kind of Trouble*
an emotional roller coaster as well as
a fast-paced romp."
—*Romantic Times BOOKclub*

"*Her Kind of Trouble* succeeds on so many levels.
The story exemplifies all that is exciting about
Silhouette['s] new Bombshell line....
Ms. Vaughn provides non-stop action
that will keep readers engrossed...."
—*www.writersunlimited.com*

Dear Reader,

Thank you for picking up *Something Wicked,* the third
Grail Keepers book for Silhouette Bombshell! If you've
already read *A.K.A. Goddess* or *Her Kind of Trouble,* rest
assured that we're nowhere near through with Maggi Sanger!
But I think you'll find Kate Trillo's kind of grail keeping an
interesting alternative.

While Maggi came at her goddess quest through
academia, and was surprised by the magical aspects, Katie
of *Something Wicked* is the opposite. As a nurse, she's not
uneducated—but neither has her blue-collar background
included much about comparative mythology. What she
knows about goddesses, she knows from her family tradition
of witchcraft—Hekate worship, to be exact. And while she's
resisted that tradition, for reasons even she doesn't fully
understand, it will turn out Katie's packing a little something
wicked herself!

I've tried not to imply that Katie's practices are characteristic
of all goddess worship, or even all worship of Hekate! Fifteen
years study of Wicca has shown me that neo-paganism is
wonderfully multifaceted. So I mean no insult to the true
ethics of the Craft, especially when Katie starts flinging
around magic that has nothing to do with "Harm None!"
Hopefully you'll agree that it works out in the end…more
or less.

In the meantime…blessed be!

Evelyn Vaughn

Something Wicked

Evelyn Vaughn

Published by Silhouette Books

America's Publisher of Contemporary Romance

SILHOUETTE BOOKS

ISBN 0-373-51391-7

SOMETHING WICKED

Copyright © 2006 by Yvonne Jocks

This edition published by arrangement with Harlequin Books S.A.

® and TM are trademarks of Harlequin Books S.A., used under license.
Trademarks indicated with ® are registered in the United States Patent
and Trademark Office, the Canadian Trade Marks Office and in other
countries.

www.SilhouetteBombshell.com

Printed in U.S.A.

EVELYN VAUGHN

has written stories since she learned to make letters. But during the two years that she lived on a Navajo reservation in Arizona—while in second and third grade— she dreamed of becoming not a writer, but a barrel racer in the rodeo. Before she actually got her own horse, however, her family moved to Louisiana. There, to avoid the humidity, she channeled more of her adventures into stories instead.

Since then, Evelyn has canoed in the East-Texas swamps, rafted a white-water river in the Austrian Alps, rappelled barefoot down a three-story building, talked her way onto a ship to Greece without her passport, sailed in the Mediterranean and spent several weeks in Europe with little more than a backpack and a train pass. All at least once. While she enjoys channeling the more powerful "travel Vaughn" on a regular basis, she also loves the fact that she can write about adventures with far less physical discomfort. Since she now lives in Texas, where she teaches English at a local community college, air-conditioning still remains an important factor.

In 2005, Evelyn won a prestigious RITA® Award from Romance Writers of America for her first Bombshell book, *A.K.A. Goddess*. Feel free to contact Evelyn through her Web site, www.evelynvaughn.com, or by writing to: P.O. Box 6, Euless TX, 76039.

The more I write, the more certain I am that this magic is a group effort. For this book, I owe special gratitude to:

- Tashya Wilson for her patience and encouragement
- Paige Wheeler for her encouragement and support
- Several incredibly helpful priestesses of Hekate
- Maggie Shayne and the folks at WitchesinPrint.com
- The Madonnas (and their agents) for keeping me sane last April
- And Juliet Burns, Cindy Dees, Kelly LaFata and Toni Telligman for keeping me going

In memory of my beloved Simone, 1986–2005

Chapter 1

I can tell you exactly when I became a bad guy. I can describe it down to the very moment, as abrupt as…

As the blow of a hammer.

My knees squelched in blood-soaked carpet where I'd landed, trembling, beside my older sister's body. At that moment, the shock was too fresh even for tears. My mouth gaped into a scream beyond sound. Not Diana. No….

But I'd been a hospice nurse for three years; I was no stranger to death. Although I hadn't embraced our family tradition of witchcraft like Diana had—witchcraft as in goddess-worship, I mean, not that fantasy TV stuff—my instincts were solid. And despite my sister's mottled face, now caked with blood, I knew her too well to find any comfort in denial.

She'd been my constant in life. My guide. My friend. I'd once badly braided that long, golden hair, so different from my own, now streaked with more blood—we'd laughed, and posed and taken pictures. I'd often held those now broken hands, still wearing their ever-present silver rings. They'd held me, countless times, especially after losing our parents. And Diana's necklace…

Most witches wear pentagrams, point-up. The women in my family wear an overlapping circle design that our *nonna* called a *"vesica piscis."* It's nowhere near as common.

The pendant hanging limp from this dead woman's throat looked just like Mom's had. Just like the one lying forgotten in my bureau drawer.

This was her.

Somehow, impossible as it seemed, I now existed in a world where my big sister did not. Was not. Would not.

Sound, ugly and hurt, moaned from my throat. The room around me shrank—our small home's living room where we'd sat up to watch movies, to play games, to trade gossip.

I should be doing something, right?

In that moment, I didn't know or care what that might be. Diana….

Our belongings littered the floor. CDs and remote controls mixed with the detritus of my sister's magical interests—tarot cards, rune stones, crystals. A tapestry of Greek ruins fluttered, half-torn from the wall—she'd always wanted to visit Greece. A tumble of tools, screwdrivers and pliers and a scattering of cup hooks and nails, looked incongruous amidst calligraphed pages ripped from her Book of Shadows. All the tools had pink plastic handles. We'd gotten the kit a few years earlier. *Magic can't fix everything,* I'd joked. Now, blinking past a blur of tears, I found myself counting pieces. Screwdriver. Wrench. The one most obviously missing was…

The hammer.

Perhaps instinct warned me, or common sense, or even Diana's lingering spirit.

With a gasp, I threw myself away from her body as the bloody hammer arced down at me.

Metal bit into floorboards the carpet couldn't protect. I rolled through blood and tarot cards and stumbled to my feet. My crepe-soled shoes squelched in the damp, and my arm felt sticky and cold. The air smelled metallic, deathly.

And a stranger, *a killer,* straightened to full height not three feet from me. His dark eyes shone. His angular face was speckled with Diana's blood.

Right there, he stood. *This was real.*

"Katie, right?" His friendly grin chilled me, even more than his easy, urban voice. "The kid sister. Wow. You should have driven slower tonight, Katie. This, you know…it complicates things."

"Because now you won't get away with it?" I barely recognized my own, flat voice. Emotion hurled itself against the lingering wall of my shock, a battering ram of pain—but it hadn't gotten through yet. The amount that whimpered from my throat and burned in my eyes was nothing next to what fought to escape.

His grin widened, showing dimples. His hair, cut neat and short, was as dark as mine, and his charisma was like a spell. If it weren't for a prominent nose, he'd be gorgeous. How could I even notice that, past all the blood?

And past the dead sister. *No….*

I felt sick.

"Like that's going to happen." He raised the hammer to shoulder height and waggled his heavy eyebrows, downright playful. "Sure, you're trouble, but let's not get above ourselves. Face it, Katie. You're as good as dead."

Numb or not, I acted. Pretty sure I couldn't outrun him, I backed away, sweeping my arm out to find something, anything for a weapon. Magazine? No. A throw pillow? Hardly. My hand closed on our answering machine, and I threw that instead. He laughed as he dodged. The phone bounced after the machine—

The phone! Scooping it up, I started to punch the magic numbers, 9-1—

In a rush, the killer reached me. The hammer caught my hand so hard that I didn't even feel it at first, just saw the receiver fly across the room and only then, as if on a time delay—

Pain. Like, broken-bone pain.

Once that burst through, the rest of my horror swept after it. The sound escaping me became an ungodly, animal-like wail. I grabbed a floor lamp, sparks flying as the cord jerked from an outlet, but it made a lousy one-handed weapon. His pink-handled hammer, *our* hammer, knocked it aside—

Then the killer had me against the wall, one forearm hard across my throat, his thigh pinning my legs, his minty-fresh breath in my face. My right hand throbbed, agonizing, with every clutch of my heart. I wished I were one of those women who knew martial arts or kickboxing. I wasn't. He had me too tight to slip loose, and I was too short to head-butt even someone as average height as him. And damn it, my sister was dead.

My sister. My sister. My sister.

In that moment, as the madman's bright, long-lashed eyes laughed down at me, even survival barely mattered. But justice...

Suddenly, I knew how people became ghosts. Because not even death would stop my need for vengeance.

I only had two measly weapons left. One was my femininity. I'd already guessed that much from the flush of heat off of him, the way his breath caught in his tanned, clean-shaven throat. *He was turned on by this!*

So I tipped my face up toward him and parted my lips as if I was as twisted as him. I tried to keep my voice from shaking. "At least tell me your name."

"It's…Ben," he offered, eyes gleaming at my unspoken invitation. "Benny Fisher."

That had been awfully easy. But hey, he didn't mean to leave me alive. Why wouldn't he tell me?

Except that his name added ammunition to my second weapon.

My sister's blood. And my own.

My good hand went for his face. He caught me by the wrist, I'm not one of those warrior women, remember? But I wrenched my shoulders sideways, smeared my elbow—wet with Diana's blood—across his slanted jaw.

And I said, "I curse you, Ben."

The rush of strength that flooded me in that moment—even coming from a family of witches, I'd never imagined magic to be like that. It wasn't special-effects fantasy magic, of course. But my spine straightened, and the throbbing in my hand faded under a stronger focus. My body shuddered with power. The power of anger. The power of vengeance. The power of standing up for myself. All aimed at him.

And something else. Something far, far older. *Waking.*

Whether from that power, or just surprise, Fisher drew back and blinked.

The words came like a recovered memory. "I wish you *agony*, Ben Fisher," I hissed, my voice thick with dark hope. When I took a step forward, he fell inches back. "I wish you *despair.* I wish you a long, lingering death that lasts forever too long until you scream for it to be over and still it goes on and on because release is too good for you."

He shook his head with an uneven laugh, unnerved but quickly recovering himself. "Shut up, Katie."

"Before that comes, I wish you a lonely, empty, suffering life where nobody loves you and everything you care about shrivels and dies." I was practically shouting my curse, now, glorying in it and in the desperate hope that it might work, that there was justice after all. When he killed me, I wanted to die believing in justice. "For every moment of happiness you've stolen from my sister and me, Ben Fisher, may you know lifetimes of misery."

"Damn! You're as crazy as she is!"

Was, I thought, and bitterness gave me the strength to pull the magical trigger. "I call upon Hekate, the Dark Goddess, to oversee your downfall, Ben Fisher. In Her name, *I curse you!*"

He attacked with a panicked swing of the hammer, right at my face. Since I'm as bad at dodging as I am at fighting, he hit. The world reeled around me, or maybe that was me reeling. I heard as much as felt myself fall against the wall, a muffled thud. I slid down it, tasted my own blood, then blinked dazedly upward. The killer with the expensive haircut and dark, pretty eyes stepped closer, lifted the girly, deadly hammer—

And the door slammed open.

Maybe I hadn't securely latched it behind me when I'd found Diana's body. And this was February in Chicago, the Windy City itself. But as a hard wind pushed through the room, tossing bits of snow and whipping my black hair across my face, Ben Fisher's surreally pleasant expression faltered.

"I curse you," I repeated a second time, through a mouthful of my own blood, and I spat a tooth at his crisply ironed trousers, for good measure.

Blood makes for classic curses.

The icy wind moaned, tarot cards somersaulted across the floor and Fisher had had enough. He turned and ran, though not before grabbing something from the cabinet Diana had used as an altar. I surged forward to follow—

Or not.

I fell to my side, tried to catch myself with my injured hand, screamed in the resulting pain. Tears weren't the only thing blurring my vision. *Head wound,* some part of me noted clinically. *Possible concussion. Call an ambulance. Put the teeth in milk and maybe they can be saved....*

But he was getting away! And really, there's not that much magical power in reciting something twice.

If I did nothing else right, in my whole life, the shock and pain and fury that choked me at this moment meant this had to be correct. And yeah, I knew the dangers. I knew the rules. Just because I hadn't seriously studied the Craft like Diana had didn't mean I hadn't picked things up.

Feeling myself list, darkness tunneling my vision, I fumbled for the closest piece of paper. I found the back of a page from Diana's Book of Shadows. I scrubbed my good hand across the bloody carpet by my sister's corpse, and I wiped it across my own blood-slick chin, and I used my finger to write, in her blood and in mine, *"Ben Fisher."*

I rolled the page into an uneven tube. I found a nail. Since Fisher had taken the hammer, I grabbed a remote control.

"In the name of Hekate," I mumbled, dizzy now, hurting, weeping. "The Dark Goddess. Queen of the Night. Goddess of the Crossroads. In the name of Her, my namesake, I curse thee, Ben Fisher, to everlasting torment!"

And I used the remote to slam the nail through the page, completing the spell.

I felt the nail drive home just as the remote hit the injured hand with which I'd steadied it. At that, I passed out.

That was it.
That's when I turned to the dark side.
For one thing, magic has consequences. Better to smack someone across the face than work a spell against them, Diana had always said, because the spell will come back at you with three times the strength. In cursing the man who'd killed my sister, I'd cursed myself.

Which, on its own, might have been so worth it.

But the rest of it…the rest of it didn't become clear right off. I came to. I phoned for help. I dealt with paramedics, cops, doctors. I dealt with my aunts and uncles and surviving grandparents. It was awful. A decade hadn't been long enough for us to get over my parents' loss, and now this?

A death in the family is bad enough, but murder guaranteed a nightmare. After my parents' death, only a tight grip on Diana's hand had gotten me through the funeral arrangements and the paperwork and the obituaries. Now we added yellow crime-scene tape, and unrelenting calls from reporters and, as an extra fun-time bonus, a next-day lineup.

"Him," I said immediately, as soon as the six suspects filed into the room beyond the glass partition. I didn't feel evil, yet. I didn't feel much of anything except dizzying grief. Shock. Anger. And no small amount of pain. "Number four."

My jaw still hurt, where I'd had two of the three injured teeth replanted in an emergency trip to my family dentist, resulting in a dental splint that made my tongue sore, and the promise of a bridge where my first molar couldn't be saved. My broken hand, now cast in plaster, still throbbed. The doctor had actually said I was lucky, that "the ring metacarpal shaft fracture was stable, with no rotation of the bone fragments or secondary nerve injury." Very lucky.

Like I was in any mood to count my blessings.

My sister was dead! That bastard, right there, had killed her.

"You're sure?" asked some guy in a suit. Lawyer?

As if I could ever forget that balanced, compact stature, that angular face, those dark eyes. That nose....

"You," said my cousin Ray, who's a cop, to the suit. "Shut it."

Except that something didn't fit. Maybe it was how his black hair, so neat the night before, now fell in unruly curls across his face. His dark, haunted gaze swept from one side of the room to the other, as if thinking hard or memorizing it.

"That's the man I saw," I insisted. "Ben Fisher." The name felt extra significant in my mouth, and I knew I was right. Except... "He looks sad."

Cousin Ray said, "Yeah, well, getting arrested for murder can be a real bummer. Let's get you home."

On the snowy ride back to his parents' place, where I'd be staying for the next few days, I silently tasted the killer's name and thought about the curse. Was that why they'd caught Ben Fisher so easily? Because I'd cursed him? After years of abstaining from magic, *could it be that simple?*

Problem was, I'd cursed myself, too. So I shouldn't have been surprised when Ray had to bring me back to the station the next day for a second lineup, this time with moral support. Aunt Maria scolded him from the backseat the whole way there—wasn't it enough that the bastard had murdered my sister without me having to face him over and over? From Ray's tight expression as he drove, though, I knew something else was wrong, and I told him so.

"The good news is, we found the murder weapon," he admitted. "The bad news is, Ben Fisher's fingerprints don't match."

"But…that can't be right. It was him."

"And he's got an alibi."

"No."

"I can't tell you anything else," he insisted, pained. "Just…wait and see."

So again, I got to stand in that cold, dark room, waiting for the lineup. The same lawyers from the day before were there, plus a new one whose suit probably cost more than my car. The suspects filed into the room, and this time, Ben Fisher was number one. His hair seemed to get curlier the longer he was in lockup. Shadows smudged his dark eyes, and his mouth was set.

"It's still him," I insisted. Aunt Maria was right. We shouldn't have to do this….

Then I saw who filed in as number five, and a chill of recognition raised goose bumps.

What the hell…?

It was the same man. But this version didn't have shadows under his eyes. This version had a neater haircut, and he was still clean-shaven. He looked impatient, but he also had an edge of deliberate charm about him that number one did not.

Other than that, they were identical.

"Two of them," I whispered, feeling sick. "Twins."

"Ms. Trillo," said the captain, "we realize that this is difficult, but is there any way you can point out the man who attacked you on Friday night?"

My gaze darted from one man to the other, ignoring the rest. Identical freaking twins.

"Katie?" prompted Ray.

I swallowed unsteadily. "Have them…have them smile," I whispered. Just in case.

The captain gave the command over the intercom, and the six suspects each attempted a smile. Number one's eyebrows angled in momentary shock before he reluctantly bared his teeth, clearly repulsed by the very idea. And number 5—

Number five smiled earnestly enough to reveal dimples, right through the glass. Right at me.

I spun away from the window and threw up, right on the floor.

Ray caught my shoulders with his hands. One of the lawyers gave me a handkerchief and the captain sent someone out of the room for water. Eyes watering, I looked back at the lineup, where the forgotten suspects had let their compulsory smiles fade into confusion. All except one.

He was still smiling, like a proud host at a frat party.

"It's him." I pointed. "Number five."

"You can't be sure," insisted the most expensive suit. I guess I knew who was whose lawyer. "They're identical."

He wasn't referring to the other four guys in the lineup, either.

"No, they're not." I accepted the paper cone of water that someone handed to me. "I remember that snooty haircut. Unless that first guy has brand-new extensions…."

The lawyer made a note, maybe to check suspect number one for hair extensions. "But yesterday you said it was—"

"Are you trying to talk a witness out of her identification?" demanded the suit who'd been there last time; three guesses whose lawyer *he* was. And the fight was on.

"We're finished, right?" demanded Ray over the bickering, and the captain nodded. We were finished.

"You did good." Ray put a supportive arm around my

shoulders. "He doesn't have an alibi, his fingerprints match and now you picked him out of a lineup against his own freakin' twin brother. We've got this bastard dead to rights."

But it wasn't time to roll the end credits, not just yet. What you'd think would be good news was barely a consolation prize, for one thing. Diana was still dead, no matter what happened to her killer. And for another...

That part stood out for me, more than anything else in those first few days.

"Which one's which?" I demanded, setting my feet against Ray's attempt to lead me out to Aunt Maria. Beyond the window, the suspects began to file away.

"The one you ID'd yesterday? That was the real Ben Fisher," Ray explained tightly. "Turns out the killer is his brother, *Victor* Fisher."

His words sounded far away as I watched number one—the solemn, haunted Ben Fisher—search the mirrored window one last, tired time before he left the room. He'd been falsely arrested for murder. That, at least, could be reversed. But more than that...

I'd cursed the wrong guy.

Chapter 2

Nobody could see Victor Fisher pacing except for Leon, his cellmate. Leon sprawled back on his metal-grill bed, his beefy arms folded and his feet extended. He had nothing else to stare at. Nothing except the peeling paint, the bars, the steel sink and toilet...and the cockroaches.

Fisher and Leon wore the same outfit, Cook County standard, but Fisher's white D.O.C. T-shirt was pristine, as opposed to the food and bloodstains on Leon's, and Fisher's khaki pants were still creased. And clearly he was thinking, his dark gaze constantly skimming the room, constantly searching. Sometimes he muttered snatches of words—"dropped the damned hammer" and "Hekate." He only stopped when he stumbled from exhaustion. He dragged his hands down his face, only to look around again, spread his arms and scream, *"Fuck!"*

The word bounced off the cement walls. Laughter from

other cells seemed to echo forever. Other inmates mimicked him, some with cruder versions. They were bored, too.

Leon just rolled his eyes. "What the hell's wrong with you?"

Fisher's dark gaze cut to him, shocked, angry. For a minute, it looked like he wouldn't deign to answer. Then, maybe recognizing that Leon was his only option, he shook his head—and smiled, as if at a joke. "Do you believe in curses?"

"I know," I admitted, at Diana's solemn look. I'd always hated her solemn look. "We're not supposed to curse people. I'm sorry."

"I'm not." She widened her eyes to mock my obvious disbelief. "Victor Fisher would have killed you if you hadn't stopped him. Hello? I should know."

My eyes began to heat with more tears. Mere days, and I was already exhausted from crying. "Then why didn't you stop him? You're the real witch."

"Okay, one? He hit me from behind; that's why I didn't stop him. And two? You've always been better at magic than me. If you hadn't scared yourself off of it when you were a kid—"

What? *"I was never that into magic."*

She dismissed that with a wave of her hand. "Whatever. My point is, you did what you had to do. Now it's all just…damage control."

"Because curses go in both directions."

She went solemn. "It's more complicated than that, Sis. You called on Hekate. It's not like you can say, 'Oops, never mind,' and take it back."

"I never said I'd take it back." And yeah, I knew that I was

embracing the darkness. But Fisher—Victor Fisher—had murdered her. *If anybody deserved cursing…*

Diana paused, cocking her head at the distant sound of a man's voice. "Ooh. You should catch this."

I opened my eyes, still swollen from crying, and tried to reorient myself. It's not like these dreams of my dead sister were making the week easier. They only reminded me of what I'd lost.

Where was I this time? I'd been staying with Aunt Maria's family since the murder, but this place was new.

For some reason, my mother's simple chant whispered from my lips. "One, two, three, protected be."

After years of practicing no more magic than the occasional knock-on-wood, I'd now done two spells in under a week.

It was anyone's guess if this one actually worked. Still, when I pictured a circle of blue light around me, some of the worry that had chewed at my gut for the last week eased… And that's what counted, right?

Then I remembered. I was in the spare bedroom of my and Diana's neighbor, Mrs. Hillcrest. She'd offered to let me and Aunt Maria hang out while the crime-scene cleanup professionals did their magic next door. You have to have a responsible party there to let them in, and for consulting and stuff.

As soon as she saw how exhausted I looked, Mrs. Hillcrest had led me to the back bedroom and commanded me to nap. I hadn't thought I could and lay down just to be polite. But to judge from the fading winter light filtering through her Swiss-dot curtains, I'd slept through the afternoon.

It was the kind of sunlight you get at the edge of darkness.

Outside, dogs barked. From deeper in the house came the strangely familiar voice Diana had heard, in my dream….

I mean, the voice *I* had heard. I guess.

"...partners for a long time now," the man's voice continued. It was a good voice, earnest, with just a rasp of city bluntness. "But I've got to draw the line somewhere, Al. 'No comment.'"

"But surely you want to set things right," protested... Al? This voice *was* affected, deep and clearly playing to a microphone.

Some kind of radio interview, then. I sat up in bed, pushed back the crocheted afghan someone had draped over me, and took a deep, painful breath. *Set things right....*

I was sore in too many ways, my face bruised purple, my hand still cast in plaster, my heart permanently broken. And Diana's absence felt a lot more obvious than my missing molar.

"A woman was murdered. There's no setting that right," agreed the voice I'd liked.

Just as I stood up, Al said, "But you were falsely accused. Arrested. As if that's not everybody's nightmare, Ben, the murder victim wrote your name *in blood* at the murder scene!"

I stopped dead still, my heart kicking back into overdrive. No wonder the voice had sounded familiar...but *likeable?*

"Nightmare?" challenged Ben Fisher, with a sharp laugh. "Look, Al, if you want to do the Conspiracy Catch-up, like we do every Friday, I'm happy to do that. But as for recent current events? *No comment.*"

"Then let's look at this event as a conspiracy. You were arrested for murder, picked out of a lineup. Yes, you passed a lie-detector test, but so did your brother and frankly, he has a better reputation than a conspiracy guru like you."

"Thanks a lot, Al. And shut up."

"If you didn't have an alibi, not to mention different fingerprints from your twin brother—and who would have guessed *that* could happen—you could be facing death row right now."

Instead of pointing out that the case had only made it past the bail hearing, Ben simply said, "Bye, Al," followed by the shuffle of someone pushing back from the console.

"Okay, okay, you win." Al's voice might be deeper, but he'd sure blinked first. "We'll do our Conspiracy Catch-up. For those listeners just tuning in, our guest tonight is a Friday regular. He's my partner in crime—wow, that sounds worse today than usual...."

"Al," warned Ben's voice, not as near the microphone.

"My partner, and sometimes on-air guest, Benjamin Fisher. But from the way our phone lines have lit up, I'm guessing you folks already know that. I'm Al Barker, and this is the *Superrational Show* on WP—"

Mrs. Hillcrest screamed.

She'd come around the doorway from the hall, nearly ran into me and leaped back with a startled screech.

What's even more surprising is—*I didn't.*

I didn't jump. I didn't flinch. I just stood there, looked at her and felt...strong.

But not necessarily in a good way.

"Good heavens, Katie," my neighbor gasped, a hand going to her chest. "What are you doing, standing here in the dark? I was just coming to check on you...."

I continued to stare at her for a long, weird moment. Then I asked, "Where's Aunt Maria?"

I felt fairly sure from the radio's volume, not to mention its channel, that my aunt wasn't still in the house.

"The, er...the *workers* are finished. They needed someone to do a walk-through and to double-check their inventory list."

"*I* need to do that. It's our house."

The sympathy in her gaze when I said "our" instead of "my" felt like cold water on my face. The last, lingering weirdness from the dream evaporated. For now.

"I'm sorry," I murmured, veering around her. "I really have to be there."

I broke into a run, grabbing my coat as I went, leaving Mrs. Hillcrest and her knickknacks and the loud radio commercials behind me with the slap of a screen door.

The houses in our neighborhood were the squat, brick style called Chicago bungalows. Working-class homes from the early twentieth century, they weren't overloaded with yard space. Only an alley with a walkway separated each home, so narrow that the kids used to dare each other to jump from one house to the next—and do it. Not in the winter, of course, even with the winds blowing the roofs clean. But still...

Anyway, it didn't make for a long walk from Mrs. Hill-crest's. I barely had time to see that the big white truck was still parked in front but that the workers—the "crime-scene cleanup specialists"—were already stripping out of their masks and biohazard suits to reveal jeans and sweaty T-shirts despite the February cold. They were pulling blankets over their shoulders, swigging water and joking with each other. They stopped when they saw me, not all at once but bit by bit, only hitting full awkward silence as I wrenched open my own screen door.

I only noticed the reporters, farther down the block past a single cop car, because of the glitter of camera flashes as I wiped muddy snow from my feet and strode inside.

For the first time since Diana's death.

This was my home—but it wasn't. It smelled of powerful

cleaning agents instead of the mix of candle wax, incense and Mediterranean cooking that had always filled it before. A large square of carpet had been cut away to reveal old wood floors I'd never seen. Diana's "magic cabinet," as we'd always called the big oaken armoire in the front room where she and Mom had kept their altar, stood open, which it usually never did. But its shelves looked strangely bare.

And of course, Diana was gone. Forever.

I took a deep, trembling breath to resist crying again.

"—complete list of the items we've taken," a man was saying in the kitchen, just down the hall from the entryway. "Some of it—for example paper products like books and, uh, playing cards—had to be disposed of. That's for health reasons, you understand. Anything nonporous that could be cleaned, we cleaned. We've sorted the loose or broken items by—"

When he saw me, he abruptly cut off.

"Katie!" greeted Aunt Maria. "You're awake."

"You should've gotten me up." I noticed how rude I sounded even as I said it, as if Diana herself had tugged the edges of her mouth down with two fingers and lisped, *Look at Miss Pouty Pants!*

Diana could be a real wise-ass, sometimes.

Still, I didn't apologize. Neither Aunt Maria nor Mr. Page— the crime-scene cleanup specialist—seemed to take offense. It's amazing what you can get away with on the excuse of grief.

"You're right," said Maria simply. "I should have."

"As I was telling your aunt," said Mr. Page, "we'll dispose of everything that couldn't be cleaned, as a biological hazard. But everything else has been disinfected and itemized. We kept an inventory of what we took and what we've left. Any loose or broken items are in those bins on the table."

He continued talking, but I began looking in the bins.

Assorted screws and nails. Pink-handled tools from the toolbox although not, of course, the hammer. CDs, though some of the jewel cases no longer had their liner notes. And items from the magic cabinet. I found pieces of jars that had held healing herbs or oils, now neatly scrubbed. I found a black-handled knife, called an athame, which had belonged to Mom before it was Diana's.

It all smelled like disinfectant instead of magic.

As if from a distance, Mr. Page said, "If you'll sign this, agreeing that I've gone over the lists with you and that you're aware of your options should anything prove to be missing…"

There's something I need to find first. I wasn't sure where the urge came from, but I felt it as surely as I felt my sister's absence. *Something important.*

"Perhaps I should sign," suggested my aunt, as I reached awkwardly over the edge of another bin and shifted its contents with my good hand, frowning. *Something vital.*

"No, wait." I found the terra-cotta disk, carved with leaves and grapes, now broken into three roughly pie-shaped pieces. That was Diana's pentacle, to honor the element Earth. I found her willow wand. But not…

After taking and glancing at the papers Mr. Page offered, I felt increasingly sure.

"The chalice," I said, and turned to Mr. Page. "The Hekate Chalice is gone. Couldn't you clean it?"

Give the man credit; he wasn't easily fazed. Then again, look at what he did for a living. "The *what* what?"

"It would have been with this other stuff, the witchy stuff." I put down the inventory to tip the bin and spill out a mix of crystals and jar fragments. Aunt Maria laughed a little nervously; she'd married into the family and, even though she knew of our traditions, she didn't practice. But hell—Mr.

Page had just spent hours cleaning up not only blood, but tarot cards, candles, incense and pages torn from the family Book of Shadows. He wasn't in the dark, here. In his line of business, he'd probably seen worse.

Besides, even the newspapers had gotten hold of the fact that Diana had considered herself a witch. It made for gripping copy, you know?

"I'm talking about a cup," I insisted. "A sand-colored goblet with three woman's faces carved into the sides of it. Hekate…" The strange word came to me as if someone had whispered it in my ear. "Hekate Triformus?"

Mr. Page shook his head. "Doesn't sound familiar."

"Not even pieces of it?" So many of the other magical items had been broken, after all. And this was important.

Vital. Even if I wasn't sure why.

"Perhaps the police took it as evidence?" he asked.

But the police had given me an inventory list, too. Everybody's watching out for lawsuits.

I turned and went back to the living room, with its chemical smell and its missing carpet, and I narrowed my eyes to concentrate.

The scene played out in front of me, in slow motion.

I back away from the killer, throw the answering machine, grab at the phone that trails after it.

Victor Fisher breaks my hand with a hammer.

Behind me, Aunt Maria said something about "…very hard on her."

Mr. Page said something about "…part of the job."

I continued to watch my memories. *I swing the lamp.*

He pins me against the wall.

I begin my curse. The door flies open. He hits me in the face, turns, flees. But…

He takes something with him.

I remembered.

"Victor Fisher took Diana's chalice," I repeated. "YaYa's chalice."

YaYa had been my mom's mother. While Dad's mother, Nonna Trillo, considered herself a *strega,* YaYa Pappas hadn't even had a word for what she was, so we all just said "witch."

None of us even knew how old YaYa's chalice was. We knew she'd brought it to the States as a war bride, in the 40s. We knew she'd given it to my mother. And we knew it was wicked old.

And now it was gone.

"That bastard took the Hekate Chalice," I repeated. "Damn him to—"

But I'd already done that part, hadn't I?

"I'll be going now." Mr. Page was backing toward the door. Aunt Maria must have signed his release form for her crazy niece. "My colleagues and I are truly sorry for your loss, ladies. I hope that in some small way…"

Aunt Maria thanked him for us, and I returned to the kitchen to dig through the bins one last time.

But I knew it wouldn't be there. I *felt* it.

I wondered…since when had I begun *feeling* things, and seeing memories, and dreaming about dead people?

Since I'd cast my first curse.

I definitely had to talk to Nonna about that. She would be angry; me casting a curse was about as stupid as a toddler trying the high wire. But she was also my best chance for advice about the spell's negative consequences toward me and the real Ben Fisher.

It sure didn't feel like it had fizzled. Every time I thought of the curse, I felt a surge of strength, of dark anger. I still wanted Victor Fisher to suffer everything I'd wished for him, all that and more.

I just didn't want to be responsible for any innocents being hurt in the crossfire.

Talking to Nonna could come later, though. Same as my job could. Same as my life could. I still had to bury Diana, as soon as the medical examiner released her body. That took precedence over everything else, curses and missing goblets included.

Didn't it?

Against Aunt Maria's protests, I insisted on spending the night there. I'm sure she wasn't the only person who might find that disturbing. But this was my home, had been all my life. Our parents had owned it outright before they died. Over the last five years, Diana and I had restored parts of it back to its 1911 condition, which got us some federal tax credits, a conservation grant and some quality sister time in the bargain. *I wanted to go home,* desperately. Even if I never could, because Diana wouldn't be here, at least I could have the rooms, the location. I wouldn't let Victor Fisher take that, too.

Most important, though, was the question of whether I should be afraid. Lonely, sure. Freaked out? Depressed as hell? Check and check, no matter where I slept. But afraid?

Victor Fisher was in jail, may he rot there. And if Diana became a ghost, she of all people would be a friendly ghost.

To me, anyway.

Besides, I desperately needed some alone time. There are some kinds of crying you just can't do without freaking out the people who love you, you know?

For the first few hours after Aunt Maria's goodbye hug, I fought it. I went through most of the belongings Mr. Page had left. I went through a week's worth of mail, which Mrs. Hillcrest had kindly been collecting for us. For me, I mean. Most of it was sympathy cards, some from as far as distant relatives in Greece. I had a little, private buffet from food that neighbors brought by after Page's crew left. But I knew what was coming. I'd done the grieving thing ten years ago. I was already a member of the club.

It started innocently. I was annoyed by the barking dogs from down the block again. I was putting away a disposable tray of pasta casserole—one-handed, because of my cast—when it bent under the weight and spilled spaghetti and tuna onto the floor.

And like that, I snapped. *Damned casserole!*

With a howl, I threw the whole thing onto the floor and stomped on it, barefoot, as hard and as thoroughly as I could. By the time I'd finished stomping, I was crying for real, crying so hard I couldn't see.

I threw things. I broke things. I fell to my knees with a wail, and sank to the floor, and pounded it with my good hand, and yelled the filthiest words I knew, along with a misery-slurred question of, "Why? Why? Why?"

I'd learned to live without my YaYa. Then without my parents. Now my sister was gone, too? *Why?*

She was being talked about in tabloids and on stupid radio shows. I'd had to unplug my phone, after all the calls from reporters. *Why?*

Diana had been good, and kind, and loving. A florist, she always sent flowers to the families of the patients I lost, and there were a lot—hospice nurse, remember? Diana had been about life and springtime, color and magic, and now some bastard had come into our house, *our home,* and smashed her head in with a hammer! *Why?!*

We hadn't done anything to deserve this. Had we?

Finally, finally, I lay on the floor—half on chemically cleaned hardwood and half on remaining carpet—and... I was done. Oh, not for good.

I had a murder trial to get through. I had no more sister. This wasn't done for good.

But I'd moved a little closer to something improved. Maybe not peace. Maybe just a little necessary...stillness.

With my mind clearer than it had been in days, I thought the question again, this time without the drama.

Why?

I inhaled a wet, ugly gulp of a sniff and sat up, frowning. That was the one thing that still didn't make sense. Why would a stranger choose this house, this sister? Could it really be random?

My wet gaze lifted to the now-closed armoire. And I thought of the one item missing from the house.

The Hekate Chalice.

What the hell? It was a ceramic *cup,* for pity's sake!

But it was also gone.

I squinted toward the clock—too late to call my grandmother, since Nonna was an early-to-bed, early-to-rise type. Too late to call cousin Ray and have the cops question Victor Fisher about the cup. I'd have to wait until morning and torture myself with the question instead.

Why?

I'd just stood up when I heard the thump, vaguely familiar from my childhood.

Someone had just jumped onto our bungalow's roof.

Chapter 3

You know those movies? The ones where the stupid heroine goes to check out the noise in the basement or attic instead of calling the cops and *leaving?* Normally I'd be throwing popcorn at the screen with the rest of you.

This time was different, and here's why.

For one thing, my give-a-damn level was about the lowest it's ever been. My parents were long gone. My sister was newly dead. While I wasn't exactly suicidal, I wasn't anywhere near Safety First mode either.

For another, my rage levels were about as high as my give-a-damn level was low.

If someone was screwing with me and my house tonight, then only one of us was walking away. I didn't much care which one, as long as someone got hurt in the process.

Preferably the intruder.

Wiping my feet on old carpet, I glanced around the room for weapons. I wasn't any better at it than I'd been a week before.

So I opened the armoire.

And there sat the newly cleaned athame.

An athame is a knife, but it isn't used to cut anything physical—no chickens, no babies. It's used to direct energy in rituals. See, magic works by affecting things on the energy level in order to change them on the physical level. This idea is so basic that even after refusing the training that Diana got from our mother and grandmothers, I knew that much.

Point being? The athame, marginally sharper than a nail file, didn't make the most practical weapon. Not if I used it right.

But I took it anyway.

Since I had only one good hand, I tucked the black-handled knife into my back jeans pocket. One careful thrust cut the blade through the denim, making a kind of sheath.

Here's hoping I remembered not to sit down.

I headed, still barefoot, to the open area off the kitchen. On one side of the niche was the door to the attic stairs. Opposite was the door to the basement stairs.

I listened at the attic door.

Nothing. Or a city version of nothing, anyway. A plane flew by overhead. A siren warbled in the distance. Dogs continued to howl—who owned those damned dogs, anyway? Wind shook the skeletal branches of the sycamore tree next door. But the intruder stayed silent.

I reached for the crystal doorknob, then hesitated. What if it was another killer?

What if it was the *same* killer, somehow escaped or freed on bail, come to take out the only witness?

The idea should have scared me more than it did. Instead, it gave me a grim satisfaction.

Welcome to the world of the dark side.

What should have scared me more? The fact that the knob then, slowly, *turned in my hand.*

Quickly, I ducked behind the opposite door, the one that led down to the basement. I barely pulled it closed, with just a crack to see through, before the door from the attic opened.

Someone stepped into the areaway between the two doors. I only caught a glimpse of a man's hefty shoulder, a glance of reddish hair.

In my kitchen.

Mine and Diana's.

That's all it took. I threw my whole body against the basement door. I slammed it open and into the intruder with all my strength.

Hardwood smacked into him with a satisfying jolt—and grunt—before bouncing listlessly back at me. When I kicked it open again, into him again, the intruder began to swear.

He also yanked open the attic door and ran up the stairs, three at a time.

I went after him.

He had a head start, and his stride was longer than mine. Even when I tried to lengthen my stride, the athame poked me in the back of the thigh. But I knew the attic better than he did. The intruder tripped over our Christmas bins and knocked over Mom's old dress dummy before he even reached the windows that led out onto the dormer roof.

This was a big guy, shoulders like a linebacker, waist like an armchair quarterback. But damn, he moved fast.

He'd squeezed out the window and onto the roof by the time I'd safely vaulted the now-prone dress dummy.

I grabbed the top sill with my good hand and swung out after him, barefoot, into the bitter Chicago night. I was in time to see him navigating the skirt roof toward the chasm between my house and Mrs. Hillcrest's. He picked up speed, regardless of possible ice patches, and hurled himself into space.

"Fall," I whispered into the wind, but he landed solidly, feet, then knees, then hands against her shingles.

No wonder I'd heard him on mine.

He looked over his shoulder while I bent past the dormers onto the skirt roof, and I saw his face in the glow of the streetlight from across the road.

He was a complete stranger.

A complete stranger with a camera slung around his neck. *The hell!* He was a reporter.

Instead of circling the horizontal skirt out front—too visible from the street, I guess, or not steep enough to have dropped ice—the reporter began to climb the slope of Mrs. Hillcrest's gable roof. I took a deep breath and ran across my skirt roof. My bare feet held to the cold, rough shingles for my last few, deliberately stretching strides. One, two—

Three!

Like riding a bicycle. But fifteen feet in the air. And without a bike.

I flew over the snow-drifted alley, landed, and was scrambling up Mrs. Hillcrest's roof with my next steps. I swung over the peak just in time to see my intruder gaining speed on the downslope. He vaulted across the next alley.

"Fall," I said again, through my chattering teeth.

But he made it. Barely. One of his feet skidded off Mr. Lane's roof, despite its dark shingles being snow-free. The intruder had to drop to his hip to keep from losing the other foot, too, and he probably scraped the hell out of his hands.

"Damn!" he grunted, loud enough to hear over the wind.

I was already gaining speed in my race down Mrs. Hill-crest's house.

The intruder crawled up Mr. Lane's roof now, on his hands and knees, as I launched myself over the gap between the houses. I scraped a big toe on impact. My feet already felt burnt from the friction of the shingles and frozen from the temperature. As I crouched into my wobbly landing, stretching my good arm out farther to compensate for the weight of the cast on the other, the damned athame poked at my calf again.

The athame, I thought, scrambling upward as the reporter hauled himself more laboriously over the roof's ridge. I reached the peak moments after him. But instead of vaulting it, I dropped to my knees, supported myself with the elbow of my cast hand, and slid the athame free of my back pocket.

The intruder gained speed, his legs barely able to keep up with his hurtling form. Just as he reached the gap between Mr. Lane's house and the Milanos', I pointed the athame at him.

"Fall," I commanded, loudly and clearly.

A small cloud of erratic squeaking, fluttering birds darted by. He tried to wave them away...and dropped like an anvil.

An anvil with a dirty mouth. But he shut up when a door slammed out front.

Mr. Lane appeared in the drift-covered front yard, his flashlight sending a zigzag search across his roof.

I rolled backward along the slope, once, twice. Shingles scraped my free hand and my feet, but I managed to roll out of his line of sight, into the shadow of the dormer windows.

My hand curled tightly around the athame as I remembered my mother's standard warnings. *Never use magic to control another person's actions. What you send forth comes back to you three times as powerful. Harm none.*

Not only had I directed the reporter to fall, I was glad of it. I hoped it *was* my doing.

Sorry, Mom.

"Who's out here?" demanded Mr. Lane, sounding more belligerent than concerned. "What kinda nonsense are you kids up to? I'll call the cops!"

Yes, I thought, easing over the roof's ridgepole, still hidden in the shadow of his oak tree. *Good idea, Mr. Lane. Call the cops.*

But I didn't point the athame in his direction; no need to go power crazy. Instead, I peered over the edge of the roof, where I'd last seen the reporter.

He was hiding, crouched in a high drift where shadows had caught the snow behind a big plastic shed.

I watched Mr. Lane and his aggressive flashlight follow the alley path closer to the shed.

Closer...

I pointed the athame toward the scene below me, just in case. Maybe the reporter fell on his own, not because I suddenly had magical powers or anything, but...

It was either this, shout a warning or jump on top of the guy. Those last two choices could work against Mr. Lane's bad heart. But I wasn't letting the old man get attacked.

Luckily, I didn't have to make that choice. That same erratic cloud of zigzagging birds shot around the house, and Mr. Lane backed up. "Damned bats," he muttered, turning around and heading toward his front yard.

Bats? Ugh!

A moment or two later, his door slammed shut.

The big guy's shoulders sank with relief, and I hated him. I hated him for breaking into my house. I hated him for feeding this morbid need people had to be entertained by my sister's murder. I hated that people like him were alive, and she was dead.

"You're lucky," I said grimly, pillowing my chin on my cast hand. "Mr. Lane used to work as a prison guard."

The reporter spun and stared up at me, mouth open.

"That, and I didn't break my damned neck," he said, his voice surprisingly deep. Deep and...familiar. "And you aren't armed."

I didn't bother to show him the athame. Instead I wondered, how did I know that voice? And why else did I hate it?

"You're Kate Trillo, right?" he demanded, extra proof of his profession. I'd avoided the press. Only people who paid close attention would recognize me as the witness—though it probably helped that he could connect me to my house. He blew on his hands, then said, "Ms. Trillo, are you willing to help the country learn the truth about your sister's death? I'll pay you five hundred dollars."

Recognition clicked. "You're that radio guy, Al...?"

"Al Barker," he agreed, clearly proud that I'd heard of him. "The *Superrational Show*. Okay, a thousand dollars."

"Go to hell." I sat up so that I could pound on the roof. I was too damned cold, numb cold, to linger. Especially if there were bats. "I'm having Mr. Lane call the cops."

"You can do that," Barker agreed. "But then you wouldn't hear my theory as to why one of the Fishers killed your sister."

One *of the Fishers?* Was there still any question of who had murdered Diana?

Now I hated him even more, for hooking me.

He sensed his advantage. "Talk to me," he urged. "Off the record, if you must. There are some things you need to know about all this. You're being played by the system."

The system hadn't killed Diana. Victor Fisher had. "You have no reason to help me."

"Sure I do. That's what my show's about—the truth. Fighting the good fight."

I made a rude noise.

"Okay then. I'm hoping that once you trust me more, you might give me some kind of scoop. I don't even need to attribute it to you. I could say, 'an anonymous source close to the family.'"

He must have read my expression even in the shadows, because he added, "Or not."

I sat there shivering and wondered again, *one* of the Fishers?

"Come on, Ms. Trillo. Don't you owe it to your sister to learn the truth? What have you got to lose?"

He was right on that account, but I still hated him. Deeply. "Stop playing me."

"You choose the time," tempted Al Barker. "You choose the place." It sounded like a dare, all the same. I hated dares. But...

"Midnight," I decided, to a background of distant, howling dogs. That would give me time to clean up. Besides...

Midnight was the witching hour.

"I was under the impression," I said by way of greeting, "that you and Ben Fisher were friends."

I'd actually agreed to meet with Al—off the record—at a 24-hour diner a few miles from my neighborhood. It didn't offer great decor, mostly framed travel posters of Italian sights with fake grapevines draped across their tops. But Joe, the guy who ran the diner, was an old friend of the family.

I felt safe in his diner. Even without my athame. Carrying a knife with a six-inch blade on the streets of Chicago is frowned upon.

"We *are* friends," said Al in that deep, radio-announcer voice of his. He slid into the booth, opposite me. "Which is why I need to clear his name."

"Ben's name *is* clear." Except for the fact that he shared his last name with his psycho-killer twin brother, anyway.

"Not even close." Al signaled Joe's one night-shift waitress for some coffee, then continued. "Think about it. Vic's an up-and-coming political consultant. He's well-spoken, well-liked, and well-off. Ben, on the other hand, is a professional student. He's a genius, don't get me wrong, but people would rather believe an advanced degree, which he never completed. He's a loner. He's also what people call a 'conspiracy nut.' Which brother do you think John Q. Public will most suspect?"

I wasn't real sympathetic to the bias of John Q. Public. "But Ben has an alibi."

It felt weird, referring to a complete stranger by his first name. But it would have felt even weirder to use his full name. I'd already used that one three times too often, the night I cursed him. Them. *Us*.

"True," Al conceded, about the alibi. "But so does Victor."

I stared, a sick feeling knotting my stomach. "He does?"

"Yeah, his girlfriend. She swears they spent the night together, that she didn't say anything before because she was angry with him. She says once she realized how serious this was, with Vic being held without bail, she had to come forward." He smiled. "Any comment?"

Vomiting on the table between us would have been an excellent comment, but I wasn't giving him the satisfaction. I picked up a spoon from the trio of cutlery before me and turned it in my fingers. It's harder to fidget with one hand. Less natural. "No," I said firmly, finally. "No comment. What about the fingerprints?"

"You mean Victor's finger*print*. Singular. That's a good piece of evidence." Al paused to thank the waitress for our coffee, then to add sugar to his. "It's also the only evidence, except for your ID. And there's evidence against Ben, too."

He took a sip and winced. "Good coffee."

My gut twisted. Ben Fisher wasn't the killer. I'd seen both brothers together, in the lineup. I'd seen how Victor smiled. *I couldn't be wrong...could I?*

True, I would have cursed the right man. On the downside, he was wandering free this very night! And that couldn't happen. Not if the world had any rightness left.

Looking disappointed that I hadn't taken my cue, Al kept talking. "I don't know if you're aware how much publicity your sister's murder is getting."

I stared at him grimly. "Because that has nothing to do with why you're talking to me?"

"Yeah, well... Because it's so high-profile, a lot of evidence is being collected from public tips. Supposedly Benny has been interviewing local magic users. You know, covens, occult shops, that sort of thing. Authorities figure that's how he found your sister. Word is, he seemed particularly interested in tracing one magical tool more than any others."

I thought I knew what he was going to say. Still, I didn't want to prompt him.

"Chalices," announced Al, and I was right. "Especially chalices used in goddess worship."

The Hekate Cup. I was sure Aunt Maria had mentioned its absence to cousin Ray by now. But its theft shouldn't be public knowledge yet, not even to a nosy faux reporter like Al Barker.

Could that really be why Diana had died? For a stupid

goblet? Okay, yes. A sacred goddess goblet. But it was still a *thing,* like a rosary or a crucifix. Just a symbol.

"Why would he be after those?" I asked, putting the spoon down. Cold weather or not, I didn't want coffee.

Al shrugged. "Ben says it wasn't him, the assumption being that Victor used his name. But Ben's made a living out of explaining all things mystical. He's got a real knack for it. Why would a political consultant be networking with the area pagans instead?"

"I don't know." I challenged. "Why?"

I should've guessed his answer. "It's a *conspiracy.* Victor's obviously set Ben up. If you hadn't interrupted him, he could have cleaned up his fingerprints and nobody would be the wiser. So what I need to know is, what's so important about witch chalices? Did your sister even have one? If so, what's so special about it?"

I hated him using the word "need" that way. We need air to breathe, water to drink, food to eat. Anything you can survive without, you don't *need.*

"No comment," I warned.

"Come on." He spread his thick hands. "Katie. Sweetie. You owe me something, here."

The anger was creeping back, a tension in my bruised jaw, a burning in my chest. That happened pretty easily, lately. "You jumped onto *my* roof and broke into *my* home."

"I thought the place would be empty. Who moves right back into a murder house?"

This time I picked up the fork. Not that I would stab him with it or anything, fun though that might be. I just needed something in my hand. "I haven't called the cops on you. You could tell me ten times as much about the Fisher brothers, and I still wouldn't say we're even."

"You've got to tell me *something*. Don't you want the truth to come out? Aren't you willing to do whatever you can to bring the real killer to justice?"

Another voice, beside me, asked, "And how, exactly, will polluting the jury pool accomplish that, Al?"

The voice had a vaguely familiar rasp of city bluntness, and my stomach knotted as I lifted my face to see him.

The panic hit first, instinctive and immediate. I wished I had my athame.

I'd dropped the fork and fumbled for my butter knife before I noticed the dark-haired man's long curls, his untucked shirt under his jacket, his obvious concern about our discussion.

The face, the eyes—those, I'd never forget. But the concern confused me.

Then I really recognized him.

My recognition of Ben Fisher went way beyond him having the same face as Diana's murderer. What I felt was a connection to him, deep down.

I curse you, Ben Fisher.

Oh, hell. I'd bound us together with my spell casting.

All three of us.

Chapter 4

Ben's deep brown eyes searched mine for a long moment, as if he felt something similar. Or maybe the bruises ooked him out. Then he seemed to realize he was staring. He dipped his attention to my makeshift excuse for a weapon.

His brows quirked into fleeting amusement. "Kinda possessive about the cutlery, huh?" he joked, with a lopsided smile, before his gaze darted back to mine. "Hi. I'm Ben. Have…have we met? That sounds like a pickup line. I didn't mean it that way, not that you're someone I wouldn't…" He shook his head, wincing and half laughing at his conversational train wreck. "You look familiar, is all. Al?"

I didn't take Ben's hand, and not just because my good hand was still curled tight around the handle of a butter knife. He didn't seem dangerous. In fact, he had the kind of unassuming keenness that used to attract me to mathletes and chess-clubbers in high school. Really. It did. I come from a blue-collar family. People with a chance at real college degrees are cool.

But my broken hand throbbed and my jaw ached just from seeing him, all the same. Even without having met, we had more baggage between us than he could begin to guess.

His quick expression stilled as he let his hand drop, untouched. A shrug and a head tip indicated Al. "Just be careful of this guy, okay? He's got a good heart, but he'd sell his mom for the publicity. No offense, Al."

"None taken, Benny. Thanks for meeting with us." With that, Al explained in full the coincidence of Ben Fisher's presence. My gaze shot over to that smug bastard—what the *hell?* But Al was scooting over to make room for his partner in the booth.

Apparently we'd both been set up. If I thought I could talk, at that moment, I would've ripped Al a new one. But the clutch in my throat almost blocked breathing, much less speech.

With a suspicious glance from Al to me and back, Ben took a single step back. He had no intention of joining us.

Good!

His gaze met and then veered from mine, another smile there and then gone. I braced myself for the same reaction I'd had in the police station, when his brother grinned right at me.

Instead, I found myself noticing his dark lashes, the angle of his jaw and the slope of his tanned neck into his T-shirt collar. Though not a big man, not beside Al anyway, Ben Fisher had the tight build of a runner or a swimmer, and *did I find him attractive?*

Damn, I was one sick woman, wasn't I?

Luckily, Ben had turned a more direct stare to his business partner. "Considering what you were discussing when I got here, I'm not thinking it's something I should involve myself in. No offense, Ms.…."

His gaze darted back to mine—and stuck. The only thing that nudged me out of my silence was that Al was about to speak. I was suddenly so furious at Al Barker for manipulating us that I didn't want to hear his voice or his excuses, radio-quality or not.

"Trillo," I said sharply. "I'm Kate Trillo."

Ben's olive complexion went pale. "Oh, my God. That's where… *Oh,* God. Al…!"

I was already turning on his friend. "Stay away from me, Barker. Stay away from my family. Don't talk about us on your sorry excuse of a radio program. And *on* the record? Go to hell."

I stood to stalk out, but Ben Fisher followed. "Ms. Trillo, I had no idea. I'm so sorry. I mean, I'm sorry for your loss, too."

"Not as sorry as I am."

Some young women who'd been giggling in the back corner booth fell suspiciously silent. I think they were checking out Ben's butt.

"No, I'm sure you're right," he agreed. "I won't assume to know what you're going through, but I didn't know about this. I wouldn't have imposed, if I'd had any idea what Al…"

I spun on him. But my fury ebbed at the distress I saw in his intense eyes, on his open face. No, he couldn't be as sorry as I was. He hadn't just seen the last of his immediate family wiped out. But neither had he done anything wrong.

I *felt* his innocence, in whatever energies connected us. And damn it, I couldn't hate the guy.

His brother was still fair game. But with Ben, I'd already made one hell of a mistake. Words from the week before echoed back at me. *I wish you agony, Ben Fisher. I wish you despair….*

Not good.

His expression asked me to believe him, even as he backed

away to give me space. A shrug seemed to say that I could take my time, that he was sorry for pressing me.

The person I'd been barely a week ago, the nurse, the healer, responded. Why did I have to have cursed a nice guy?

The person I'd become needed to know more about whether it had even worked. About curses in general.

"You're some sort of expert on the supernatural, right?" I asked suddenly.

His head came up. "I don't know if anyone could be classified as an expert, the subject's so fluid, but sure, I've got a working grasp of the theories."

Uh-huh. "Why do you call your Web site Superrational?"

"Our viewpoint is that there's a rational explanation for almost everything that's considered supernatural," explained Ben, squinting slightly as if studying something I couldn't see. "The natural in supernatural. The normal in paranormal. Finding it takes some of the fright factor out of it."

"So you're one of those debunkers?" I folded my arms. I hated skeptics and debunkers with their single-minded cynicism. They always seemed so…mean.

"No! Not at all. Debunkers are pessimists about human nature. They tend to think that everything's a con. I'm more of an optimist. I think it's all real—ghosts, magic, reincarnation, you name it." Ben relaxed as he spoke. His hands tried to shape ideas in the air, and he had no problem at all holding my gaze. "I mean, people have believed this stuff for millennia! To think differently…isn't that fairly conceited? Our ancestors may not have had our science, although even that's increasingly debatable. But they had basic human intelligence. Even now, statistics show the average adult believes in at least something that's been labeled 'supernatural,' so—"

Ben stopped himself then, as if embarrassed.

Even Joe had looked up from his paper by now. The girls were whispering among themselves. Two lovebirds sitting near them had stopped snuggling to stare.

"I'm—" Ben swallowed back what I suspected would have been yet another apology and set his shoulders. "That was, er, the long answer. Why do you ask?"

I need to know more about curses.

But asking that in front of Al Barker had to be its own kind of stupidity. Better to keep track of Ben through the press, make sure nothing happened that could conceivably bring him a lonely, empty, suffering life or a long, lingering death… or anything else I'd wished on him. Them.

Hekate had to understand who I meant.

"You know your brother's guilty, right?" I asked instead.

Ben's brightness faded. "Yeah," he admitted, the word squeezing from his throat. "I just wish I knew why."

"I don't give a damn why." I turned away to the glass exit. *As long as he goes down for it.*

I didn't see anything except for a blinding wash of high beams. I didn't hear a warning. But with a sudden body blow, Ben Fisher tackled me to the floor.

Then the place exploded in noise. Crashing. Shouting. Screeching. And my only thought, as my shoulder blades slammed onto the linoleum and Ben Fisher slammed onto me, was a strangely calm and foolishly childish, *One, two, three, protected be.*

Please.

Safety glass hailed down on us even as we skidded from the force of the tackle. Red booths and a table launched themselves into the air. Right behind them a broken headlight, a crumpled fender, a thick black tire loomed over us—

We rolled. Somehow, Ben Fisher and I rolled faster than a car could fly.

The red sedan ground to a stop amidst debris, its near wheel spinning inches from our heads.

As suddenly as it had happened, it was over. The sedan now sat in the middle of Joe's Diner. Through the ruined front of the diner, icy winter air washed across us. The back of the diner looked freakishly normal. A dangling picture labeled Bay of Naples dropped off the wall with a smash. Steam hissed from the car's gaping hood, above us. Someone moaned behind the air bag.

And Ben Fisher slowly sat up, one arm still tight around me, lifting me with him, and I didn't even think to mind.

"My God," he muttered, more than once. "Oh, my God. Are you okay? Kate, are you hurt or—"

"I'm fine." I tipped my head to meet his wide eyes. Then I forced my gaze to the wreckage. "I'm…wow."

We were close enough that I could see the tiny pits and scratches on the car's undercarriage, the kind left by winter road salt. If either of us hadn't moved…

But how *had* we moved that fast? Even with Ben jumping me like that. *One, two, three?*

Oh, hell. "The others," I gasped, struggling to my feet. Ben helped. "I've got to see if anyone's—I'm a nurse—"

To my immense relief, Joe was already on the phone calling 911. The lovebirds seemed unhurt, although when the woman stood, staring, she began to wobble.

"Sit down!" I commanded loudly, pointing. "Have her put her head down. Put her coat on her."

Ben was pulling at the driver's door. "It's locked!" He circled to the passenger side while I made my way across glass and rubble to check on the girls in the back booth. One had passed out, but her pulse and breathing were strong. I left her friends piling their jackets over her and went to check Al.

He had minor lacerations from flying glass. After getting Joe to toss me an unopened box of rubber gloves, I put one on and found that only one of Al's cuts, over his forehead, looked deep. I pushed the edges together with my good hand and pressed a clean napkin to the wound. "Keep pressure on it. Head wounds bleed like crazy, but you should be fine."

A nervous glance over my shoulder showed that Ben had stopped trying the doors and instead knelt on the hood, pulling broken safety glass from the windshield with a jacket-wrapped hand. His T-shirt clung to the length of his back, to the strain of his shoulders. Smoke billowed through the opening he created. Oh, hell....

"I've got to get shots of this," Al argued, reclaiming my attention as he fumbled with his camera.

"No." As I protested, I felt the strangest thrill of power—and I looked at my hand in its oversized, neon-yellow rubber glove.

Al's blood smeared the fingertips.

Words came to me, almost audible in their clarity. *Take no pictures, feed no press. Sit in silence, nothing less.* With one smear of blood and one weird, whispered rhyme, I might just...

No. I stripped off the glove as I left Al to hemorrhage or not, as he chose, and ran to join Ben. Bad enough that after years of normalcy, I was suddenly turning to magic. Why was I so drawn to dark magic? *Blood* magic?

This wasn't my family's way. But it seemed to be mine.

"What's burning?" I demanded, as Ben cleared the last of

the pebbled glass from the now gaping windshield and hopped down to the rubble to make room for me.

"Nothing. The smoke's a mixture of combustion and talcum powder. It's a kind of lubricant, to keep the air bag from sticking to itself. Kate —stop!"

I paused, one knee already on the side of the car to boost myself closer to the open windshield. I'd already turned the unused, left-hand glove inside out and fumbled it onto my right hand, We could hear a groan from behind the driver-side air bag. "He's hurt!"

"Just give me a second." He tried to lift the crumpled hood, but it wouldn't stay up. Though unsure what he meant to do, I ducked in to support it with my shoulder.

With careful, quick movements, Ben disconnected the negative battery cable. "So none of the other air bags deploy into you," he explained shortly. "That's the plan, anyway."

"How do you know all this stuff?"

"I, uh, come from a smart family."

After taking care of the positive cable, he held the hood so I could step back. Then he dropped it with a hollow thud.

I hitched myself up onto the hood and braced my cast arm on the roof to hold me. I reached through the gaping windshield and pushed the deflating air bag out of the way. I glanced for other passengers—none. I quickly checked the driver's seat belt—fastened. His steering wheel wasn't bent. Then, more hopeful that he'd avoided internal injuries, I turned to the driver himself.

He was regaining consciousness. Good sign.

So was the sound of sirens approaching.

I kept the guy talking and tried to hold his head steady in case of neck injury until the EMTs arrived. Since they were the professionals at emergency response, I was glad to let them take over. After that, everything became a confusion of cops and firemen and strobes of red and blue and white lights.

I ended up standing next to Ben Fisher, who had a blanket draped loosely over his T-shirted shoulders since he'd gotten glass in his jacket. The concern on his angular face as his dark, bright eyes followed the EMTs was either genuine or Academy Award worthy. How could identical twins be so different?

"Thanks for pushing me out of the way," I said.

He smiled fleetingly at me. "Anyone would have done the same."

"No, they wouldn't." Victor, for example.

He shrugged.

"So how *do* you know about disabling air bags?" I asked, to change the subject.

"It's kind of weird, actually. I've had three accidents this last week. Nothing too serious, obviously, but I sure got some firsthand, up-close experience with air bags."

This week? "Three accidents including this one?"

"I guess I should start taking the El."

Except…as goddess of the crossroads, Hekate had powers over all transportation, even the elevated train. Not just cars.

"Here, you take the blanket." He shrugged it off to drape across my shoulders before I could protest. It was warm from his body. It smelled good, too, like some kind of spicy soap. I still had long sleeves on and so didn't need the blanket as much as he did. But I couldn't bring myself to protest.

"How was your driving record until this last week?" I asked, instead. Just because I'd cursed him a week ago didn't mean anything, right?

"It was great," admitted Ben. "I can't imagine what my insurance rates are going to do now. Why?"

Well, hell.

I had to talk to my grandmother.

The witch.

Chapter 5

"What do you mean, it's not the real grail?" Victor Fisher pushed back in his chair so suddenly that the nearest guard glanced through the reinforced, Plexiglas divider that created a soundproof wall. "Do you have any idea of the hell I've been through for that damned thing?"

His attorney, a man who'd already known Victor well enough to recommend him to several local candidates in recent elections, could probably guess. Victor had arrived at their latest consultation with a black eye and a swollen lip. He'd limped to the table they now shared. His jail khakis were no longer creased, and his shirt sported its own bloodstain. Still, Sherman Prescott hadn't become the best criminal defense attorney in Chicago by feeling sorry for clients. "You undertook that quest on your own, Fisher. Not because any of us requested it."

"Only because you never recognized me as one of you. But

I am! By blood, and by temperament. You admitted as much when I said I have the Hekate Cup."

Prescott's smile was plastic. "But as it turns out, you don't. We had it analyzed. The chalice you…acquired…is barely a hundred years old. It's nothing. You got yourself arrested for nothing."

Victor leaned onto the table, his gaze sharp. "It's not my fault. I had no way of knowing that it wasn't the right cup, that the sister would come home. I wanted—"

But apparently he was still smart enough to shut up when Prescott raised one silencing hand. "However, despite those disappointments, you've at least impressed us with your perception. My colleagues and I like to believe that our society's existence is all but invisible. But you not only found us, you identified individual members and gathered enough information to deduce our goals, never once tipping your hand until this particular…complication. If you hadn't thought you really had the grail, I doubt you would have given yourself away even now."

Victor's chin came up. "I didn't mean to kill her."

"And let me guess. You feel terrible about it?"

"No." At his lawyer's look of surprise, Victor added, "It was her fault. If she'd just let me have the damned cup…."

A smile spread across Prescott's face. "This is why we have decided to support you through this unfortunate situation, Fisher. You understand the true use of power. Given a second chance, do you believe you could find a real goddess grail? Not just some New Ager's altar dressing, but an actual cup of ancient power?"

"Of course I can."

Prescott waited, clearly intrigued.

"I've found an actual witch of ancient power," explained Victor bitterly—and touched his swollen lip. "And I sure as hell owe her payback."

* * *

"Hekate is a dark goddess," warned my grandmother Trillo, her parchment skin nearly translucent in the candlelight. Her aged, accented voice wavered like the water in the black scrying bowl she held. But her half-sung words held a strength beyond volume—the strength of a priestess. "She is the powerful Queen of the Night. It is She who stands at the threshold between life and death. She is not to be called lightly."

Lightly? I could remember every word of my curse. *I wish you a lonely, empty, suffering life in which nobody loves you and everything you care about shrivels and dies....*

"Don't worry, Nonna. 'Lightly' isn't a problem."

We were in the parlor of Nonna's apartment, her blinds drawn firmly against outside light and prying eyes. She'd draped an embroidered altar cloth across her coffee table, with magical tools arranged on it—green candles, a censer, an athame, a beautiful old cypress wand from her homeland in Tuscany...and the bowl she now held.

A bowl black as night, filled with melted snow. It was in this that she looked beyond our world to someplace else, maybe to the will of Hekate herself.

To do this, Nonna stood very still.

I did not. It was my job to move, to walk with slow spins, clockwise, around her. It's not as strange as it sounds. A lot of traditional dances move in circles, for long-forgotten reasons. Even kids sense the rightness of it, from "Ring around the Rosie" to "Duck, Duck, Goose."

Movement raises energy. And circles within circles hold triple power. I was weaving myself into and out of the scent of incense and candle wax and something more—the tingle of magic in the air. Trancelike, I didn't even have to turn on my own. The growing magic turned me.

"The Goddess," Nonna continued softly, "is not ours to be summoned or ordered about. We are Hers. You especially, *cara*, are Hers." She meant because both sides of my family worshipped Hekate—and because of my name. Kate isn't short for Kathryn. "You called out to Her in your time of greatest need, and She answered."

"I think She…" But here was no place to doubt why the door had flown open as I spoke my curse, or why Victor Fisher had fled. Yes, it *could* have been coincidence. But I knew it wasn't. "The Lady saved my life."

Nonna's focus remained on the scrying bowl and on whatever she saw reflected in it. It sent a fluid mask of light across her aged, timeless face. "Would you have spoken the curse had you known the price?"

I would have sold my soul to bring justice down on the bastard. Still would.

But would I have sold someone else's?

Her sharp gaze lifted to mine. Her penciled-in eyebrows arched questioningly.

"I used the wrong name," I reminded her.

She nodded. "Half the name you spoke was correct. It bound the curse to the killer as well." To judge by the newspaper articles I'd collected since last night's accident, she spoke the truth. *Victor Fisher Attacked in Jail. Lawyers Request Solitary Confinement for Witch Killer's Safety.*

I'd read each article, and I'd thought, *Good*. But…

"But what about his brother?" I whispered.

Her tsk-tsk sound wasn't hopeful. "Can you unthrow a handful of rocks because one of them struck an innocent?"

The answer to that was probably *no*. Damn it. "There has to be something you can do to fix it. Please."

Nonna shook her head. "This is not for me to change,

cara. It is yours, and Hers. For this, you will have to ask He-kate yourself."

"Like…pray to her?" Could it be that easy?

"Write your request."

When she handed me a small piece of parchment and a silver pen, I considered, then wrote, *Help me make this right.*

Meanwhile, Nonna studied the water. Some witches can see visions in anything that puts off reflections—mirrors, crystal balls and black bowls of liquid. Eventually, she uncorked a vial on her altar and poured a clear liquid into the water. I barely noticed that it smelled alcoholic until she took my request, folded the paper into a triangle, lit it from a green taper candle and, once it had half burned away, dropped it into her scrying bowl.

Whoosh! A ring of blue flame danced, eerie and elflike, across the water's surface.

"No." Nonna stared into the magic fire. "There must be a way. Ah, yes." Magic was about willpower. To know, to will, to…*something*—I always forget that ingredient—and to stay silent. When Nonna looked up at me, her old eyes shone with the blue fire. "A pilgrimage. You must find Her source. Only then can you right your wrongs and fulfill your destiny."

Okay. I suspected there was more, but one crisis at a time. "So where's Her source?"

"Where She is most remembered. Where She was once worshipped. I think perhaps the old world…" The flame had quickly burnt out, leaving only water and a curl of ashy paper. Nonna drew a cloth of black silk over the bowl. "Never have I sensed so strong a calling, child. You have much to do."

"The old—you mean Italy? *Greece?* I can't! We've got the funeral, and then there's all the court stuff." The preliminary hearing was scheduled for the next week.

I'd already made arrangements to cut my hours and take night shifts until Victor was imprisoned for good, hopefully for life, hopefully with abusive cellmates. Was I supposed to leave the country, on top of all that? Sorry, Queen of the Night, but *no*.

"I've got to be there for Diana."

"Give me your hands," commanded Nonna.

When you grow up in a family of witches, you don't argue things like that. She laid her old, worn hands palm up on the altar cloth. I put mine in hers, the cast one, too. Her fingers embraced me.

Outside, those same noisy dogs howled.

"It is time you resume your training, *cara*. It is time you let Her speak to you, and not through me."

"But Ben Fisher—"

"It was your curse. Only you—or She—can deflect it."

My stomach knotted, but I felt the truth through my fingertips. "You mean I should train as a witch."

"You say She saved your life." Nonna released my hands with a final, comforting pat.

I nodded. Dark or not, deathly or not, that much felt too true. "Yes, Nonna. She did."

"Then your life is Hers."

I took a deep, shaky breath full of incense and candlewax—and magic. Time to get that *vesica piscis* pendant out of my drawer.

As long as Victor Fisher's life was Hers as well, it was a deal I could live with.

The next week felt unreal for so many reasons. For one thing, I found a toad in my house. Twice. In February.

The medical examiner released Diana's body. It seemed

like half of Chicago showed up for her burial alongside our parents' graves, but not all of them were there to express sympathy. The crowd trampled the snow to mud, and her true friends seemed lost among them. Diana's funeral had become an event, not about her life so much as her sensational murder.

Like I didn't have enough reasons to hate Victor Fisher.

Valentine's Day passed, barely noticed. I went back to work—part-time, at an inpatient facility instead of driving to my patients—and the normalcy of wage-earning felt like a betrayal of Diana. It wasn't. I was on automatic pilot, doing the old fake-it-till-you-make-it thing. My job also drew me deeper into that "threshold between life and death" that Nonna had mentioned as one of Hekate's realms. Hospice work had never been about saving lives, after all. My patients were already dying. My job, which I'd been drawn to after watching my mom go through YaYa's lingering death, was about making them comfortable, keeping them company and being there for their loved ones after they passed.

And yeah, that part also felt weird now. The blind leading the blind.

Nonna began training me in magic. Intensely. I was surprised by the déjà vu, by how much my mother must have already taught me in my early childhood—the importance of candle colors, of moon phases, of rhyme. I knew more than I'd remembered I did.

I received a package from my second cousin Eleni in Greece—or maybe she was my first cousin once removed? Her grandmother had been my YaYa's sister. The package included a blue glass disk with a golden eye painted on it, and the note simply said, "Perhaps this can help."

Strange. But YaYa had hung a similar disk in her front window when she was alive, so I did, too.

Finally, I got my cousin Fran, Ray's sister, to help me look up everything possible about the Fishers on her computer.

I didn't like what I found.

For one thing, they were orphans, too. But instead of an accident, like the one that had claimed my mom and dad, Ben and Victor had lost their parents in a home invasion. The actual newspaper reports about the stabbing deaths gave me chills. The twins had been six. The killers had never been brought to justice.

For another thing, Al Barker hadn't lied. Victor had a *much* better reputation than Ben did. Victor had gone to Yale. He'd worked at Prescott & Sons, one of the leading law offices in the city, before expanding into political consultation. His old firm proclaimed his innocence and offered a reward for information implicating the *real* killer. Victor had a wealthy girlfriend, who now stuck to her story of having withheld a valid alibi until she realized the weight of the charges.

In contrast, Ben Fisher had no degrees. And he was self-employed, studying conspiracies, secret societies and the occult.

By the day the preliminary hearing started, exactly ten business days since Diana's murder, I was half doubting my own sanity. What if Ben *was* the killer? What if *Victor* really was the innocent victim?

Then I saw them together. Victor stood by the defendant's table. Ben waited in the gallery immediately behind him with an older couple, probably the grandparents who'd taken them in after their parents' deaths. The immediate resemblance between the two brothers was remarkable. *Identical.* But Victor had a fresh shave, his hair had been gelled neatly back and he wore a three-piece suit; the whole dog and pony show for the hearing.

Ben's attempt at formality meant khakis instead of jeans and a brown corduroy blazer over his maroon T-shirt. His hair still flopped in easy curls over his forehead, curls he occasionally pushed back with one impatient hand.

I couldn't see auras. But if there's one thing magic teaches, it's that there's a definite reality beyond what we can see and hear. And whether I could name the source of my certainty or not, I could see the innocence in Ben and the through-and-through evil in Victor as clearly as if each of them radiated neon signs.

Ben's eyes brightened when he spotted me, and he started to smile, then turned back to his grandparents with one last, sidelong glance.

I saw him touch his brother's shoulder, saw Victor flash Ben his charismatic grin—and saw Ben give his brother a bracing squeeze before removing his hand. *They really were a pair,* whether Ben had helped that stupid drunk driver the other week or not.

I felt sick all over again. I hoped everything went quickly. This hearing, choosing the jury, the trial, the sentencing. I needed closure. I needed to see Victor Fisher convicted.

Then the lawyers got started.

As Mr. Jennings, the prosecuting attorney, had explained it, a preliminary hearing exists to try out the charges against the accused. It's a lot like a trial but with two big differences. One is that there's no jury; the judge alone makes the decision. The other is that, instead of finding guilt, the judge only has to find that there's enough evidence to warrant the case going to a full trial. Clearly, in a case like Diana's, this was just a formality.

That first day, in which Mr. Jennings walked us through Diana's murder, was both disturbing and encouraging. Di's head had been smashed in *with a hammer,* after all. How could anyone hear that and not see the need for a trial?

One day down, so far, so good. I went to work that night satisfied that at least we were doing *something.*

The next morning at the courthouse, I ended up in line for the same elevator as Ben. Today he wore a beige blazer over his T-shirt. We exchanged quick, polite smiles. It didn't feel like we were mere acquaintances. But that was probably due to the spell work. I'd been doing regular protective spells for him since Nonna showed me how.

That's not wholly legit in our tradition—doing magic for people without asking their permission, I mean. It goes against free will. But since my recent magic was to protect him from my earlier magic, and since I had no intention of mentioning the curse, I was willing to take the karmic risk.

It's not like I had a spotless karmic record, since the curse. What's another pound to an elephant?

When we ended up squished close to each other in the same elevator car, I just had to ask, "How's your car?"

Ben smiled, shrugged. "I'm taking the El a lot, lately."

"Other than that, things are…?"

"Fine. Yeah." He bounced slightly on the balls of his feet. "You? I mean…other than your sister, of course…."

"I'm taking it day by day."

He nodded. "I get that."

We arrived on the third floor.

"You're testifying today, right?" he asked as we got out. When I nodded, he said, "Good luck with that. I mean—God, that's not…" Then he reconsidered. His chin came up, as if he'd made a decision. "Really. Good luck with that."

He sounded sincere—and his dark gaze sure looked it— but… "Even when it puts your brother away?"

"I'm hoping it gets my brother some help."

I stopped dead. People had to veer around us like a river parting around a boulder. "You aren't saying…" I had to swallow, hard, to keep down a surge of anger. "He's not going to say he's innocent because he's crazy, is he?"

"What if…?" But I'd already known Ben wasn't stupid, and he proved it by not going there. "No," he admitted instead, holding my gaze. "Victor would never say that."

But Ben might? Unwilling to even consider that, I ducked past him and into the courtroom. As long as Victor went to prison and never left, I didn't care whether shrinks tried to "help" him or not. But I wasn't about to see him go free.

No matter what it took.

Other than the expected stage fright, up there in the witness box in front of everyone, my testimony went fine—as long as I was answering Mr. Jennings's questions. I haltingly described how I got home, what I'd found, what Victor had done and said, and how I recognized Victor in the lineup. I even got to point at him when Jennings asked if the killer was in the courtroom, like on a TV show. For the briefest moment, I saw pure loathing in Victor's gaze. I met it, hatred for hatred.

I never mentioned the curse to the authorities. Apparently he hadn't, either.

"Nothing more," said Jennings, and I foolishly relaxed. *For every moment of happiness you've stolen from my sister and me, may you know years of misery.* Life in prison would be an excellent step in that direction. Victor was going down.

Then I got cross-examined.

"The intruder said he was Ben Fisher?" asked Sherman Prescott, Victor's attorney. I remembered him from the second lineup. He reeked of self-importance, and not just because of his sideburns.

"He lied," I said.

His snapped "Objection!" made me jump.

The judge gently told me to answer yes or no.

"Yes, he *said* he was Ben Fisher."

"And when you participated in the first of two lineups, whom did you point out as—and I quote—'the man I saw?'" asked Prescott.

Jennings had prepared me for the questions, but not the outrage I'd feel. "I didn't realize they were—"

"Objection. Nonresponsive."

"Ms. Trillo," prompted the judge.

I became more aware of the whole crowded courtroom watching me. Some people were actually *sketching* me as I sat there, losing my cool in inches. "I chose Ben," I admitted through my teeth. "That time."

I could tell Prescott didn't like that addition. "Now Ms. Trillo, will you share with us what your sister was?"

What? I narrowed my eyes. "A blonde. An Aquarius. An organ donor. A florist."

"I'm referring to her occult interests…?"

"Objection!" At least that one came from our side. Mr. Jennings stood, saying, "Irrelevant."

But Prescott had a way around that, too. "This goes toward the victim's lifestyle, Judge."

"The victim is not on trial here!" Jennings looked as stunned as I felt when the judge allowed it.

Prescott continued, "Is it not true that Diana Trillo was a practicing witch?"

"Objection!"

"Counsel," warned the judge—*to Jennings!* "You aren't playing to a jury, here. Tone it down."

I remembered something Diana used to say when people

got snarky about her beliefs, and I said it. "Goddess worship is one of the fastest growing religions today."

"Nonresponsive," said Prescott. "Move to strike."

I noticed Ben Fisher frowning. He leaned forward and said something sharply to Victor, who shook his head and grinned. Damn, I hated that grin. He'd stolen all Diana's smiles forevermore. He didn't deserve more of his own, not a one.

But by now, I knew the drill. "Yes. Diana was a practicing witch."

Prescott smiled evilly. "And as such, with what manner of people did she normally associate?"

It went downhill from there, despite Jennings's damage control on redirect. Prescott was lucky I had to go to work so soon after the hearing, while I was still in full temper, or I would have seriously considered doing another curse. On him. The *bastard!*

The next day, it was Ben's turn. Jennings called him up first, to establish that Ben had attended a small gathering of friends that night and that no, he'd never asked around about goddess cups and no, he didn't know Diana.

Then Prescott went after him, too. "Mr. Fisher, do you work?"

"Objection!" protested Jennings. "How is this relevant?"

"Please, Judge. A little leeway here?"

And the judge nodded. I saw Jennings's fingers dig into the table in front of him.

Ben leaned forward to the microphone. Despite being awkward one-on-one, he seemed far less intimidated by the crowd than I'd been. "I work all the time."

"Let me rephrase. Are you currently employed in a salaried position?"

"No."

"Why not?"

"When would I find the time to work?" Ben seemed startled when some people in the gallery laughed. Apparently, he hadn't been joking, and he tried to explain. "I'm self-employed."

"About how much do you earn?"

Ben made a guess based on royalties and ad revenue off the radio show and the companion Web site. It was about twice what I earned, so I was particularly annoyed when Prescott said, "Not much, then."

"I also have a trust fund."

"That you share with your brother, right?"

"Objection," protested Jennings. "How is *any* of this relevant?"

Again Prescott said, "It goes to credibility, Your Honor, and to motive." *Motive?*

"I'll allow it," said the judge.

"Why?" I whispered, but Jennings just shook his head, his jaw clenched. Aunt Maria—who'd managed to come today—patted my hand in a way she thought was comforting.

It wasn't. *Hurting something* would be comforting. Hurting Victor and Prescott would be even better. Me. Bad guy. Remember?

I sure as hell did.

Prescott continued. "You live with your grandparents, don't you, Ben?"

If I'd needed proof that Ben Fisher didn't have a poker face, I was getting it now in his obvious annoyance. "On their property, yes. Not in—"

"And—" started Prescott, but Ben forged on.

"Not in their house."

"Move to strike," said Prescott. "Argumentative."

"You're making me sound like some crackpot," Ben protested. "This shouldn't even be about me."

It went downhill from there, too. On redirect, Jennings was able to establish that Ben had his own home on his grandparents' property, that he was considered an expert in his field, and most important, that he'd never met Diana in his life. But it didn't sound as powerful, after Prescott's hatchet job.

When Ben finished testifying, he left the courtroom. I thought he'd left the courthouse, too, and wouldn't have blamed him. But when I excused myself to head to the restrooms, there he stood, brooding against the wall by the water fountain.

I couldn't just walk past him without saying, "Hey."

"It's not the way he made it sound," he told me, an edge to his tone as if I'd made accusations, too. "I live there so that I can keep an eye on them. It's not like I live in their basement, or my old bedroom. Not that—"

"Prescott's evil," I agreed.

"And real education consists of more than degrees." Prescott had also brought up Ben's hit-and-miss college career. "I've got more hours than Vic does."

"He twists everything. Diana's not some blood-drinking, orgy-having Satanist, either."

"Doesn't he realize that even the U.S. Army recognizes Wicca as a legitimate religion?" Ben shook his head, frustrated. "But he just cares what will win the case for him. That's his job."

"Because he's evil," I said again, wanting an amen.

But Ben shook his head, still scowling. "No. Evil is something people do, not something they are. Otherwise, Vic...." He trailed off.

Not soon enough. "Victor's evil, too!"

"I'm not saying he didn't kill your sister!" Ben shoved a hand through his unruly hair. "Or that he should go free, or even that he didn't *do* something evil. But how, Katie? How can someone become that, do that? We had the same parents, the same opportunities, almost identical DNA. Doesn't it make more sense that he was influenced by something outside himself? That maybe he's a victim here, too?"

"The only thing that makes sense is for him to be put behind bars. Forever."

"Do you hear me arguing with that?" He spread his hands and, since he couldn't take a step back, took a step sideways, as if to distance himself from me. "Look, I'm trying to get my own brother put into prison. Maybe for life. What you've been through is horrible, but—" Again, he shook his head. "He's still my brother."

I didn't like this conversation. I couldn't hear Ben say anything kind about Victor, anything at all, without imagining that it would somehow lead to his brother's release.

Hadn't we started out by agreeing on something?

"The judge can see through Prescott's lies," I said, after a long moment. "Right?"

"I hope," said Ben, glum and tired.

So at least we were on the same side there. Sort of.

Maybe too much so.

I was surprised to be called back on the stand that afternoon. For the defense.

I was even more surprised by Prescott's triumphant first question.

"Just how well do you know Benjamin Fisher?"

Chapter 6

Prescott murdered Diana all over again.

"Did you not meet with Ben Fisher just last week? Before you answer, let me remind you that there are accident reports at a certain diner—"

"I never said I didn't meet him last week. But it wasn't planned."

"And we should believe you why?"

"Objection!" protested Jennings. Like that helped.

"Is it not true that you and your sister were the joint recipients of a rather large inheritance?"

What? "Mom and Dad left us the house and a life insurance policy."

"Both of which are now yours. And speaking of life insurance, how much do you receive from your sister's murder?"

"Objection!" yelled Jennings.

I couldn't believe Prescott had actually asked that. I had

to have imagined it. And yet when my gaze found my aunt's, in the gallery, her wide eyes showed similar shock.

No, I wanted to scream. *You don't understand. Diana was everything I had left!*

But I could barely draw enough breath to stutter, "I don't know, but—"

"Your Honor," continued Prescott, as if I hadn't spoken, "the greatest weakness in this case—and it has many—comes down to motive. My client had no reason to know Diana Trillo, much less to kill her, while the only so-called eyewitness, her own sister, stands to gain a great deal from her death—"

How did I gain anything but misery?

"*Objection!*" insisted Jennings. "Your Honor!"

"—just as Victor's twin, his *identical twin,* stands to profit equally from his brother's ruin. The fact that the witch's sister—"

Lady help me, I thought—and my breath returned with a whoosh. "Her name's Diana! Stop calling her 'the witch!'"

Prescott smiled, as if to say that I'd admitted there was something wrong with being a witch. "Judge, add the fact that the witness and the defendant's brother are well acquainted—"

"*Objection!*"

"But we aren't!" I protested. "We barely even—"

The judge's gavel interrupted me, and Prescott, and Jennings, and even the people in the courtroom, who had burst into excited murmurings. Reporters scribbled frantically. Ben, who'd stood toward the end of Prescott's rant, was pulled slowly back down by his concerned grandmother.

Victor looked stunned, hurt, outraged. It was as fake to me as if he had another neon sign over his head that read, *Acting.*

"Enough!" insisted the judge. "Don't make me clear this courtroom. Counselors, approach the bench."

The bailiff helped me down from the witness box. Aunt Maria met me with a hug, just as she'd met me at the emergency room over two weeks earlier. And I felt no less in shock now than I had then.

Me and Ben? Conspire to kill my sister and frame his brother for it? And people called a belief in magic crazy!

Jennings and Prescott were arguing animatedly with each other, falling silent only as the judge spoke sternly to both of them.

I looked across the gallery and found Ben Fisher watching me. He still looked as stunned as I felt. He shook his head, as if to say, *I didn't know....*

Somehow I managed to nod. I believed him.

Then Prescott returned to the defendant's table, and Jennings came back to his. The judge pounded his gavel once more, to get everyone's attention.

Jennings said softly to us, "I'm sorry. I tried."

What? Still numb, I couldn't begin to process what he meant until the judge began to speak.

"It is the finding of the court, based upon the facts presented, that there is not enough evidence at this time to warrant a trial of Victor Fisher for the death of Diana Trillo. The district attorney's office is welcome to refile charges if and when more evidence comes to light at a later date. Until then, Victor Fisher is free to go."

And that was it. It was over.

As abrupt as the strike of a gavel.

The courtroom erupted into chaos, but the judge was leaving, so he didn't bother to stop it. Me, I barely heard anything at that point. How could this happen? As inconceivable as it was to live in a world without Diana, it was even more incomprehensible to live in a world where her killer could so easily go free.

Aunt Maria asked Mr. Jennings the questions I couldn't— what about the fingerprint? What about the eyewitness testimony? But apparently there'd been a technicality with how the print was recovered, and now my testimony left too much room for reasonable doubt. Jennings tried to be encouraging. Because this hadn't been a trial, double jeopardy wouldn't apply if we found more admissible evidence. But his glumness contradicted his encouragement.

What were the chances that more evidence would show up, if it hadn't been found by now?

I felt dizzy. Sound seemed distant. Images weren't focusing. This wasn't real. Damn it, I'd *cursed* him!

But I'd also cursed myself.

"Ms. Trillo?" said someone through the mist. Like on a time delay, I belatedly turned. Then I felt more confusion, to be standing so close. *Ben…?*

But—suit. Gelled hair. Absolute poise.

It wasn't Ben.

"I just wanted to assure you that there are no hard feelings," said Victor, loudly enough that the waiting reporters could hear. "You've suffered a terrible loss, I know how that can distort a person's perceptions. Good luck finding your sister's real killer."

He sounded so very sincere. He even offered his hand.

I didn't take it.

"I'll be raising a cup to her memory," Victor assured me softly with a dimpling smile, and held my gaze just long enough to make sure I *got it* before he turned away, into the arms of his lying girlfriend and the back-slapping, cheering company of his colleagues.

Raising a cup? A *goddess cup,* maybe?

"Why did you take it?" I demanded, loudly enough that he would hear me. "Nothing was worth her life. What could you have wanted with some stupid chalice?"

But Victor and his lawyer friends exchanged confused, *damn, she is crazy* looks, and kept going.

He thought he'd won. He had literally gotten away with murder, and there was no real justice in this world…

Unless I wielded it.

A deadly calm overcame me, then. I'm sure I managed a few "No comments" to the press who crowded around me as Aunt Maria and I left the courthouse. I must have responded to whatever comforting things my aunt was telling me, on the way to my car, or she would never have let me leave alone. Apparently I managed to drive without breaking laws or hurting anyone.

But inside, I was planning darkest magics.

So being witches hurt our credibility? I'd show them a witch! What good was it to reconnect with my magical heritage if I couldn't even avenge my murdered sister? Maybe I'd botched the first curse—it had felt damned powerful at the time, but how else could Victor have gotten off? This time I had a better idea what I was doing. This time, I would use the right name, I would use the right ingredients.

Hekate was Queen of the Underworld? Good. Then I would call down on Victor's head all the powers of hell.

I'll use my own blood, I thought, taking the closest available parking spot to my house, in front of Mr. Lane's. *I'll use the little ring of braided hair Diana gave me, that time she donated hers to Locks of Love. I'll use the black candles in her magic cabinet. I'll cut one of the pictures of Victor out of the newspaper, so that every bit of horror falls directly onto him, him, him.*

And if I have to take the magical backlash?

Bring it on.

I barely noticed that it had started to snow again, a light dusting of white across the sidewalk and the yards. I was too busy ignoring the tiny voices protesting my plans.

One voice sounded like Nonna's. *The Goddess is not ours to be ordered about.* But Nonna had also said that we were Hers. And if that was the case, why *wouldn't* Hekate want to make Victor Fisher suffer for the destruction of Her priestess? Hekate wasn't known for her sweetness and light. She would probably welcome the invitation to rain misfortune down on Victor's head.

Another voice sounded like Diana's. *Victor Fisher would have killed you if you hadn't stopped him. But this time isn't about self-defense. It's about revenge.* To which my answer was, *Yeah, it is.* I'd tried playing by the rules, letting the Fates couch our revenge in the no-real-justice system, and it hadn't worked. Now he would reckon with me.

The whole damned world had turned out to be a place where evil thrived. So why the hell not join it?

But as I headed up my front walk, a third voice—one I didn't recognize—said simply, "Circle to circle."

What? I stopped, confused…and realized that I was standing in the middle of a circle that had been drawn into the snow, just before my front steps.

That, and the voice hadn't been in my head.

I looked up—and took a step back, out of the snow circle.

My first, crazy thought was, *the Goddess!*

But of course the woman who separated herself from the shadows of my brick stoop was human. She wore a deep blue cape with an attached hood that half hid her face, and she held a thick cane. When the wind caught a flurry of snow onto my stoop, her cape flew out like wings. Her hood blew back, re-

leasing a halo of medium-length brown hair and revealing a
solemn face far younger than the cane had me expecting.

She couldn't be much older than Diana was.

Than Diana had been.

"Hello, Kate Trillo," said the mystery woman.

"Go away." I sounded childish, I knew, but *hello*—I
needed to call the darkest powers I could command down on
Victor Fisher while my fury was fresh. "You have no idea
who you're dealing with."

I liked saying that. I almost wanted to say it again. Instead,
I mounted the stairs and started to shoulder right past her on
the stoop. But...

She turned sideways as I passed her. Somehow I ended up
farther from the door instead of closer. *What the hell?*

"I think I do," she answered evenly. "Your name is Kate
Trillo. Your sister was a priestess of Hekate. And her grail was
stolen by the man who murdered her. Is that about right?"

I stared.

The stranger took a deep breath, her blue eyes somehow
both sympathetic and respectful. "I am so very sorry for your
loss. I wouldn't have intruded if the need weren't great." She
reached out, as if to put her hand on my shoulder—and the
rage in me broke. I slapped her hand away, then shoved her
backward, as hard as I could with one hand, toward the
steps—

Or that had been the plan. When I shoved outward, it's like
suddenly she wasn't as close as I thought she was. *I* was the
one who ended up stumbling, with nothing to brace against.
How had she done that?

However it was, it pissed me off. I bodychecked her—

Or that was the idea. Again, with a simple turn, she stopped
being immediately in front of me. I hit the cold brick pillar

and spun. I glimpsed that another strange woman had gotten out of a car across the street and was approaching the house. Backup. They were ganging up on me. All my damned helplessness—on the witness stand, against Victor, against death itself—screamed out of me.

"What the hell do you want from me?"

The first woman shook her head toward her backup and put her hand on my shoulder—not to push me, or direct me, just to touch me—and something happened. *Magic.* I felt stronger. I felt less alone. I even felt the tiniest hint of something that, before I'd turned to the dark side, I might have called hope. Like maybe everything wasn't lost yet, after all.

I didn't like that feeling. It was a lie. But instead of pushing the crazy lady off the stoop—or trying to—I caught back a sob.

Before I knew it, she'd dropped her cane and had a grip on my other shoulder. "Kate? Kate, I'm so sorry for your loss...,"

I know this sounds crazy. It *was* crazy. But it felt as if my sister held me, and I missed her so badly, and I felt so guilty that her killer was now free....

The next thing I knew, I was in this stranger's arms and I was crying. The whole story spilled out—the murder, the hearing, Prescott's attacks, Victor's freedom. She held me, and made the right sounds of horror or outrage at all the right times, and somehow the weight on my shoulders eased a little.

I wasn't just crying. I was being comforted—and healed. By a complete stranger.

"Shhh," she soothed, petting my hair, rubbing my back. Her tummy pressed roundly against mine—was she pregnant? "Shhh. You aren't alone, Kate. You don't have to do all of this alone...."

I finally managed to catch my breath enough to snuffle, "Katie."

"Pardon?"

"My sister used to call me Katie."

The stranger drew back far enough that I could see her face, and she smiled. She wasn't classically pretty, but damn, she was somehow beautiful. *The Goddess,* I thought again.

"Maggi," she said, by way of introduction. "I'm Magdalene Sanger-Stuart."

And since we were no longer strangers—not on the soul level—I invited her into my house.

Waving her backup back into the car, she accepted.

"You really have no reaction when I say 'Circle to circle,' huh?" she asked, as I took her cape and scarf from her. She was taller than me—no surprise there—and what looked like seven months pregnant. Thank heavens I'd never actually connected with her, when I'd tried to shove her off the porch! She wore a pendant like mine, the *vesica piscis,* overlapping-circle thingie. She also wore a stunner of a wedding ring set on her left hand.

"What kind of reaction should I have to it?" I asked. Like this meeting wasn't weird enough.

"It's a rhyming game that some, uh, friends and I learned as children," she explained. "'Circle to circle, never an—'"

It clicked, then, and I finished, "'End.'"

"Yes!" Maggi seemed awfully pleased.

It had been a clapping game that Diana and I would play as small children, like "Pat-a-Cake" or "Miss Mary Mack." *Circle, circle, never an end.*

I said the next line as I'd known it, "'Cup-cup-cauldron—'"

"'—Ever a friend.' You *do* know it!"

"You're pretty excited about a nursery rhyme." I led her into the kitchen to put a pot on the stove. "Would you like coffee or tea? I have decaf."

"Tea, thanks. And…it's not just a nursery rhyme. Katie, what I'm going to tell you may sound strange."

"I'm a witch." I think that was the first time I'd spoken those words out loud. They kind of shivered through me. I really was, wasn't I? "I think I can handle strange."

"Did your mother or grandmother ever tell you a bedtime story about a queen and her daughters?" Maggi settled herself into Diana's chair, either by accident or instinct. I didn't mind.

Instead, I considered her question, and I remembered my mother's near-forgotten voice. *Once upon a time, there lived a great queen who had thirteen beautiful daughters.* "She sends her daughters away, right? And she gives them something…."

Whoa. I'd just remembered the rest.

My gaze met Maggi's. She nodded, encouraging.

"Cups," I finished, pretty sure this was no coincidence. *"Pour your powers into these cups,"* the queen instructed. *"Share them all you want. But if you end up in danger, or if people plot against you, hide the cups so your powers will be protected."*

"First nursery rhymes," I challenged, "and now fairy tales? What is it with cups? Who *are* you?"

"I'm a professor of comparative mythology in Connecticut," she admitted, which made me and my community college nursing degree feel a little inadequate. "And I'm a Grail Keeper. I think your sister was, and you are, too."

I just waited, because—I mean, really. A *what?*

"It's my belief," Maggi continued, "the belief of many scholars, that goddess worship was once the norm, long ago. That was a good time for women, apparently for most people. But as patriarchal rulers and religions took over, the goddess culture slowly had to go underground. They hid their most sacred objects—their grails—to protect them until it was safe, until it was time for them to reemerge. In order to keep the locations secret, they passed the information on to their daughters in a form that most men wouldn't find the least bit interesting. Mainly because women have always been in charge of children."

"Nursery rhymes." I got it. "And bedtime stories."

Maggi nodded. "If you know the rhyme, and/or know the bedtime story, and/or wear a chalice-well pendant—"

I must have looked confused, because she indicated her necklace. The *vesica piscis*. I nodded.

"—then you may be descended from some branch of these priestesses. I think there may be hundreds of them."

"So you think that the cup Victor Fisher stole from Diana is...some kind of grail? Like the Holy Grail?"

"*A* holy grail, in any case." Here, Maggi frowned. Up until now she'd had a kind of confidence to her; I wasn't surprised that she was a college teacher, she seemed to know so much. But she also seemed to dislike *not* knowing things. "There's no way to be sure, except to drink from it. But in the last year, a secret society of powerful men have begun seeking out and destroying goddess grails."

"Wait, wait, wait," I interrupted. It all made a great story, and watching Maggi Stuart tell it, I could believe too easily. But... "A secret society?"

"Businessmen. Politicians. Telecommunications magnates.

They already destroyed the Kali Cup, in India. And they went after my ancestral grail, the Melusine Chalice. This Fisher—he's in politics, huh? Attended Yale Law? Rubs elbows with VIPs?"

Okay, so that made me suspicious. "How do you know all this?"

"The Internet. I subscribe to a service that searches for different word pairings. Anytime a news story comes out that combines goddesses and cups, I'm sent a notice. He is, isn't he? One of those big power-broker types?"

I nodded and, reminded of my sheer hatred for Victor Fisher, scowled. I had to leave for work in about an hour. It didn't leave a lot of time for calling all the powers of darkness down on his head. "Not for long, if I have anything to say about it."

"Then he fits the profile of the old Comitatus. The secret society," she explained. "They've realized the power of these grails, maybe because it's time for the goddess's power to return, and they want to stop it. If your sister's cup was a true grail, it's a direct line of communication to your goddess."

"Hekate," I whispered.

"One of the most powerful goddesses there is," Maggi agreed. "Which means that if Her cup is kept safe, and its power joins with that of other goddess grails, their combined force could improve the situation of women a hundredfold. I have reason to think it's time. But if it's destroyed…"

Then—women's rights might go backward? It was a lot to swallow, especially since I'd never felt sexism was that big a problem anymore. But it was even more to dismiss out of hand.

"That's what I came to tell you," Maggi Stuart explained. "That if it was a goddess grail Fisher took, he took more than a repository of your family's power for generations back."

"No," I agreed. "He took Diana, too."

Maggi nodded. She really seemed to understand how that was the worst. But she wasn't going to linger there.

"But the cup, you might be able to get back."

Chapter 7

The Fisher family used to say that Victor had good days and bad days. Their grandparents, in particular, preferred to focus on the good days and pretend the bad ones didn't exist.

Today was apparently one of them. "Come on, Benny," Vic insisted, scooping up the keys to his BMW. "The party won't be the same without you."

Ben, who'd hung back for the whole visit, just stared at his brother. Then his grandmother said, "That's a lovely idea. It's so good to see you two doing things together again." Ben turned the same shocked, silent gaze on her.

Victor rolled his eyes. "It's not like we're celebrating that poor woman's death, Benny! Just that her family wasn't able to pin those ridiculous charges on us."

Their grandfather snorted at the idea of anyone thinking such evil about either of his grandsons, as if they truly were identical.

Hurt crept into Victor's dark eyes at his brother's continued silence. "My God. You believe it? You believe that I'm capable of—God! Never mind. Forget I asked."

Shaking his head, he backed toward the foyer.

Ben gave up on silence. "Why *wouldn't* I believe it, Vic? She picked you out of a lineup."

"Benjamin!" exclaimed his grandmother. Of course.

Vic waved back her outrage. "What, Kate Trillo? She picked *you* out of a lineup first. And her sister wrote *your* name in blood at the crime scene. But do I think you committed the murder, or even that you and Kate conspired to frame me? No. And do you know why? Because you're my brother. Because I know you. I thought you knew me, too, but…"

He shook his head, scowling, just a little…hurt.

It was a great act.

His grandmother put her hand on his arm. "Ben doesn't mean it. He's just confused. Tell him you're just confused, Ben."

"*I'm* not the one who's confused."

Victor gave their grandmother a loud, blatantly affectionate kiss and grinned, to show he was fine. "Look, walk me to the door at least, okay? I need to ask you something."

With a last, questioning glance at the grandparents who had raised them, Ben headed out with his brother. Only after they were alone did he ask, "Why would she lie?"

"Why would *I* lie?"

"*Because that's what you do!*" Despite keeping his voice low, Ben's words shook with intensity. "I don't know why. I wish I did. But this wouldn't be the first time you claimed to be me."

"What, you mean when we were kids? Years ago!"

Ben shook his head. "When you were caught shoplifting. When you trashed Gran's car. When you slept with Amanda. When you—"

"I've explained all that. More than once. What else can I do? And if you want to believe some grief-stricken witness from a whacked-out family over your own brother? Fine. Be that way, Benny. Excuse me for wanting to make sure you're okay."

Ben barked out a laugh. "That *I'm* okay?"

"It wasn't *my* name written in blood at the murder scene. I'm not the expert you are, but doesn't your name in blood mean the witch cursed you or something before she died? Or let me guess. You don't believe in curses."

Ben refused to answer.

"I guess it doesn't matter anyway," Victor continued, shrugging into his expensive coat. "Even if it were real. The witch is dead now, so her curse is dead, right? That's how it works, isn't it? I mean, if curses work at all. Once a witch dies, her spells die with her?"

Ben's gaze raked his brother's face, speculative, before he deliberately answered, "Not…always."

Victor's eyebrows rose. "No?"

"No. If the curse required sustained focus, then sure—the death of the magic user ends that focus. But if Diana Trillo wrote the name as she died, then the energy of her death might linger, continue to feed it."

"Wait. Now that she's dead, there's no way to break the damned curse?" Victor laughed, clapped a hand on Ben's shoulder. "Should I be worried about you, here?"

Ben shrugged off his touch. "Even if it was a curse, I'm pretty confident it wasn't aimed at me."

"But why the hell take chances? What are you going to do about this? How do you protect yourself?"

Ben studied him for a long, tense moment, before turning away. "Let me worry about that."

But behind him, Victor's narrowing gaze indicated otherwise.

* * *

"Well…" Diana spread her arms to indicate the scope of what Maggi Sanger-Stuart had told me that afternoon. *"That was unexpected."*

The really odd part was that I'd begun to "dream" her—to imagine her?—without even being asleep. If I was doing something quiet, like now, it felt like I was really listening to her. Despite that she'd never followed me around work before.

A lot of hospice care is provided in the patient's home, but since my hand was still cast—now in lighter fiberglass—and I'd cut my hours for the trial, I was working at a nine-room, inpatient facility called the Crossroads. The stately building had once been a private residence, before its donation to an area hospital for the purpose of "palliative care." That means making incurable patients comfortable as they die. It was an elegant and surprisingly peaceful place, for all its sadness. Graveyard shift was doubly so.

I was mainly there to keep an eye on things and to put people at ease. Making rounds, I checked in on Mr. King, who was in the end stages of lung cancer. His divorced daughter had two jobs and three children, so he'd come here to die.

"I mean, really," insisted Diana, trailing me. *Chatting around patients would probably seem more insensitive if she, too, weren't dead.* *"Who would've thought we had a* destiny?*"*

Mr. King's breath was ragged, despite his oxygen mask, but otherwise he seemed as comfortable as possible. I looked around the floor until I found the toy dog his daughter had given him to stand in for his real dog, which she sometimes brought to visit. I tucked the toy under his bruised, aged hand. He sighed with what seemed like satisfaction, and his hand closed slightly around the fake fur of the plush guardian.

"Watch over him," I whispered to the toy. Many witches believe inanimate objects can hold guardian spirits. I couldn't help but feel like the real dog could somehow be with his master through the toy.

And if that was possible, why couldn't a goddess store power in a goblet used in her worship?

I said to Diana, in my head, *You could have mentioned all this while you were still alive.*

"What, you think I knew? Hello! If I had any idea that we were part of a long line of Grail Keepers, with a divine mission to help restore womanly power, I think I would have mentioned it."

"How could you not know?" I asked her, charting Mr. King's numbers before moving on to check Miss Parkhurst. *"You're the superwitch."*

"Okay, one? I know you've only been back in training for a couple of weeks, but you know darned well magic isn't a free ride. It's a way of..." Diana extended her hand as if to grab some invisible prize. *"Of reaching beyond the ordinary to access hidden energies. Like with Mr. King's dog back there, and how he sleeps better with it. And two? Listen to me this time. You were always the super-witch of this family, not me. I did okay, but you..."* Her expression softened with what looked like pride. *"It's good to see you back in the game."*

Miss Parkhurst moaned. I blinked, and the image of Diana's soft, proud expression faded back into fantasy. No surprise that I was obsessing over what Maggi had told me that afternoon. Part of me couldn't help but wonder if it was some kind of snow job. Sure, I believe in magic, but goddess grails? Secret societies? The chance to restore female power?

Frankly, I'd never felt particularly *dis*empowered—not from being female. Despite being short. Grrrl power, and all that.

Still, if this grail thing was true...

I petted Miss Parkhurst's remaining hair back from her sunken face, and her moaning softened. Since I'd already looked in on the others, I pulled a chair closer to the bed, sat and held her frail hand with my good one. Her eyes didn't open, but her lips curved faintly.

Maybe that had been the most shocking thing about Diana's death. People tend to come into hospice care with a life expectancy of less than six months. But death rarely comes as quickly as you'd think, and life tends to put up a damned good fight, even when everyone involved wishes it would give up and let go. For Diana's young life to have been ended with one blow of a hammer...

It was unnatural. And it said something terrible about Victor Fisher's powers of destruction.

If that grail stuff is even true, I thought. *Maggi seems smart and all, but I just met her. If I knew someone who might understand all this, someone I already trusted....*

But...there *was* someone else. Someone who would know better than anyone if Victor Fisher was in a secret society. Someone I trusted more than made sense—unless you counted our magical bond. It was a crazy idea, but knowing him had already set a killer free. Shouldn't some good come out of it, too?

What if I asked Ben? I thought to Diana. She didn't say anything, being dead and all. But the idea felt...right. *Ben.*

If that Grail Keeper stuff is true, I thought to Diana, *then Ben Fisher may know. This sort of thing is right up his alley.*

*I'll ask him to meet us for lunch tomorrow. I'll have a better
idea where I stand on all this, then.*

I spent most of the night making Miss Parkhurst comfortable as her diseased heart finally gave out. Toward the end,
she kept trying to lift a hand as if reaching out toward something. She nodded. Then she just…stopped.

Outside her window, in the Illinois winter, an owl hooted,
low and poignant. Me and Hekate.

Guardians of Death.

Ben nodded when he caught sight of me waving him over
to my and Maggi's table. He headed in our direction.

"Are you sure we should even be meeting?" he asked, looking
suspicious. "After the allegations Vic's attorney made…."

"They were bullshit allegations," I said. "I have no intention of giving that asshole any more power over me than he
already took. What about you?"

His dark eyebrows lifted—and I didn't blame him. My
attitude would have surprised me, too, the afternoon before.
But…calling down the powers of darkness would still make
for a legitimate Plan B.

With an approving nod, Ben sat. Then he noticed Maggi.

"Magdalene Sanger-Stuart," I said. "This is Ben Fisher.
He's…" Hell, what was he? "He's the good twin. Ben, this
is my friend Maggi Stuart. She teaches—"

He lit up. "Comparative Mythology at Clemens College? My God, what an honor. I just received an advance
copy of *The Faerie Goddess in Early Gaul* to review for
the site."

"That's more my aunt's work than mine," said Maggi
modestly, while I stared. She was a writer, too? Of *books?*

"I doubt that, especially the English translation. Your

theories relating feminine divinity to an appreciation of the everyday sacred is inspiring. And yet it makes so much sense!"

And to think, I'd warned Maggi he might be quiet.

"Thank you. Katie tells me that you're one of the creators of the *Superrational Show?*"

"My partner Al's the spokesperson," Ben insisted. "I just do the research."

"If you're reading *Faerie Goddess,* that's some pretty deep research," Maggi agreed.

Our waiter showed up to interrupt the lovefest. Maggi and I had chosen a Greek restaurant for our meeting with Ben. She said Greece was a great place for goddesses. A man at a synthesizer played some strange, plodding music, and the walls were painted as if pieces of brick had fallen away to reveal a sunny island landscape.

Then Maggi leaned forward—as much as she could over her protruding belly. "So, Ben, what do you know about the Holy Grail?"

And they were off, talking about "illusory quests for perfection" and "sacred bloodlines," and referring to places and authors I'd never heard of. We'd ordered our lunch and eaten half our appetizer before I got up the nerve to ask, "But what about goddess cups?"

I'm not sure what bothered me more—that Ben looked as surprised as he was impressed for a minute? Or that both expressions quickly faded into suspicion and maybe…hurt? "You think I've been after goddess cups, too?"

Surprised, I shook my head. I didn't like that jolt of connection I felt as he studied my face, like he was maybe too smart for comfort, so instead I asked, "What kind of knives killed your parents?"

Maggi choked on her water.

Ben's gaze narrowed, and he tried his word twice before forming it. *"What?"*

"We think your parents might have been killed by a secret society," I explained. "A society that wants the goddess cups. Maggi told me that they use knives in their attacks."

"With people they respect, anyway," Maggie added.

That had explained her carrying the cane, which had turned out to be a sheathed sword. As I'd suspected already, she also had a female bodyguard with her, a competent black woman now seated at another table. *For my husband's peace of mind,* she'd explained. *Until the baby comes.*

"And you…" Ben shook his head as if to clear it. "That is… *What?"*

"Then I remembered reading that your parents were stabbed, and…" Damn. I really had turned evil, hadn't I? Or at least insensitive.

These were his *parents* I was talking about!

"That's what I read," I said weakly. "Anyway."

At least I managed to stop talking. Maybe Maggi *should* take over, here. If she'd just stop wasting time.

"We've started at the end," she said tactfully. "I'm sorry for ambushing you. It must be a painful subject."

"It's been almost twenty years." Ben looked from her to me and back, and his dark eyes seemed almost too sharp for comfort. "I'm just wondering why it's anybody's business what happened."

That was a good point. So why did I get the feeling he was hiding something?

Maggi said, "Let me tell you a bedtime story."

By the time we'd had our dessert—baklava—Ben knew as much about the Grail Keepers as I did. But he was still resisting the idea of secret societies of evil men. Especially the idea that he and Victor had any connection to one of them.

Interestingly, when he argued, Ben Fisher completely forgot to be reticent. He was dogged. "So Ms. Sanger—"

"Stuart," I corrected.

"Call me Maggi," she insisted.

"These Grail Keepers may or may not be real. But even if the mythology were valid—" He tapped the table with three fingers, in case his intense gaze and shifting weight wasn't emphasis enough. "It doesn't mean there's also some group of powerful people—"

"Men," Maggi corrected firmly. "Powerful *men.*"

"Men, then, who are running the world without any of us ever catching on. People aren't that easy to control, and secrets have a way of leaking out. Yours is a contained mythology. You understand?"

I really, really didn't. Maggi seemed to, and nodded, but Ben's the one who explained it.

"Mothers passing on knowledge to their daughters, that kind of secret can be kept because you aren't trying to control anybody else. You aren't trying to direct other fates or lives. So it's really nobody else's business. Even if the secret got out, immediate interest to unaffected parties may not be high."

Now I thought I got it. "So if someone else found out, they'd go, 'Huh, nice story,'" I said. "They wouldn't go, 'What the hell do you mean?' because they aren't involved."

"Exactly. And—"

I interrupted because, really, waiting for him to take a breath didn't seem to work. "But what about increasing feminine power a hundredfold?"

Ben considered that. He had a really animated face when

he debated things, his lips pressing or relaxing, his eyebrows rising or his eyes narrowing as different thoughts shot through his mind. He had a brain I was only beginning to get the enormity of. "I assumed we were talking personal power, not dominating power. Am I wrong?"

And like that. Lost me again.

"You're not wrong," said Maggi. "And bless you for knowing the difference."

"But *I* don't know the difference." I sounded sulky. But I couldn't do more damage to my image that I had with the question about his parents' murder, so why not be clear about it?

"Personal power means power over oneself," explained Maggi. Okay, like magic, changing the world by changing one's perceptions. That I got.

"But some believe that one person's gain must by definition be another's loss," added Ben. "You see this all the time when a successful person becomes an object of ridicule or envy despite the fact that his or her success doesn't come from us, in no way hurts us, or may even help us. That's a dominator belief, that there's a limited amount of power out there and one person's advancement is by default another person's deficit. Understand?"

I nodded. Slowly.

"Dominator power is power over other people. But personal power accepts that one person's gain isn't necessarily anybody else's loss. If that's what the Grail Keepers are about, more power to you." He smiled a lopsided smile. "So to speak."

"So you can believe in the Grail Keepers—or at least not actively disbelieve," Maggi clarified, "because our secrets don't limit people. But a society of powerful men running the world…"

"Especially a hereditary society like you described," he agreed. "Wielding power over others, *dominating*. It's not in human nature to be perpetually dominated. So, yeah. That would be one hell of a tough secret to keep."

Drawing a breath, he looked sternly at both me and Maggi. As stern as he could look, with those long, loopy curls. "Especially from one's own family."

"But what else makes sense?" I insisted. "Why would Victor steal our Hekate Cup unless he believes it is worth killing over? And why would he believe it has power unless he's part of this society?"

"No." Ben shook his head several times. "No. Because for him to be part of this group, our dad would have to have been part of this group. By blood. Right?"

He asked Maggi that. Then again, she knew more about this group than I did.

As soon as she nodded, Ben kept going. "Am I supposed to believe that after murdering our parents, these people sought Vic out to bring him back into the fold? Or that Vic knew about this even as a kid? That he's kept this secret all these years?"

"Because Victor's big on the sharing," I challenged.

"I keep telling you, I'm not saying he's a good guy! But he's my brother. My responsibility. My *twin*. How could he know something this huge and keep it from me?"

Maggi and I exchanged a quiet glance. She said, without conviction, "You may be right."

"This is a secret that, according to you, killed my parents and your sister. And that's not something that can be kept quiet indefinitely."

So…that was that, right?

Ben's scowl softened. "Hey, maybe this is an indication

that Victor *didn't* kill your sister. If there really is a murder-
ous secret society after goddess cups, by not being part of this
society, Victor's less of a suspect, right?"

"Except for the him-trying-to-kill-me part," I noted,
annoyed. "And *taking our cup.*"

"You didn't initially say he took a cup. You said he took
'something.' It was only later that you noticed the cup missing." Bastard.

"And the him-trying-to-kill-me part?"

Ben's gaze held mine, almost pleading. "You're *sure* it was
him?"

"Yeah." But my annoyance faded. I'd lost my sister, but at
least I hadn't lost my faith in her.

"Because the accuracy of eyewitness recall is notoriously
flawed," Ben insisted. I was starting to notice a pattern with him.
Get him upset, and he retreated into data. "It can be affected by
numerous factors, including outdated police procedures."

"Ben," I said.

"In fact, recent studies show that the mood of the eyewitness alone can seriously—"

"Ben." I reached across the table and covered his hands—
which were tearing at a napkin—with my good hand. "It was
either him, or you. *And it wasn't you.*"

He dropped his gaze, scowling. "I want it to be a mistake."

"I know."

"I knew he had problems. I was even afraid he might be
dangerous. But your sister…it just doesn't make sense."

Maggi said, "Especially if he's not Comitatus."

Ben blanched. His gaze flew to her. "What?"

"Comitatus," she repeated. "That's the secret society trying
to destroy the goddess grails. Actually, they've recently split,
so there are two groups using that name…not important."

"Why?" I asked, and waved away Maggi's attempt to answer about the split. "No, I mean Ben. Why are you looking like that?"

"I've got to go." He pushed his chair back.

"You recognize the name," guessed Professor Maggi. Well, *duh*.

"I've got to check this myself." He stood, dug out his wallet, dropped a twenty on the table. "I'll get back to you."

"I'm leaving town in a few hours." Maggi caught Ben's arm before he could leave. "Listen to me. See if you can take Kate into your brother's house, maybe his office. Safely, of course. Sometimes I can sense when a goddess grail is nearby—since this one's hers, I bet Katie will have the best chance of finding it. Will you at least do that?"

"I don't know. I don't—" He stopped himself and took a deep, troubled breath. "I'll try to help. But I have to go now, do you understand? I have to leave. Now."

Maggi let go of his arm.

Ben met my gaze once more, then left the restaurant.

"What do you think that was about?" asked Maggi. But beyond him recognizing the name, I couldn't have guessed.

I mean, I *really* couldn't have guessed. I went with her and her bodyguard, Sofie, to the train station—Maggi wasn't flying in her third term—and saw them off to New York. I went home. I went to work. Still feeling helpless, I began to take inventory of Diana's—my—magic cabinet. One night passed. Then another.

Then Ben Fisher called.

"Is your passport current?" he asked, his voice strained.

What? "I don't have a passport."

"Then you should probably get one. I'll meet you in Athens."

This time I said it. "*What?* Ben, you're not making sense.

I've never even been to Canada. I have a job. Why would I want to go to Athens?"

"The word Comitatus," he explained.

"Yeah. You recognized it because…?"

"Because my brother has used it as his computer password for years. He didn't know I knew, but…anyway, I hacked into his system."

"You can do that?" Wow.

"And he really is involved with it. All of it. The Comitatus. Your…cup. And now he's gone to Athens."

Something about Ben's voice, a waver of concern, said that this was about more than just the secret society. Something was wrong.

I braced myself. "Uh-huh…?"

"Kate, I think my brother might go after your cousin Eleni next."

Chapter 8

I can tell you exactly when I stopped thinking of Victor, however briefly, every single time I saw Ben Fisher.

It was when Ben met me at the Athens airport.

I've sometimes wished I was one of those women who speaks three languages and regularly jets off to exotic places. I wasn't.

I'm Greek on my mother's side, but it's not like she spoke the language, and YaYa and Papou only used it for secrets. Now we were in our approach to the Eleftherios Venizelos International Airport, which I'll just call the Athens airport because it really *was* all Greek to me.

I stared out my thick airplane window at a sprawling white, distant city beside an impossibly blue sea, sunlight spilling across me despite my watch saying it was the middle of the night. We must have flown into morning.

I was in Greece!

And since I apparently have a hard time sleeping on airplanes, what with all the usual worries about hijackers and crash landings, I was exhausted.

Once we touched down and taxied to a really modern terminal, I simply followed the other passengers—and tried not to worry about all the soldiers standing guard with machine guns. First came baggage claim. Despite the big purple bow I'd tied onto my red suitcase, at Nonna's suggestion, I missed it the first time it went around the luggage carousel and had to wait, worried that someone else would take it, for it to circle back.

Then came customs, and more guards with machine guns. I got into the blue line marked EU, because it was moving fastest, but a nice lady noticed my United States passport and directed me to the green line. Apparently EU was only for the Europeans.

The first stamp in my brand-new passport was in Greek.

Finally I escaped into the arrivals area, with people shouting in all kinds of different languages, and I thought, *What the hell am I* doing *here?*

Which is when someone called, "Katie! Kate Trillo!"

I turned, and Ben was pushing through the crowd to reach me, and I could have hugged him. I *wanted* to.

Except for the looked-like-my-sister's-murderer thing. Even that didn't stop the twinge of magical recognition between us before he looked away. "Here, let me take that."

I was glad to let him have custody of my suitcase. And me. Traveling with one hand in a cast is a bitch, and at least he seemed to know where he was going.

He said, "I've checked a lot of the major hotels, starting with the kind Vic's most likely to frequent, but so far no go."

"That took you a week?" I asked.

"Do you know how many hotels there are in Athens?"

I considered the huge sprawl of city that I'd seen from the air. "Good point."

The Athens airport had to be the shiniest airport I'd ever seen, with clean white floors, white walls, white ceilings, high windows, and lots of lights. Our way out was lined with bright shops and Internet kiosks. Not exactly what I'd expected from listening to YaYa's stories of the old country.

"They built a new airport for the Olympics," Ben explained, noticing my distraction. Then, because he was Ben, he had to continue. "They've got a new metro system, too, which is incredible—marble floors and walls, escalators, glass displays of museum pieces. But it's taking a lot longer to finish than they'd hoped. You see, every time they dig, they find urns or graves or temples and have to call in the archaeologists."

He'd retreated into lecture mode. Did *I* make him nervous?

Anyway, it was mind-boggling, this melding of the supermodern and the superancient. Also mind-boggling? The weather. I'd worn a coat and scarf and mittens to O'Hare when I left...was it only yesterday? The coat was still draped across my bad arm, partly so nobody saw me as weak. But when sliding doors spilled us out into the springlike sunshine, I could tell I wouldn't need it.

Definitely not the mittens and the scarf.

We stood in line for a taxi, and I scanned the crowd. There were a lot more dark-haired, dark-eyed, olive-skinned men around here than I was used to, and I hang around Little Italy. Victor would blend in way too well for comfort. I stood closer to Ben. "Have you seen my cousin?"

"You asked me not to approach her," Ben reminded me.

I'd only spoken to Eleni Pappas once, over the phone, to let her know I was coming and beg her to be careful. Luckily, she spoke okay English. "I couldn't think of any way to describe you without describing Victor. I didn't want her thinking he's safe."

"I've seen her," Ben admitted. "I've been keeping an eye on her when she goes to work and back. I haven't seen Vic."

"But he's here all the same, isn't he?" I asked, looking up into the cloudless blue sky. *I could sense it.*

"Yeah," agreed Ben, and then it was our turn for a cab. It smelled of cigarettes. "Yeah, I can feel him."

He told the cab driver to take us to an address in "the Plaka," and for most of the very long drive into central Athens, I stared out the window, still amazed that I was here, wondering what the hell Victor Fisher would want with my cousin.

A cousin I'd never even met.

I knew Eleni Pappas was a few years older than Diana. Than Diana had been, I mean. The families kept in touch with Christmas cards for the holidays and sympathy cards whenever someone died. Sometimes we sent pictures. But that was about it.

And now Victor was after her?

"Tell me again what you found on his computer," I said, and was startled to see how closely Ben had been watching me with his dark, intense eyes. "Please."

"Not enough," he said, but looked quickly away, like maybe he was lying. "Nothing that we could take to the police, even if I'd found the information legally, which I didn't. He'd recently made a list of all your and Diana's relatives in general, and collected a bunch of information about Eleni in particular—her address, her job, a handful of pictures from her driver's license and college records."

"Those are available for download?"

"Not all of them. But I'm not the only one who can hack into a computer."

Oh.

"Maybe I overreacted," Ben said, though the fist he tapped against the cab window didn't agree. "I hope so. But him researching her, coupled with the fact that he'd just flown to Athens himself, and…"

And the fact that he'd already murdered Diana?

But I didn't expect him to say that part. Neither of us had forgotten, would ever forget, that part.

"No, it's worth coming," I agreed. "I don't know exactly what we can do, but we had to do something."

"Telling her in person will help. Showing her pictures of Vic. Maybe convincing her to get some protection." Ben was doing that thing with his eyes again, that thing where he focuses on nothing, on something in his head. "If we can figure out what Vic's really after, that would sure help."

The farther we drove into Athens proper, the worse the traffic got. At times it snarled up completely, and the rest of the time we went really, really fast, as if to make up for the gridlock. All the chaos and congestion and concrete weren't exactly what I'd imagined Greece to be. Every once in a while we would pass an ancient church, or a vacant lot full of white-columned ruins—but they were crowded on either side by apartments or shops, and the blue sky was dulled with smog. Anyway, it was hard to sightsee with all the lane changes and sudden turns, with other cars going against traffic and with scooters and motorcycles zipping along between lanes and darting in and out of traffic and even onto the sidewalk.

"I'm glad I'm not driving," I gasped.

Our driver, who'd introduced himself as Panos, let out a

bark of laughter but said nothing. The string of blue and white worry beads on his rearview mirror swayed dramatically as the cab hurled itself across lanes to avoid stopped vehicles in front of us.

"Me, too." Ben shook his head, and I thought he looked tired even without the transatlantic flight. Something seemed different about him. Not Victor-different, but...something. "I don't know what it is about me and cars lately, but I've had more close calls in the last week..."

The curse, I thought.

"Close calls like back home," I murmured. Something niggled in the back of my jet-lagged mind. Something I was supposed to do. "You were taking the El a lot."

"Even as a pedestrian I'm doing pretty badly, here," Ben admitted, watching me closely. "Just yester—"

But he broke off.

I looked, just in time to see a big, black dog standing on the street in front of us, staring at us with yellow eyes. *Like a dare.*

Panos braked and yanked the wheel at the same time. A sudden impact accompanied the boom of us clipping another vehicle. We bounced off of that into an out-of-control spin.

Panos swore, fighting the wheel. Strange storefronts whirled by my window. Gravity pushed me hard into Ben as the whole world of high buildings and smoggy sky and utility wires swooped around once, twice—

The car lurched as we jumped a curb. People screamed.

"One, two, three," I whispered through my teeth, and visualized a bubble of safe blue light, like a force field, around us. *"Protected be."*

And suddenly we stopped. Horns blared from the street. People shouted from the sidewalk.

"My God," muttered Ben, yanking his door open.

I struggled one-handed with my seat belt, which felt like it was cutting me in half. *No....*

Panos continued to swear—at least I assumed that's what he was shouting, to judge by his gestures and how hard he punched the wheel. If he was hurt, it wasn't his lungs.

No, no, no. My sense of panic had less to do with the damned seat belt, and my damned cast hand, and more to do with what I'd forgotten. But the belt wasn't helping. "Ben!"

He glanced back, then quickly leaned through the open door and across the backseat to unlock my belt.

"Nobody seems to be hurt," he assured me, helping me out of the cab. His hands felt solid on my shoulders.

Not this time. "But where's the dog?"

"Was that thing huge, or what?" Ben also looked around. No dog. "I would have swerved to avoid it, too."

But I wasn't thinking of the size of the black dog versus the size of the cab, or the way it had stared at us as if laying down a challenge.

I was remembering all the howling that had been bothering me for almost a month, back in Chicago.

I was remembering that dogs were one of Hekate's totem animals. Especially black dogs.

And I was remembering that I hadn't done my protection spell for me and Ben the night before. I'd flown through the night, remember?

The curse still haunted me, haunted Ben. It's not like what I'd done with Nonna could fix it permanently.

A pilgrimage, Nonna had said. *You must find Her source. Where She is most remembered. Where She was once worshipped....*

And look where I'd found myself. Freaking *Greece.*

On a pilgrimage without even knowing it.

That made me shiver—the shiver that goes with something happening beyond my normal perception. Like somehow Victor and Hekate had worked together to get me here. I didn't like being manipulated. Not by either of them. Not by anyone.

Panos was in a screaming match with the driver of the car we'd clipped, all in Greek. One of his many gestures was to point toward the road where the dog had stood, then to throw his hands in the air.

For a moment, I considered hailing a cab and returning to the airport, returning to the United States of America. Katie Trillo was *nobody's* pawn.

Except…

I looked over at Ben, who had unloaded my suitcase from the trunk of our wrecked taxi and collected my coat without me even asking. He was an innocent in all this, despite his scowl. So was Eleni. Victor was the one who'd dragged them both into it. And through my curses and my genes, I'd helped.

I sure had no faith that Victor would do anything to see anyone out the other side.

So I guess it was up to me.

Chapter 9

When I'd talked to her, my cousin Eleni had described the "flat" she shared with two other women. Ben and I locked my luggage at his hostel and set off in search of her address.

Tired or not, I thought we ought to find her right away.

"She said the building was once a mansion, before it was converted to apartments," I read from the crumpled notes I'd scribbled. As we hiked, I could see why the narrow, twisting streets of the Plaka were closed to cars. They were a maze of great old flagstones. Some of them even had steps.

"I can find it," Ben assured me. International travel sure played with your values. That he spoke English seemed especially wonderful, just now.

At least we were safe from traffic, though at least twice a motorbike buzzed too close by us.

"It should be three stories high," I continued, "and a reddish brown, with white trim and a blue door."

"I've seen it." Ben stopped at an intersection to study each quiet direction. He headed left. "I can find it again."

I didn't see how he could. The area was a jumble of quaint tavernas with outdoor seating and souvenir shops with bright T-shirts flapping in the breeze. How a Greek-speaking, tourist-crowded neighborhood could feel so damned *peaceful,* I had no idea.

Maybe it was all the potted plants. Or all the cats. Potted geraniums and cats were everywhere.

"Up there, I think," Ben said.

I looked up—and my stomach sank to see a crowd milling in front of a three-story, reddish-brown house with white trim. "Oh, hell," I said and ran.

The incredible weather and flagstone street weren't the only signs that I wasn't in Chicago anymore. The cluster of almost a dozen people were all talking, and I couldn't understand a word. Had something happened to my cousin? Was she upstairs, lying dead on *her* living room floor…?

"Pappas?" I called, shouldering into the crowd. That was her last name. "Eleni Pappas? Is she all right? Does anybody here know Eleni—"

"Katie?" a woman responded, and I turned. And stared.

Eleni Pappas looked like Diana.

I'm not kidding. If she'd had blond hair, and a longer jaw, and stood maybe an inch or two taller, they could have been twins.

"You are Katie Trillo, yes?" she asked, while I stood there gaping in front of the bright blue doorway to her building. When I nodded, she threw her arms around me and gave me a big hug. Then she kissed me on both cheeks. Then she hugged me again. She smelled of sunshine.

"It is good to meet you at last! Our little Katie, come home to Athens."

Home to Athens? "But…what's going on? When I saw all these people, I thought… I thought something had happened to you…." Oh, hell. My eyes actually started to burn with concerned tears. And I barely knew this woman!

But the tears weren't exactly for her, were they?

She made a friendly, dismissive sound. "My neighbors, they see a trespasser in our building. Because of your warnings, I ask the men to, um…" She made a circular motion with her hand.

"Check it out?" I asked.

She laughed, nodded, and gave me a sideways hug, leaving her arm over my shoulders. "Yes, check it out. Do not worry, Katie! You are like my family, so concerned about single woman, but all is well. This is a safe place."

I realized that the crowd included housewives still wearing aprons, children and stooped old men who probably would be playing the Greek equivalent of checkers this time of day. Several dark, burly men emerged from her doorway with shrugs and shaking heads. Even without understanding Greek, I could tell they'd found nobody.

A boy of maybe seven years old was talking quickly and getting a lot of attention.

"Milos sees the intruder," translated Eleni. "He sees this man before. He sets up a shout, we all run down to the street. But the man, he is gone."

I had my suspicions, even before young Milos suddenly pointed past me and began "setting up" another shout, this time with recognition.

In barely a moment, poor Ben was surrounded by glowering Greek shopkeepers, housewives, children and senior citizens.

"No!" I protested, wedging myself in to stand beside him, my shoulder pressed against his. "No, you've got the wrong guy. He was with me!"

Ben may have done more good when he said, *"Ohee,"* and *"Parakalo."* Or something like that. Who knew the guy spoke Greek? He even managed a strained smile.

What was even more unsettling, though, was when Eleni cocked her head in recognition. *"Ben?"*

I looked from her to him and back. "You know him?"

"We meet at the market," she insisted. "Two days ago. You ask me if I know where to find the good ceramics."

The crowd was moving in on us again. Pressed against Ben in response, I barely had to turn my head to catch his gaze, confusion solidifying into dark realization.

"Victor," I guessed. The flip-flop in my stomach had nothing to do with jet lag, my foreign surroundings, our recent accident or even the growing mob surrounding us.

"Victor," he agreed in a bleak, defeated rasp.

"No," I repeated, loudly. "Eleni, *this* is Ben Fisher. His twin brother is the man I warned you about. His *identical* twin brother. That must be who you met. And Ben couldn't have been the intruder—he's been with me since I arrived. Ben's trying to help. It has to have been Victor."

Much of the crowd must have spoken English; they backed off a step or two. Eleni's quick translation earned us a cease-fire from the rest of them.

"I meet Victor," she repeated. "But he says he is Ben?"

"Yes," Ben and I said, more or less in unison.

"And you believe Victor trespasses on my home, and not Ben?" she asked.

We both nodded.

She considered that, then turned to talk to her neighbors. Though suspicious—especially skinny young Milos, who apparently liked the attention—they seemed to take her word for it. But instead of bringing us inside, Eleni took my hand and drew me down the street with her. "Come," she said. "Both of you. We have much to do, much to discuss. The others, they keep watch on my home."

So we followed. Wherever we were going, it was uphill.

Eleni gave me another sideways hug and soft kiss on the cheek. "You are very much my cousin, this I can see. We are like sisters, yes?"

Since she looked like Diana, she looked like me. More so, since we were both dark-haired. And we'd both been drawn to medicine. "Yes," I agreed, unsteady from more than jet lag.

"And you are like a sister to worry about me. But how do you know this is Ben, and not Victor?"

I managed not to shudder at the idea. "Part of it's his attitude. Victor's more polished. He dresses a lot better, too."

I felt Ben's gaze on me and turned to meet it.

"Thanks," he said. Not that his maroon T-shirt was tucked into his jeans. His sneakers were scruffy, too.

"He *is*." I shrugged. "Then again, he's evil."

"Dangerous," Ben argued. "He does evil things. And he needs help before he hurts anyone else."

"Ben, on the other hand, is laid-back," I continued, since Victor's need of *help* was something we wouldn't agree on. Ever. "And his hair's longer."

Only after I'd reached out and fingered one of Ben's loopy black curls—and caught his sharp black gaze from under it—did I realize what I was doing. *Damn* that jet lag!

Sorry, I mouthed, but he seemed intrigued.

Then I asked Eleni, "What did he want? Victor, I mean."

We turned up an even steeper, narrower street. Shops and houses on either side of us made way for green trees.

"He asks about pottery," my cousin said. "Pottery for the goddess. I tell him shops that are reputable, and he asks if I do not perhaps have some myself."

"Bastard." I was starting to breathe hard—and not just because of the climb. Not for the first time, I wondered how Victor had approached Diana about *our* chalice. I wondered why she'd fallen for it. I wished she hadn't.

Ben asked, "*Do* you have anything yourself?" At Eleni's arch reaction, he added, "What I mean is, what did you tell him?"

"I tell him not everybody in Athens wishes to sell to tourists, and I leave him there." She shared a smile with me. "But I remember him, because he is so good-looking."

Good looking? *Not* how I would describe Victor. But I snuck another glance at Ben, all the same. Maybe…

He'd pulled out his PDA and was oblivious as he split his concentration between jotting some notes and not slipping on the smooth stone street. Low-key, definitely. But yeah… good-looking, too. "So he's after more goddess grails," he muttered.

"Diana's wasn't enough for him?" He'd killed my sister for it, and it *wasn't enough?*

"I guess that's what we have to—" But as we came around another turn, Ben interrupted himself to say, "Wow."

I looked up. "Holy wow."

Across a stretch of open pavement, shaded with scrubby trees on either side, stood a roofed gateway into more trees. Nothing special. But far above and beyond those, high atop limestone ramparts and white against the blue sky—

The Acropolis.

I, Kate Trillo, was really standing at the foot of the Acropolis.

Eleni looked delighted by our reaction. "You wish to pay respects to the Lady, yes?" she asked, and indicated my *vesica piscis* necklace. "Circles…um…beyond all endings?"

She drew a similar pendant out from under her blouse. Damn. I really shouldn't have been surprised.

She was a Grail Keeper, too.

"'Cup, cup, cauldron,'" I finished, slowly recognizing her version of *Circle, circle, never an end.* "'Ever a friend.'"

She gave me another quick hug. "Then you do nothing in Athens until you pay respects to the Lady. Wait here. I know Costas, at the ticket booth. I get us a good price."

Ben said, as we waited, "So that pendant means you're a goddess worshipper? I mean, I assumed you were—your sister being one—but I'm not familiar with this particular symbol. Pentagrams, yes. Renditions of the moon, sure. Not the overlapping circles."

"This one's specific to Grail Keepers," I explained, staring at the white ruins that towered above us. "But Ben, I don't know what Lady she means. The Goddess, of course, but… why here?"

Ben laughed, like at a joke. Then he must have seen from my expression that I wasn't kidding. "This is Athens," he reminded me, stuffing his hands into his pockets.

I folded my arms. "Duh. And…?"

"And… Athens is named after Athena. Goddess of wisdom and war?" Ben's eyes widened at my ignorance. "You didn't know that? Katie, the Acropolis may be the largest goddess temple in existence."

A goddess temple?

Eleni came dancing back with our tickets. "Come, come," she urged, delighted in her role as tour guide. "We go to the head of the queue, and I will bring you to the Lady."

In all fairness, there wasn't much of a line. March must not be a big tourist season. She gave the guard—Costas, I assumed—a kiss on the cheek as she ushered us through the gate. Then came a lot more winding and climbing, surrounded by dry rocks, olive trees and even marble blocks and column sections just lying around. And always, above and ahead of us, beckoned the beautiful, ancient columns of a truly blatant goddess temple. Huge. Unmistakable.

I'd just assumed that witches always hid their beliefs behind secrets and nighttime. For safety, if nothing else. A major ingredient of magic was secrecy. To know, to will, to…something…and to *keep silent.*

But this…!

Bless Ben for all his questions and information. Apparently more than one of the columned structures above us belonged to Athena. The biggest one, the Parthenon, represented Athena *Parthenos,* the virgin goddess. Another smaller temple was for Athena *Nike,* goddess of victory. "Outside the gate," said Eleni, "there is…*was* a statue of Athena *Promachos.* This means guardian of the city. She stands so tall, ships at sea can once see the tip of her spear." Or, I assumed, they had at one time.

"So the one goddess," said Ben, barely short of breath despite our increasingly steep climb, "can symbolize many things. Is that why you worship Athena, although Diana worshipped Hekate?"

She laughed. "I worship Hekate also. My name, it means 'torch.' For Her, the torchbearer. But Hekate is a, how you say, common goddess? Many homes once have—had—stat-

ues of Her by their doors, for protection. Now She has no
great temple nearby, and Athena does. So…" She shrugged.
"All are faces of the Goddess."

"Sort of a one-river-many-wells concept," mused Ben.

"All paths are Hers," agreed Eleni.

Me, I just listened and enjoyed the mild warmth of the day.
This path took us even farther up through a big stone gate and
up more stairs into a vast dreamscape of dry rock, low stone
walls, scrubby wildflowers and fluted white columns.

We were on top of the world.

With the Goddess.

Feeling hushed, like in a cathedral, I started walking,
closer and closer to the Parthenon. In some areas lengths of
chain had been hung between metal posts, to keep tourists on
the paved pathways. In others, we could clamber over the
rocks and ruins at will. To one side of this high plateau, the
blue-and-white Greek flag flew over the city, but other than
the tourists, that was all the color there was. Even the tiny
wildflowers were white and yellow, like the age-stained
stone.

Eleni and Ben talked about how these temples had been
destroyed, and when, and by whom. They discussed
someone named Lord Elgin, and whether he should give
back some statues he'd taken—apparently that was a pretty
big issue around here. I barely listened. And when they said
something about going to see *caryatids,* whatever those
were, I told them to go ahead, and I sat down on a sun-
bleached stone wall at the edge of the ramparts overlooking
what seemed like all of Athens, far below into the hazy
white distance.

Usually I connected goddess worship with the moon, and
shadows, and night. But with the gritty, hewn stone warm

beneath my jeaned legs, I closed my eyes, held up my arms, and felt sunshine caress me. I wished my left hand weren't still encased in its fiberglass cast, so that I could spread both hands wide and capture whatever essence it was that bathed this magical place. But more...

"Oh, Diana," I silently said. "I wish we'd come here together, while we still could."

"How do you know we haven't been here together?" I imagined her answering. Because Diana always had to be contrary—it was a bossy, big-sister thing. "How do you know we weren't priestesses in a past life, living here on the sacred rock, bringing silken robes and golden jewelry for the Lady's statue?"

"The statue," I murmured, sleepily opening my eyes to a world without Diana and scanning all the scaffolded temples. It was nice that so few tourists were here; it gave me privacy for my communion with the Goddess. And my sister.

Sort of. Ben got back in time to hear me. He sat beside me and said, "There used to be a statue of Athena in the Parthenon, made of gold and ivory. It was huge, maybe forty feet tall."

"But she's not there anymore?" I asked, my gaze moving to the columned temple in question.

"Oh, no. Please. Her time's long gone. The site was turned into a Christian church, then a Moslem mosque, and Athena got melted down for parts. Pollution's slowly taking the rest of her rubble. So much for her so-called power, huh?"

Even as I began to turn, began to question why Ben was suddenly being such a jerk, part of me must have guessed.

I even imagined, very clearly, Diana saying, "Katie, *look out.*"

Then I was nose to hawkish nose, not with Ben, but with Victor Fisher. Same heavy brows. Same sharp eyes. Same angular face.

No soul.

"So about that curse," he said, and I scrambled backward, farther onto the wall. I would have swung to the ground's safety, taken off in the direction Ben and Eleni had gone, but Victor easily closed the space between us. So the wall made for my only escape. I stood, to better react.

On the plus side, it made me taller than him. And Ben and Eleni were more likely to see me. These were huge, solid ramparts, so even the top of the wall was as wide as a good sidewalk.

On the minus side? The wall dropped beyond, hundreds of feet down the wall to its rocky foundation. Wind whooshed past my ears and blew at my hair. When I backed away from Victor, I did so *very carefully.* And yet…

Remember when I startled Mrs. Hillcrest, but didn't scare myself? This felt kind of like that. I was a creature of darkness, of power. And he was my enemy.

"Whoa there, Katie," Victor cautioned—which would have been a lot more credible if he didn't also spot me, staying between me and the only safe way down. "You aren't much use to me dead."

Much use to him?

He grinned, so very friendly. "Just ask your sister."

"Stay the hell away from my family." My mind searched for ways to protect myself, like one of those logic puzzles I've never been good at. Luring him up here with me just to push him off seemed risky. And while screaming for help might work, the magic of this place, the power of the Goddess, still flowed through me.

It was time I took care of this guy *my* way. Mine, and Diana's, and Hekate's.

"I call upon Hekate," I warned him, and spread my arms.

"Stop it," he protested. "That last mojo hex you put on me is bad enough. If you want me to play nice, maybe leave Eleni alone, you'll take it off me, not cast another one."

Or I could just finish him, here and now. "I call upon the Goddess of the Crossroads, the Queen of the Night. I ask her to be here with me, now, in this place."

Surely it wasn't just my imagination that the wind was picking up, buffeting me, whipping my hair, snakelike, around my face. This was magic, witchcraft, *power.*

"Uh, Katie." Victor's gaze fastened on something just behind me. "Whatever you're doing—"

"Be with me," I said, a second time. But there's no great magical power in doing something twice. So I lifted my arms even higher, my posture proud and strong. *"Be with me!"*

"Watch it!" Victor lunged forward. I kicked out at him, but then my foot landed on something soft. *Something that moved!*

It happened too fast. Even as I looked, saw the rearing brown snake, it struck at me. I dodged—somehow, through magic or luck, I dodged a striking snake.

But I did it by stumbling out into nothingness. Hundreds of feet above rock and ruins.

When my foot stepped into thin air, I threw myself forward, risking snake, killer and all. But you can't push off of nothingness. My knee slammed against the hard edge of the wall as I dropped. I fumbled for a hold. *Hekate, help me!*

But my good hand caught a handful of writhing snake, instead.

I threw it. My left hand skidded, useless in its cast, off

rock. Weight and gravity pulled me backward. My knee slipped, and my right hand didn't have the strength to do anything but break fingernails in a last, desperate scrabble.

The last of my balance, and apparently the goddess Herself, failed me.

I plummeted off the ramparts of the Acropolis.

Chapter 10

I was going to die.

I didn't have the wits or heart to try more magic. I was going to fall, hit the rocks…

Then two strong hands clamped around my last sliding foot. With a lurch I slammed against the outside of the rock wall. Distant treetops and orange-tiled roofs blurred at the edge of my vision. Bits of loose rock fell silently away from me, down, down, down. But I wasn't falling with them.

I was hanging. Someone had caught me.

Someone?

Trying to twist without kicking free of whoever held me, digging the fingers of my right hand into a grassy crevice between two vast white blocks, I managed to crane my neck and look upward.

It was Victor. Even upside down, there was no mistaking

his well-pressed business casual, his slicked-back hair, his sharp focus as my weight bent him over the wall.

Victor had saved my life?

"Give me your hand, Katie," he gasped, hooking my foot awkwardly under his arm to better secure a one-handed grip, then reaching downward for me with his freed hand.

I stubbornly dug my fingers deeper into the crack I'd found, pressing my cheek against the stone like a lover. But really…four fingers and a thumb wouldn't hold my weight if he let go. Would they? *Especially* upside down.

His grin widened, as if I amused the hell out of him. "C'mon, Katie. What choice do you have?"

Damn, I hated that he was right.

I released my fingerhold. With a hard twist, I swung myself upward with all my strength, reaching, straining. I felt sure he would let go. He would drop me, and the last thing I would ever see was him laughing at me over this one final betrayal.

That's why I felt such soul-deep shock when his hand clamped around mine.

Our fingers curled hard into each other's. With me hanging in a kind of U now, by one foot and one hand, he pulled. But I'd been right. Fingers weren't strong enough to hold a whole person. Even with his tight grip, my hand began to slip, bit by slow bit, out of his. My foot, still tight between his arm and his ribs, could feel his heart pounding right through my shoe.

With a lurch, my hand slipped free.

Throwing himself forward, Victor somehow caught my wrist instead. The sudden lurch of it—my drop as he moved forward, the wrench in my shoulder as I caught—made me scream. He was leaning precariously over the edge now himself.

"Not *yet*," he growled.

With him holding my wrist *and* my foot, I managed to turn

more surely and to lean upward, fighting gravity all the way, scrabbling with my free foot and my cast hand—

Other hands caught me then, fingers digging into my calf, onto my elbow, grabbing my shirt, and now two more bystanders were pulling me up and over the wide rampart wall.

My feet touched stone, and I gasped what felt like my first real breath in forever. I'd survived. But…

Because of *Victor?*

I turned on him.

"Why?" I demanded, rudely ignoring more helpful tourists who crowded close asking worried questions in languages I didn't understand. Sheer fury tore out of me in that one question. *"Why?"* But I wasn't just asking why he'd saved me, was I? I was asking about a lot more than that. Why Diana? Why Athens? Why the hell wouldn't he leave me and my family alone?

Other than that we were bound by my curse.

And why hadn't Hekate helped me this time? *A snake!*

My legs shook, but I was determined to stand on my own feet in front of my sister's killer.

"Here's my deal," Victor said, low and intense. He tried to take my shoulders, but I shook him off. The whites of his eyes seemed particularly bright against his dark, dark focus. "You cancel the damned curse, and you help me find the Hekate Cup."

"But you *have* the cup!" *You killed my sister for it!*

"That thing? It's barely a century old. I'm talking the *real* cup, Katie. The *original* Hekate Cup. *That's* what brought me and Diana together, what brought you and me together, what we're all here for!"

Still holding my gaze, he tried to skim his hand down my jawline. When I smacked it away, he drew his fingers back, a smear of blood on their dusty tips. Then he smiled the sweetest, most helpful smile—and licked them.

The world roared around me like wind in my ears, bright with white marble and blue sky and questioning strangers—and memories.

Memories of Victor Fisher and blood. *Evil.*

He leaned even closer. "And hey," he whispered gently, hot against my ear. "Take my advice, hon. Don't trust—"

I punched him, solid on the gut, my fist curled tight with the thumb on the outside just like my cousin Ray had recently taught me. It felt good. And it worked! Victor staggered back with a satisfying "Oof!"

Then he winked through his wince of pain, like, *point for you.* He tipped his head significantly to my right, and turned away—

Just as Ben himself shouldered through the bystanders and threw himself in front of me. *"Get away from her!"*

"You've got it wrong, bro." But Victor didn't even bother turning as he said that. Instead, he held up one hand as he walked away, regal and dismissive. "You always have."

Ben lunged after him—but I must have made some noise, because he looked back in time to catch me as I dropped. I didn't exactly faint. Fainting means losing consciousness, and I didn't. But it's almost as embarrassing that, suddenly, my own two legs couldn't hold me anymore.

It was okay, though. Ben's arms closed around me, cushioning my fall before I could hit rock for the second time in five minutes. He eased me the rest of the way to the ground, stronger and safer than you'd think a genius would be. His head pivoted from me to his retreating brother and back, his expression unusually dark.

Then he shouted something in Greek, apparently calling

for help. Because he could do that. As soon as Eleni arrived, pale from my near miss, Ben eased me from his arms to hers and tore off after his brother.

Damn, damn, damn.

Ben didn't return for far too long. Eleni reassured and thanked my other saviors. Guards came by to make sure I was all right and—according to Eleni—to lecture me about not standing at the edge of a drop, and about watching out for snakes.

Yeah, great advice, that. Timely, too.

I wanted to send the guards after Victor, especially the longer Ben stayed away—what if Victor hurt him? But what excuse would I use? More than one bystander swore that Victor had saved my life.

Even more confusing—Victor *had* saved my life. *Because he wanted something.*

After checking me for snakebite, Eleni sat next to me against the white stone wall, her arm soft around my shoulders. She said the snake I'd described had been a poisonous horned viper, probably come out to sun itself on the rocks in preparation for spring. But that wasn't the viper I most worried about.

Finally, thank heavens, Ben was back—mussed and panting and looking more frustrated than I'd ever seen him. "He's gone," he admitted, pacing a half circle in front of us and pushing his hair back from his sweaty face before zinging me with a full-on stare. "What happened?"

So I told them. Partway through my story, Ben finally stopped pacing and sank into an easy crouch in front of me. I don't know if his balance came from natural grace, or the intensity of his focus holding him in one spot. It seemed both odd and right that he would be that into me—even if he was just "under my spell."

"So Vic wants you to find the Hekate Grail," Ben mused, when I finished. "Maybe he thinks he can't find it himself."

"I thought he *had* the damned grail," I muttered. My words were faintly slurred. My tongue moved fine and my teeth still fit together, so my jaw wasn't broken. "Diana's."

"But yours is barely a hundred years old." Apparently, Ben had to be told a story only once to keep its details straight. "My guess is that he got into Eleni's apartment and saw her grail, too. Maybe he went back today to find an older one. How old *is* your chalice, Eleni?"

Rather than deny that she had one, the way she did earlier, she said, "Our grandmother's mother, she is a potter. She makes special cups, before the Balkan Wars." Before the *what?*

"That's 1912, 1913," translated Encyclopedia Ben. But he looked angry enough that even accessing little-known historical facts didn't much soothe him. His brows were low, his jaw tight as he threw worried glances toward me. It made him look more like his brother…but not in a bad way.

"My sisters, my cousins—we all have such cups for our altars. I think perhaps Kate and Diana do once as well?"

"*Did,*" I snarled. There was my life before Victor Fisher, and after—and they didn't have much in common.

"So Vic is after something older," translated Ben, taking a deep breath. "Maybe the original Hekate Chalice, if it really exists. Kate, didn't your friend Maggi say Grail Keepers are better at finding goddess cups than the average person?"

"He thinks I can find it for him because of who I am?" That, and he wanted the curse gone. But I hadn't mentioned that detail to Ben, for obvious reasons.

Eleni asked, "Then how old is this original grail he wishes us to find?" Because she was a Grail Keeper, too. I wasn't Victor's last chance at a grail-detector.

Ben used bottled water to redampen the handkerchief that a kindly old tourist had given us, then returned it gently against my sore, scraped jaw. Would he ever see me without bruises? He said, "Well…from what I've read, Hekate was originally a Karian goddess."

"Karian," I repeated blankly.

"Karia was a civilization in what's now southwest Turkey, from about the same time as the ancient Egyptians, and why did Vic call you Katie?"

I had to do a double take on that. "He did the night he killed my sister, too. Diana must have called me that."

"Oh. Well…" He frowned down at the rock between us. "Anyway, Hekate had become part of Greek religion by the 700s B.C. That means an early relic used in her worship could be over two thousand years old."

Eleni's eyes were big. "And very, *very* powerful."

"Well, I'm not doing it," I announced. "Victor really is crazy if he thinks I'd actually help him find something that valuable. Wherever it is, it's probably a lot safer than if I help him dig it up. Not that I'd even know where to start looking."

"You could try goddess sites," Ben suggested. "The remains of Eleusis aren't far from here. There are islands we could try, and Turkey isn't even that far, relatively speaking. So what do you suppose Vic meant when he said I had it wrong?"

"I don't know, and it doesn't matter where the grail is because *I'm not looking for it.* Not for him."

"But didn't Maggi Sanger say that it's time? That could mean the grail will be found by someone, either way."

If Her cup is kept safe, and its power joined with that of other goddess grails, their combined force could improve the situation of women a hundredfold. I have reason to think it's time.

"Maggi also warned that the grail can't be destroyed, or women would suffer. But how can I protect it without finding it? And how can I find it without endangering it?" Damn, I hated this stuff.

"If you feel better," Eleni interrupted, "we should take you back to my flat. You will stay with me, of course. I leave on Saturday for Istanbul, for a demonstration, but you may come as well if you wish? We are holding a free clinic for International Women's Day, and there is much work to be done."

I hadn't heard of International Women's Day, but that didn't mean anything. At the moment, I had more important things to consider. What could I do to stop Victor? How long could I stay away from my nursing job to protect Eleni? Would anything I did actually be enough?

And why had Hekate turned on me?

Because really, she had. I'd called on her for help, but this time I was nearly bitten by a poisonous snake.

Snakes, like dogs, are sacred to Hekate.

"Come," insisted Eleni—and from the way she held my gaze, I realized that she understood more than I'd given her credit for. "We have much to discuss."

Perhaps I could get a few answers, after all.

Nonna and Diana were not the only priestesses of Hekate that I knew.

When we went by Ben's hostel to pick up my luggage, he surprised me by insisting that Eleni and I go on alone. "I've got, um, stuff. To do," he added awkwardly.

"Stuff," I challenged. But despite his lingering frown of concern, all he did was nod stubbornly. So we went on without him. It felt strange to be separated from him, the one familiar person from home…but how wimpy was I, to care? Besides, I did need rest.

Still, I only got a few hours' nap on Eleni's sofa before she woke me again.

"It is time," she said.

Groggy from jet lag, and still shaken from the day's near misses, I just followed.

As it turned out, one of Eleni's roommates—a forty-something nurse named Thea—was also a goddess worshipper. She assured me that this wasn't common in Greece, which was mostly Orthodox Christian despite its pagan past. But Thea was a rebel, as proved by her recent divorce. The divorce rate here wasn't high, either.

Hefting a backpack full of occult supplies, we got on one of the electric trolleys outside the Plaka. When I suggested we grab something to eat on the way, Eleni told me we were "fasting." Resigned, I watched the ancient, modern, polluted, beautiful mess that was Athens out the window until we transferred onto a big orange bus for Elefsina.

Elefsina, it turns out, had once been ancient Eleusis.

"Wait," I protested as, with a slight lurch, the bus headed out. "Ben said that was a Hekate site. I told you, I'm not finding any grail just so Victor can get hold of it."

"We do not go there for the grail," Eleni assured me. "You have heard of the Eleusinian Mysteries, yes?"

I had to shake my head. Of course I hadn't.

It was Thea who explained further. "Long ago, twice a year, worshippers would make a pilgrimage from Kerameikos—the Athens community of the *kerameis,* or potters—along the Sacred Way to Eleusis. Perhaps…thirty kilometers? There they would celebrate the goddess Demeter and her daughter, Persephone."

I felt relieved to actually recognize something. "Isn't Persephone the daughter who gets kidnapped by Hades and taken to the underworld? And Mother Nature turns the whole world to winter because she's so upset."

Barely a month had passed since Diana's death. I could *so* relate to the need to make others suffer for one's pain, fair or not.

"But each year when Her daughter returns, spring comes," said Eleni. "Yes, this is the legend."

"The Greater Mysteries took place in the autumn," Thea continued, stretching back more comfortably on her bus seat. "At harvest time, when Persephone and Demeter parted. The Lesser Mysteries took place in the spring, for their reunion. This continued for perhaps two thousand years, until the Christians outlawed it."

"So… Eleusis *isn't* a Hekate site?"

Eleni laughed at my ignorance. Luckily, she had a nice, Diana-like laugh that invited you to share the joke. "Hekate, she is the guide in the legend. The one who takes Persephone from her mother each autumn and returns her each spring."

I looked out the window again, at the light edging toward sunset. The view of ugly factories and refineries was hardly inspiring. But I wasn't in the mood to be inspired, either. I was hungry. I was hurting. I was tired. And even after a month, I was still very angry.

While Hekate might still take people away to the Underworld, it's not like she ever gave them back anymore.

"So if we aren't going for the grail, why *are* we driving to Eleusis?" I asked.

It was my cousin Eleni who answered. "Is it not time we asked Hekate what *She* wishes?"

And at that, I wasn't quite as hungry or as tired. Sometimes the universe surprises you. This was it, the rest of the pilgrimage my *nonna* had suggested. This was my chance to ask Hekate how I could remove the curse from Ben! Except…

What if her answer was to cancel the curse entirely?

I thought of Victor licking his fingertips and smiling—*You cancel the damned curse*—and I knew I wouldn't do it. Not in a thousand lifetimes. Not for my own safety, and not even for Ben's. As long as I did nightly protection spells, he was safe enough. Right? Even if it *did* complicate that false, magical bond between us.

Still, maybe Hekate and I could work out something better. She owed me, if for nothing else than the snake.

I only wished the view of factories out the bus window, refineries on land that had once been sacred, weren't such a grim reminder of man's corruption of nature.

Of the Goddess.

Chapter 11

Victor didn't even hear the scooter coming. One minute he was limping along the Plaka—limping because he'd slipped and fallen on the path down from the Acropolis as he attempted to dodge Ben. He'd avoided his traitorous, bewitched brother, but wrenched his ankle. Damned curse.

The next minute, it felt as if someone shoved him hard enough that he flew four feet and crashed into a cluster of bistro tables and tall metal chairs. A woman screamed. Wine bottles smashed to the cobblestones beside Victor's head, which hit ground as hard as it had that night when his parents died and the men in the black masks threw him against the wall.

The world closed briefly around him, going red, then negative, then resolving itself into normalcy. Or what had become horribly, painfully normal for him, this past month.

This was her fault.

Victor pushed himself unsteadily to his hands and knees. A waiter shouted at the biker. The biker gestured impatiently at Victor, as if to say it was the pedestrian's fault for being in the way. Neither of them knew the truth about Kate Trillo's damned curse.

Victor struggled to his feet, against bystanders' protests. He knew he wasn't hurt badly enough to need a hospital, because that wasn't how the curse worked. The witch had wished him—him and Ben—a long, lingering death, not a fast one. She'd cursed them with years, not months, of misery. As if Diana's defiance had been *his* doing.

No, the Trillo women were asking for it.

Waving away the Greek protests of the waiter, even of the biker, Victor limped on. Every step was grinding agony. Until Kate Trillo took off the damned curse...

Hadn't she realized he was serious? Didn't she grasp that he was the only reason she was still alive?

He *owned* her now! Once he had the cup and took up the mantle his parents had so stupidly thrown aside, he'd have more than enough power to make sure the witch paid. She liked her suffering slow, lingering? Victor had entertained himself with enough small animals during his youth to know he was up to meeting her every desire in that arena.

And then some.

After what felt like unending agony—were his ribs broken, or just bruised?—Victor reached his hotel, made it to the elevator without garnering too much attention and then to his room. He half sat, half fell onto his bed and found himself staring at his hands. Especially the one that had touched Kate Trillo's bloody face, after he saved her worthless life. Her dark eyes had been wide, her olive complexion so pale....

And she was with his *brother?*

The bitch had cast a spell on Ben, as surely as on Victor. But only Victor realized it. Nothing else explained how badly he ached for the little tramp, or why Ben would betray him—*him*—like this, except for magic. Her obvious love spell wasn't why Victor had saved her. He'd done that so she could cancel out her curse and find his grail. But maybe…

Trying to catch his breath around his injured ribs, he pulled open the drawer beside the bed and pulled out a linen envelope. His hand shook as he used a business card to scrape dried flakes of Kate Trillo's blood out from under his fingernails, into the envelope.

Vic didn't know shit about black magic.

But he knew something about fighting fire with fire….

Picture the spookiest witches' circle you can imagine. Waxing moon. Howling dogs. Dancing torchlight. Wind in the trees.

Now get rid of most of the trees, and add Greek ruins.

That was the three of us at Eleusis.

Demeter's old sanctuary wasn't up high like the Acropolis—which, considering my afternoon scare, was a good thing—but it was huge. In fact, some of it sat below ground level, where it had been excavated out of the scrubby hillside. Stone courtyards spread out at different levels in front of us, connected by roads lined with low walls. Square foundations marked the places where temples had once stood. Crumbling stairways, rounded from centuries of erosion, and columns broken off at different heights interrupted the unnatural openness of an area that should've had buildings, and roofs… and people.

The people who'd originally worshipped here had been

dead for thousands of years. But I couldn't help but imagine their ghosts still lingered, all around us.

Add to that the fact that we were officially trespassing, that the sun was setting and that dogs howled in the nearby hills, and I felt unnerved even before we reached a cave. "Look, I don't want to go to a Greek jail," I protested, but Eleni only laughed.

"My friend Dimitri knows we are here," she assured me. "He is the head guard."

My cousin seemed to know a lot of guards, didn't she?

But apparently the site officially closed to visitors at three o'clock in the afternoon—"fifteen o'clock," Thea had said—during winter hours. And what we meant to do didn't exactly invite visitors or afternoon sunlight. So here we stood in the shadows, flouting legalities.

We stopped in front of a gaping cave—two large, black-stained arches into the hillside, like dark eyes. In front of it, grass and tiny yellow flowers grew over pitted, pale flag-stones. Half a low wall fronted the space, and more stone blocks lay around, as if tossed there. A final block, newer, had Greek words carved on it. Thea said it called this place the Ploutonion, the mythical entrance into Hades, after the Roman version, Pluto, of the word *Hades*.

Wow. If Hekate lingered anyplace physical, it had to be here, right?

We spent time setting up our circle—three unlit torches, a heavily embroidered altar cloth spread out picnic-blanket style, and Eleni's athame and goblet. I caught my breath when I saw the cup, it was so similar to Diana's. But the differences were as clear as the resemblance. Same potter. Different pot.

She opened a jar and sloshed brown liquid into the goblet.

"It is dandelion tea," she informed me. "Not the hallucinogens of ancient priestesses."

That was a relief, anyway.

She also set out plates of food, honey cakes and cheese and garlic. My stomach growled at the scent, but I knew from my training that this food was for after the ritual, and much of it would be for Hekate.

Thea helped me henna my good hand and the fingertips of my cast hand with sacred symbols. She drew a pentagram on both her palms, but I painted a lopsided *vesica piscis* on mine. Then she said, "This was once to symbolize blood," and my stomach twisted.

More dogs set into howling, closer to us, just over the hill. A breeze kicked through the distant yew trees.

"She comes," whispered Eleni with a smile, and my stomach turned another full twist. The sun had set, revealing a three-quarter moon in a denim-blue, darkening twilight sky. When we lit the torches, they danced and twisted in the breeze. Beyond us stretched the ruins of a long-dead sanctuary in a land that couldn't help but feel foreign to me.

I could see why witchcraft scared so many outsiders—but it wasn't supposed to be this scary for the witches, was it? Then again, the other witches seemed fine with it.

But none of them had probably been tossing curses around.

We started the ritual. First, we cast our circle, meaning we walked a slow circumference around our torches and altar cloth, marking out a physical boundary for ourselves and our magic this night. Then we called the quarters. Eleni, who started at the East, did so in Greek. But I could tell by how she spread her hands, and tipped her head back in the dark night, that she was asking the spirits of the East, the element of Air, to be with us.

Since I was in the right spot, I went next. "I call upon the spirits of the South, element of Fire, to harken to our circle. May we know your warmth, your courage. So mote it be!"

Thea went next, to call the West—in Greek—and Eleni finished with the North. That's the benefit of ritual. Like hearing a Catholic service in Latin, you still catch the important stuff.

But I.

Felt.

Nothing.

Bupkis. Zip. Zed. Nada.

Tendrils of pale cloud fingered across the moon. Dogs still howled. A dust devil rose and spun past our ritual. The dark, gaping eyes of Pluto's cave watched us with millennia of indifference.

I didn't feel magic, or powerful, or wise. I felt no different at all. Except for feeling increasingly helpless, and frustrated at being helpless, I was unchanged.

This was as witchy as you could get without a trio of old hags stirring a cauldron and chanting "Bubble bubble toil and trouble"—or whatever it is that those witches chant—and *I was no different than before.*

Hekate was giving me the cold shoulder.

We knelt on the uneven ground, each of us a point on a human triangle, inside our circle. We passed around the chalice of Eleni's dandelion tea, sipping its odd, soothing flavor. Then we bowed our heads to make our own silent entreaties to the Lady—as if She would even listen. And I'd never felt so alone. Not even—

"Hello, Miss Pouty Pants. How's it hanging?"

I looked up from my meditation, startled. And there stood Diana, alive as can be, her hands planted on her hips. I considered reaching across and nudging Eleni—both she and

Thea had their heads bent in prayer—but if Diana wasn't real, then having Eleni look would confirm that. And I guess I didn't want it confirmed.

"Hi," *I whispered, like I used to whisper to my best friend in school, hoping the teacher wouldn't hear.*

Diana laughed. "Don't sweat it, this is trance time. They won't notice. So come on, spill. What's this latest crisis of faith all about?"

It didn't help that she held up her hands and made finger quotes around the words "crisis of faith."

"Hello? I almost fell off the freaking Acropolis."

"Yeah. That rocked." *She widened her eyes at my expression.* "Okay, one? It's not like you didn't survive. And two? I'm already dead. Dying? Not so big a deal anymore. So is that it?"

"Is that it? Di, the man who murdered you has our YaYa's chalice. He wants me to help find an even older one, for who knows what reasons. He warned me not to trust Ben—I think—and even though that should probably be a ringing endorsement for Ben, considering the source, I'm still worried. And…this!" *I swept my arm out, to indicate the other two witches.* "I don't belong here. I don't get it!"

She shrugged. "If you say so."

"What's that supposed to mean?"

"Hello?" *And yes, she was mocking me.* "Magic 101, remember? We create reality through our thoughts. If you think you don't belong, you probably won't. If you say you don't belong, you really won't. Hell, Katie, why not make it rhyme, just to be absolutely sure?"

"You think I'm *choosing to make this hard?"*

"On some level, yeah! You always have. How many

times do I have to tell you? Tina Sutherland's hair was not your fault!"

I stared at her. I blinked, tensing. I asked, "Who?"

"Don't tell me you can't remember. Second grade? Tina Sutherland? She had long, red, curly, Felicity-hair, and she lorded it over you like she was Queen of the World."

I spread my fingers and shrugged. "Nothing."

But was it really nothing, or was the tension in my neck, in my shoulders, calling me a liar?

Diana plopped down on a broken-off column, eyebrows rising. "Interesting! You really are in denial."

"Di! What does this have to do with anything?"

"Okay, keep in mind that I only got this secondhand. I was starting junior high by then, thank you very much. But for a couple of weeks, you couldn't stop griping about Tina Sutherland and her hair. You used to mock how she would toss it over her shoulder." She mimicked the action. "You even asked Mom if you could dye your hair red, and she said you'd have to bleach it first, and over her dead body."

I still didn't remember, but thank goodness. Me with red hair instead of black would just be...wrong.

"So on the day the school pictures came in, you came home crying, and you begged me not to tell Mom, and I asked you what's up."

"I remember the picture," I admitted slowly—it's not like my mother and aunt and grandmothers didn't have all my school pictures, no matter how awful, displayed somewhere in their home. "I hated that picture."

My hair had been in braids, but one of them had slid half out, and I'd looked lopsided. My throat began to close at the *very thought of it…which should have been odd, what with it being* seventeen years ago.

"Yeah, well, that's not why you were crying. Sure, you hated the picture. And you hated that Tina's pictures turned out like some little fashion model's. But what really bothered you was that… you'd touched her hair? I didn't quite get that part either, but it started this whole…"

But I was starting to remember that, too. I didn't want to, but I was. I'd had the seat behind Tina. The autumn was unusually warm that year, and the air-conditioning wasn't running, so the school windows were open. A box fan wedged into one of them tried to cool the whole room. Tina's auburn curls kept shifting, shifting, in that artificial breeze, like something magical. And I'd felt so envious, I'd reached out and touched one of those gleaming curls….

Hey, I'd only been eight.

But my finger caught in her hair, and she'd spun on me. Ow! Keep your greasy hands off me, you dirty little dago!

"She insulted Dad," I whispered now. Because to insult my Italian side was, of course, to insult my father. "But why would that make me cry? Why didn't I just punch her?"

"You tried. She dodged and tattled. You had to stay in during recess."

I stared at my sister—or my sister's ghost—feeling sick as the rest of the memory shoved into place. We'd been studying magic at home, of course, what with my mom being a witch. And I knew our family rules. Harm none. Ask permission. What you send forth comes back at you three times as powerful. *But I'd been so angry, so very angry, that when I saw one single, sparkling thread of curving red hair on my desk, from where it had pulled from her head…*

I'd drawn a picture of Tina with outrageously long, curly

hair flowing out behind her. Then I taped the strand of real hair to it. And then—

Then I'd whispered, Pretty hair isn't there. *And I'd torn the hair—drawn and real—right off the picture. But the rip didn't go right, and it took off part of her crudely drawn head. That had scared me.*

Once I couldn't take it back, guilt had set in. I mean…nobody really wants *to be a bad guy. Do they?*

Then Tina showed up outside the window with her friends to laugh at me. As she spun to go, with the usual flip of her hair—it caught in the fan. And the fan kept spinning, making a horrible grinding noise. Tina began screaming, caught, wrenched backward. I began screaming, imagining her face sliced right off, her blood splattered across the classroom, across me, like the worst horror movie.

That last part didn't happen, of course. It was a safety fan. A wire cage kept her face from being sliced off, though she claimed the blades came very close to her ear before our teacher got it unplugged. But her hair…her long, curly, auburn hair was history. The teacher had to use shears to free her.

And it was my fault. In my eight-year-old mind, Tina had almost died, her hair was gone, and it was my fault.

I shuddered, wishing I hadn't remembered. "That's why I gave up magic."

Diana nodded, as if she'd remembered with me.

"I didn't want that kind of power."

Diana nodded. "You hit a crossroads, and you made your choice."

"And I was right! *Look* at what I'd done! And what was my very next spell? I cursed the wrong guy!"

"That was an honest mistake. Anyone could have made it."

"*Anyone tossing curses around, you mean!*" Anyone evil.

"*Oh, get over yourself. I had a choice that day, too. You asked me not to tell Mom, so I didn't, and that was the wrong choice. I was only thirteen. What did I know? But Mom could have helped you get through it, could have taught you spells to help fix things. She could have kept you involved in the Craft, kept you from becoming such a coward about magic.*"

"*Such a* what?"

Diana folded her arms. "*A coward. At least you made choices back then. Now you hit a crossroads and you just…stand here.* '*Do I go this way? Do I go that way? Oh woe, what if one of them's a mistake?*'"

"*I have never said 'oh woe' in my life.*"

"*Find the damned chalice, Katie.*"

"*I don't even know where to look,*" *I reminded her.*

"*Well it's not like I do—you think death makes me all-knowing or something? Ask Ben. He seems pretty smart.*"

I considered it. "*No.*"

"*Why? Because a psycho killer who clearly has his own honesty issues told you not to trust Ben?*"

"*No, because the psycho killer wants me to find the chalice for him.*"

"*So you find the chalice and don't let him have it. How's that for a solution?*"

"*Or I just* let it stay hidden."

Diana rolled her eyes. "*Coward.*"

"*No. Sensible.*"

She glanced upward and to the side, as if ignoring me, but quietly repeated, "*Coward.*"

"*And just which one of us is dead?*"

She pretended to sneeze, but said, "*Coward!*" *into her*

*hand, and I started to laugh at how stupid that was, and then
I remembered she was dead and started to cry. And then, with
a final roll of her fingers, she wasn't there at all....*

And I was sitting in our dark, torch-lit circle, my eyes still
wet.

Face-to-face with the biggest, mangiest black dog I've
ever seen.

It panted sour dog breath into my face, its tongue lolling
out, its sharp teeth exposed in a canine grin. I slowly slid my
gaze to the women across from me, one at my right, one at
my left. Neither of them was meditating anymore. They were
staring with wide, worried eyes.

It was Thea who croaked the name first: "Hekate."

Eleni's eyes widened more, if that was possible, but she
blinked then in comprehension. "Hekate," she said. Her hand
trembling, she offered the dog our plate of cakes.

The big dog twisted around to gulp our "feast," but her
body still faced me. She could turn back at any moment.

Part of me thought, *Oh, please. No wonder nobody takes
magic seriously. A stray dog shows up, and we think it's a
goddess?*

But Diana's voice—or probably just the part of me more
open to magic—retorted, *"Oh, please. An impossibly huge
animal thought to be a symbol of Hekate walks into
your witches' circle in the middle of the night, and you
think it's what, a coincidence?"*

Maybe I was rejecting the possible symbolism because of
my supposed fear of magic. But I had that right, didn't I?

The dog licked the plate across the rocky ground with her
big tongue, then gave up on the chance of more food appear-

ing on it and turned back to me. She sat and said, "Whuff!" Once. Sharply. Like she was trying to tell me something.

I could think of only one thing Hekate would be telling me. *"No,"* I said clearly. "Witches have free will, too."

The dog whuffed at me again, more quietly, then turned and padded away, and that was that. I was done. Finished. I would tell Ben my decision, do what I could to keep an eye on Eleni, and deliberately *not* do what Victor wanted, because he had no more say over me than Hekate did. Less, in fact.

Why the hell would I find an even older chalice for a man who hadn't returned the first one, just so that he could steal it, too?

On the bus ride back into the city, away from those particular ruins and everything they held, Eleni and Thea were a lot more excited about the "sign" from the goddess than I was. Afterward we grabbed a quick dinner at an outdoor Gyro stall, savoring delicious lamb stuffed in a pita pocket with a yogurt dill sauce drizzled onto it. Athens was still wide awake—if anything, it woke more as the night went on. Maybe part of it was finally getting some food, but I felt surprisingly...free. *Normal,* even.

I didn't have to be anything I didn't want to be.

Eleni and Thea told me about the upcoming International Women's Day rally. Eleni was part of a contingent of female doctors and nurses traveling to Turkey to provide education, counseling, and free well-women exams near the demonstration area, and with my nursing background I could definitely be of help. With patients who weren't dying.

And then, promised Eleni, we could go to the beach.

For what felt like the first time since Diana's murder, I began to think about something other than death. *And* this was the perfect way to keep an eye on Eleni, just in case.

We'd be leaving the day after tomorrow, so I decided to tell Ben tonight. At least, that's what I told myself; why else would I want to see Ben? Eleni helped me find the hostel where he was staying but agreed to wait outside with Thea, looking over the selection of paperback books at yet another vendor's stall, while I went inside.

I've got something to tell you, I thought as I headed into the cramped, scuffed-linoleum-floor lobby, practicing.

No. That made it sound like I owed him something.

Ben, I don't know what else to do. Yeah, Victor's in Athens, but unless we can extradite him, what good does it—

No. Too wimpy.

Or maybe I could just say—

But someone grabbed me from behind, his hand curving over my mouth, before I could even *think* of saying anything else.

Chapter 12

"Shhh," warned the man whose hand covered my mouth.

I might not be much of a fighter, but I still had the good sense to stomp down, hard, on the guy's foot.

"*Son of a—!*" He let go as he pulled away from me, drawing his hurt foot up, gasping. "Ow!" he whispered.

I knew that raspy voice, and I readied myself to try another of the sloppy but effective moves my cousin the cop had taught me over the last few weeks. This one would consist of jamming the heel of my hand into my attacker's nose. And it's not like Victor Fisher didn't present me with a damned easy target.

Luckily, his eyes widened before I could strike—and I recognized my mistake. There was no missing the immediate connection, now. "*Ben?*"

"Shhh!" he repeated, wincing. And standing on one foot. "And *ow.*"

"What the hell do you think you're—"

He widened his eyes insistently, and pointed.

I recognized the large redheaded man emerging from the bathroom right off the lobby. This time when Ben pulled me around the corner into the kitchenette so we wouldn't be seen, I let him.

"Sorry about the foot," I whispered as he leaned against me to share the best view and we peeked back out.

"Sorry about the scare," Ben whispered back, his breath pleasantly warm across my temple. "I just didn't want—"

But that part was kind of obvious. "What the hell is your radio partner doing in Greece?"

"He said he's here to help," Ben explained. "He said since he set up our meeting that night, he feels responsible for Vic getting off."

He drew a deep breath and added, "He's lying."

His voice fell hollow on that last part, and I turned from my view of Al Barker consulting a folding map to better see Ben. His dark eyes radiated accusation that I felt glad wasn't aimed at me. "How do you know?"

"I know Al. I know how he gets when he's on a story. I guess this time, I'm the story."

He couldn't trust anybody, could he?

"So you decided to follow him when he left?" I asked.

Ben nodded. "But he went into the bathroom first, and then you showed up."

"Why didn't he use the bathroom in your room?"

"You haven't stayed in a lot of hostels, have you?" When I shook my head, lost, Ben smiled his lopsided smile. "Private bathrooms aren't very common."

In the meantime, Al was heading out. So Ben and I followed—

Only to be intercepted by Eleni and Thea. My cousin brightened with recognition and started to make introductions, but I interrupted. "You go ahead," I urged Ben. "Go!"

With a guilty look toward my cousin, he did, leaving me to make our excuses. Eleni thought shadowing a radio personality through nighttime Athens sounded exciting, but I convinced her that even two of us were pretty obvious. Four was closer to slapstick than I wanted to go. So with a final, quick hug, she and Thea headed back for the flat, and I tried to catch up with Ben past all the cafés, gift shops, clubs and jewelry stores of the Plaka.

If Ben hadn't been watching for me, and caught my hand as I passed, I might not have found him at all.

Or maybe I would have. That residual energy link between us, from the curse, seemed stronger the more time we spent together. When we touched, it was like completing a circuit.

For me, anyway.

"You haven't lost him yet?" I asked, as Ben drew me through the crowd of clubbers and tourists wandering the cobblestone streets.

"It helps that there aren't a lot of Greek tall redheads," he noted wryly.

Good point. Other than Ben's slight limp, the two of us blended in pretty well, with our black hair and olive complexions. Ben's cheekbones were an added bonus, and the angle of his jaw, and his long, dark lashes…anyway, he looked Mediterranean. Al didn't have that benefit.

It also helped that Al didn't hop any public transportation. After some blocks—hard to count, in this maze—he stopped in the street and looked around.

Ben drew me quickly back into the cover of a gift shop,

still open and bright with artificial light despite the late hour. It said something about my appreciation for holding hands with him that I didn't pull loose and complain that I knew when to duck. I did know, of course. And I didn't have a lot of free hands lately. But…

Backlash, I reminded myself. *It's not a real connection; it's residual energy from the magic.*

"What did you see?" I asked instead, watching his profile.

"Al's stopped to look around." Ben leaned back out to take another look. "Oh, damn."

"I help you?" demanded the shopkeeper, who looked more like he should be herding sheep. "You wish postcards to remember your stay in Athens? Pistachios, for your friends back home?"

I looked for myself. Yeah. Al was gone.

"He was there a minute ago," said Ben. "Great."

"Worry heads?" suggested the shopkeeper. *"Matia?"*

Matia? I looked to see what he meant—and was struck by a sudden awareness of real magic, right here between snow globes of the Acropolis and dolls wearing those funny pleated tunics and pom-pom shoes of Greek soldiers. *Matia* turned out to be those blue glass disks with round eyes painted on them, like the one Eleni had sent me after Diana died, to ward off the evil eye. Mass-produced protection.

Even after saying no to Hekate—literally—I could still sense the magic, like someone seeing green and red in a mostly color-blind world. Damn it.

"I guess we should just keep walking," suggested Ben. "Maybe we'll catch up to him."

On the one hand, not an hour ago I was arguing with Diana about how badly my magic usually turned out.

On the other hand, I *wasn't* a coward. Diana might be a

figment of my imagination. This wasn't the same as finding the grail for Victor. *And what the hell was Al doing here?*

"Let me try something," I suggested. With an apologetic smile toward the hopeful merchant, I led Ben in the direction we'd last seen Al. I could do this.

Thoughts hold power, words more so, spoken words more, and rhymes even more than that. "What rhymes with Al?"

"Pal?" Ben suggested quietly. "Shall? Guadalcanal?" Then he thought to ask, "Wait a minute…why?"

I took a deep breath, let it out, and tried to concentrate. Like Diana had said, minimum effort can still bring maximum results. Magic also worked by natural means. Looking around, I located more of those ever-present pots of geraniums nearby. Crouching beside them, I collected a small handful of fallen red petals, dry and curling, from the cobblestones beneath.

Ben's gaze on me made me self-conscious.

"Wait here," I suggested, and left him to go ahead, to the last spot we'd seen Al. I took another deep breath, tried to sense the energies around me, and deliberately believed in them even if I couldn't sense them.

"We shall," I whispered simply, "find Al."

Opening my hand, I blew gently on the petals.

They fluttered off to the side of me, landing at the doorway of a narrow building called the Hotel Zeus. I shivered—but in a good way, for once.

I beckoned to Ben before ducking into the lobby.

To judge by all the shiny glass and marble and dark paneling in the lobby and the posh bar beyond it, rooms in the Hotel Zeus had more luxury than just private bathrooms. This place compared to Ben's hostel the way…well, the way Victor Fisher's clothes compared to Ben's.

Coincidentally, the concierge said, "Mr. Fisher! Is there anything I can do for you?"

Ben and I exchanged telling glances. Well, now we knew where Victor was staying, didn't we? But why did Al...?

When Ben said nothing, I stepped in. "This is kind of embarrassing," I admitted, smiling, "but Mr. Fisher? He forgot his room number. What with it not being printed on the key card or anything, you know..."

Ben's gaze cut to me, doubtful. But when I pleaded with him with my eyes, he nodded.

"Ah, yes—a security precaution," agreed the concierge, and wrote something on a memo pad. "Here you are, Mr. Fisher."

Ben took the memo, dark eyes flicking across the number on it. "Oh. Yes. That's it, all right." He wasn't real convincing, but that might have been more obvious to me. "I transposed the eight and the...uh, thank you."

"Any time," smarmed the concierge, while Ben led me to the elevator.

"I don't like doing that," he muttered, as soon as the door closed.

"Doing what?"

"Pretending I'm Victor."

"*He* pretends he's *you*."

Ben widened his eyes, as if I'd made his point for him.

"Fire with fire," I reminded him.

"Two wrongs don't make a right," he reminded me back. "Do you even have a plan here? I'd think you'd want to stay as far away from Victor as you can get."

"I do. But what are the chances that Al and Victor just happen to be registered at the same hotel?"

Ben rolled his eyes. Chances were low.

"Wait here, then," he said, as we stepped off the elevator. "I'll see if he's inside. Al's voice carries."

I nodded, and he did. I didn't like how exposed we were in this beautifully carpeted, darkly paneled hallway. But Ben wasn't outside the doorway for long before he came back to me, edgier than ever. "I can't make out what he's saying, but Al's definitely there. Why don't you go down and wait for me in the bar—"

"What? No!"

"I don't want you anywhere near Victor, Katie," Ben insisted—and maybe he saw something in my expression, because he changed that to, "He's my problem. He's always been my problem. Let me handle him."

"By what—knocking on the door and asking what's up?" From his stormy expression, that's exactly what he had planned. "Like they'd tell you the truth."

"It's a better chance than if I *don't* ask." Good point.

"Or how's this? We separate them. We'll wait in the bar for Al to leave, assuming he does. I'll run into him and ask him what's up, and…you really aren't scared to talk to Victor?"

"He won't hurt me." Maybe Ben saw the doubt in my expression, because he ducked his head, widened his eyes. "Really. He's had plenty of chances over the years."

"Then while I'm talking to Al, you talk to your brother. Afterward, you and I hook up at your hostel and compare notes. Maybe between their two versions, we can piece together at least some of the truth."

Before I leave for Turkey.

"And you won't just let me handle this?" asked Ben. But

when I folded my arms, he pressed the down button for the elevator.

That's how I ended up having a drink with Ben Fisher, at midnight, in Athens.

"So…that was pretty cool," he said after a long, awkward silence, once the waiter brought glasses of red wine for us. "The thing with the flower petals."

Observant, wasn't he?

I shrugged, watching the lobby reflected in the mirrored wall behind him. What could Al and Victor have to discuss that would take this long? Hell, what could they be discussing at all?

I thought of something Maggi Stuart had mentioned, about the kind of men who joined the Comitatus. "Would you say Al's a powerful presence in the telecommunications industry?"

"He's a well-known personality, anyway," Ben admitted, but didn't seem to be catching on to what I was thinking. He seemed distracted. "So how long have you been practicing magic?"

I must have looked surprised, because he quickly added, "If you don't mind my asking. I mean, if you've taken a vow of secrecy or something, I completely understand…."

At a loss, he took a sip of wine and watched the lobby.

My sister had attended public rituals and given continuing-education workshops on witchcraft. Secrecy wasn't the issue. "We've got witches on both sides of the family," I told him. "My mother tried to teach us, but Diana was a better student than I was. She understood so much more about the energies, about the ethics…" Maybe I wasn't the right person to discuss ethics. "And she stuck with it. I decided to become a nurse, instead."

"Are the two paths that incompatible?" he asked. "I thought a lot of witches were healers."

I remembered the second grade, and poor Tina's face

squished against the safety grating on the fan, her hair being twisted tighter and tighter…. "Not always."

He continued to watch me a little too intently. When he noticed me noticing, he smiled, dropped his gaze and took another sip of wine. This was the perfect time to confess the curse to him, wasn't it? *Hey, Ben, speaking of the dark side of magic…*

"Diana was the real witch," I insisted, instead. "I'm just doing what I can to protect my cousin, and then I'm done with it. Tell me more about what you found on Victor's computer, about Eleni and why he wants the Hekate Cup?"

"Victor's always kept journals." Ben eyed the lobby over my shoulder, but I suspected that was to avoid looking directly at me as much as to spot Al. Either that, or he seriously disliked the lobby. "Like an autobiography. Now that I've read them, the challenge lies in differentiating between what's real and what he's fantasized in order to make himself sound important."

"Like?"

"Like the business with that secret society, the Comitatus. The way Vic tells it, our father was a member but our mom convinced him to quit. She said she'd go public if he didn't get out. Vic writes that they were murdered to keep her quiet. He says…he says he saw it all."

Just like Maggi and I had guessed. The murder part, anyway. *Knives.* But— "How could he even remember? You two were so little when it happened."

"I remember some of it."

Oh. I didn't know what to say about that, so I reached across the bistro table between us and covered his hand with mine. *Connection.* "I'm sorry."

Maybe we had more in common than I'd ever thought.

Except…I hadn't been only six, when I'd walked in on a murder.

Ben leaned suddenly closer. "The thing is, I saw these guys, too—before I ran for the neighbor's, I mean, to call for help. They were thugs. They wore black ski masks, not cloaks or hoods. So the whole secret society thing could still be a figment of peoples' imaginations. Except…our parents really were murdered. The killers never were caught. And if Vic didn't find where Mom hid her alleged proof, how would he have known about the rest of it?"

"The rest of it being…?"

"Apparently he used what Mom had collected to track down other Comitatus members. He hacked into computers, bugged telephones, did everything he could to gather data, and he decided that finding a goddess cup for them would be the way to get our family reinstated. That's why he pretended to be me, doing research for the *Superrational Show,* asking around the pagan community about chalices. That's what led him—"

Ben shut up, but it was way too late.

"That's what led him to Diana," I finished for him, the taste of red wine suddenly bitter in my mouth.

Ben nodded, sympathy thick in his gaze.

"What did he say in his journal about killing her?"

"Nothing." But he was *so* lying. And that meant—

I stood, dizzy. "It's all on his computer, isn't it? That son of a bitch *confessed* in his journal, didn't he?"

Ben winced up to meet my glare. "He didn't use names. It's hard to tell what's real and what's he's fantasized."

Bullshit. "Get me a copy."

"You won't want to read it."

"I said, *get me a copy.*"

"I already asked my attorney, Kate. It's not like any of it's admissible in court."

"Damn it!" And before I even knew what I was doing, I picked up my glass of wine and threw it, smashing it hard against the mirrored wall behind Ben. He flinched away from the explosion of glass and wine, but red droplets splattered across his cheek and shoulder all the same.

So much for our stealthy stakeout. Most of the bar fell silent. One drunken tourist even called, *"Opah!"*

Ben stared at the wall behind him, then turned back to me, his gaze dark with accusation and…hurt. He reached a slow hand to his cheek and wiped away wine…and something darker. Blood.

I'd hit him with flying glass, and he was bleeding.

And heaven help me, my first instinct was to use it in magic, to force him to share whatever he'd learned about Diana's murder. *By this blood that brothers bind—*

Feeling sick, I spun and fled the bar, fled the Hotel Zeus, fled onto the crowded streets of the Plaka. Lights, bright against the night sky, disoriented me. Noise, loud with languages I couldn't translate, surrounded me. Everything blurred and tipped, and I didn't understand. I'd been raised to harm none. I'd been raised to use magic only for the good of all, only according to the free will of all. I knew that was possible—my mother, my grandmothers, my sister, all of them were kind people, good witches. It couldn't just be the magic. *It had to be me.*

What was I becoming? What kind of a horrible stereotype…?

"Katie!" I didn't even hear Ben calling me until he'd grabbed my shoulder, turned me around. And no, it definitely wasn't Victor. Wine still stained his shirt. Luckily, it wasn't a very good shirt. Blood stained his cheek. "What was that?"

I shook my head, backed away from him.

He grabbed my arm. *"Talk to me."*

"No. Let me go. I'll just hurt you."

"I'll take my chances." Despite the fact that he was bleeding because of me. And that had been *without* magic.

"You don't understand," I warned him. "You don't know what I'm capable of." Or maybe, since he'd read Victor's journal…did he?

"So tell me."

But if he didn't know, I wouldn't—couldn't—tell him. Instead, I retraced our steps from earlier, as far as the souvenir shop. I grabbed one of the *matia* and paid for it with what I hoped wasn't too much money—it was Euros, after all. *Protect this man,* I thought desperately, ignoring the merchant's offer of a bag or a receipt. Instead, I held the blue glass disk with its magical eye as tightly as any good-luck amulet has ever been held, and closed my eyes. *Protect Ben.*

From me.

But I didn't say it out loud—I couldn't bear more attention. And it didn't rhyme.

As far as spells go, it felt about as powerful as saying "Bless you" after a sneeze. Bring on the curses, and I was a regular Wicked Witch of the Lower Westside. But let me try something positive, and it fizzled.

Could I be more useless?

"Let me take you back to your cousin's, okay?" Sliding a hand warily onto my back by inches, as if he expected me to attack him again, Ben guided me in that direction.

"What about Al?" I asked. But I did start walking.

"I'll worry about Al."

"But he and Victor are up to something."

"Then they'll be up to something tomorrow, too."

Partly because I was afraid of what I'd do if I fought him, and partly because I was just so freaking tired, I stopped protesting. Just as well. I doubt I could have found my way back to Eleni's without Ben along, just now. Maybe I was just jetlagged. Or maybe I was wiped out from the ritual earlier that evening…or from my near-death experience on the Acropolis. But I wasn't in great shape to tail Al Barker any farther that night.

Better to fight another day.

In the meantime, the ancient streets got quieter and quieter. The waxing moon shed a silvery light across us and across the Acropolis high above us, making me think of a song— something about "When the moon is full and high." The air was warm for March, and smelled of flowers. And Ben's arm, which found its way around my waist, was solid, real, warm. His shoulder made a good headrest.

"I'm sorry," I whispered, as we got closer to Eleni's apartment. "I don't know what got into me back there."

"Rage, maybe?" he suggested. "My God, Kate. Your sister was murdered. Charges were dropped against the man you know is guilty. Then I tell you that there may be proof, and that you can't use it? I'd be throwing things, too. Maybe worse."

Really? I turned in the cradle of his arm as we walked, to better examine his long-jawed, hawk-nosed profile in the moonlight. Was my curse in Victor's journal? *Did Ben know?*

"How much worse?"

"You must want to kill him."

Even as I sank with relief—*he didn't know, couldn't know*—he stopped walking and studied my face with something like…anguish.

"And I look just like him," he said. "That can't help."

No, it didn't help either one of us. It couldn't be easy to know that his twin brother, a man who shared his DNA, was capable of something like cold-blooded murder.

"Katie," Ben said, the rasp of his voice becoming a whisper. "I'm so very, very sorry for everything…."

I never would have imagined wanting him to kiss me— until he did.

Chapter 13

Ben's lips were soft. He smelled really good, like soap and spices. A soft curl of his black hair brushed past my cheek. But what I noticed most of all was a now overwhelming sense of…of completion. Like a puzzle piece clicking into place.

Like we'd been meant to kiss, all along.

He drew back slightly, his dark eyes searching mine in the moonlight, making sure it was all right, longing for it to be.

Enough with the hesitance, already. I closed the space between us and kissed him back. *Click,* went that connection between us, as satisfying as the press of lips to lips, as how he slid a hand over my shoulder to loosely cup my neck, as how he gradually opened his mouth to mine. Whether he kissed a lot of women or not, facts and figures weren't the only area where this guy had natural aptitude.

I slid my good hand down the long line and curve of his

back, onto his tight butt. He caught his breath with a soft sound of approval, and wove his fingers into my hair. Despite everything, he wasn't scared of me. *Yes....*

This feeling in me was the opposite of death and destruction. This was what moonlit nights in Athens were made for.

When the moon is full and high...

Then I pulled back, eyes wide, because I suddenly remembered why we felt so connected.

The curse. The damned *curse!* When you cast a spell on a person, it's an energy bond, like loving someone or hating someone. It ties the two of you together. That was all that was happening between us, and it was my doing, and I really resented this being so artificial, because for a moment—one poignant, happy moment—I'd thought...

Yeah, me and magic. What a great pairing *that* turned out to be.

"I'm sorry," said Ben immediately—I'd never known a guy who apologized so much. Maybe he was making up for every apology his brother owed and never gave. "It's not like you've... God, every time you look at me, you must see—"

"No." I tried to press my fingers against his lips, but the round *matia* I still clutched got in the way. "You don't look like him. Not really."

Not to anyone who could really see.

"You're a good liar," he said with a smile, leaning closer. It almost broke my heart to step back from him.

He didn't know he was under my spell. And until I had the guts to tell him...

Or at least to protect him from it.

Like that, I knew what to do. "Wait here," I murmured, and turned away from him. Several steps down the quiet sidewalk, my back to him, I thrust the *matia* up into the light of the waxing moon. I willed the words, and they came in an intense whisper.

"Power of this talisman," I murmured, "protection of this seeing eye. Be with Ben and ward off danger—know my magic, hear my cry. Keep him safe within your sight whenever evil bides nearby."

Even on a whisper, fairly sure he couldn't hear me, this could have seemed too lame for words. But a burst of power ripped through me, then and there, like the amulet was a lightning rod and I was some kind of conduit between the Lady Moon and the Mother Earth.

I called the power and, unlike my attempt to contact the Goddess, it was right here in my hand. Almost as electrifying, as satisfying as the kiss had been.

Almost.

Suddenly wiped, I turned and closed the space between us, pressed the *matia* into Ben's hand. "Do me a favor," I said. "Keep this with you. All the time."

He took it on my command, though with his brow furrowed—and his long-lashed attention seemed equally divided between the charm and my lips. "It's warm," he stated. "From you?"

Yeah. My touch was why it felt warm to him, why not? "Promise to keep it on you."

"Why do I think you know something I don't?"

"You know a lot that I don't, too," I reminded him. When he frowned, I added, "All that stuff about the history of the Holy Grail, and what Hekate sites are where and…stuff. All I know is magic."

"That's all?" Ben actually smiled at that. He was trying.

"I'm starting to think it's too much." Starting? Hell, right now I wished I could end all this without ever lighting another candle or speaking another rhyme. The same magic that had lit my mother's and sister's lives was turning me darker and darker. What if I never again emerged from this blackness I'd been weaving around myself?

The least I could do was not drag this man down with me. It seemed as though all I was doing lately was endangering people, and—

A scream stabbed the night. Immediately, Ben's hands were on my shoulders, drawing me beside him, behind him.

The screams didn't stop.

I looked up, horrified to realize that we'd been standing beside Eleni's building. The terrified screams floated down to us, from what could be—

The third floor.

I've never run up three flights of winding stairs so fast in all my life. Ben tried to stay ahead of me, but I outdistanced him. Eleni's apartment house was converted from an old mansion, so it didn't have the symmetrical layout of the buildings I was more used to. Her and Thea's "flat" had once been a cluster of servants' quarters, now connected.

When I hit the door, the knob refused to turn in my hand, and I bounced off. *Locked.*

But someone inside was still screaming.

"Eleni!" I threw my shoulder against the door again— same result.

Ben banged on it, beside me. "Stand back."

The screams suddenly cut off. Neighbors appeared on the landings, looking up.

"No, wait." I took a deep breath and, despite having given magic up, like, twice in the past half hour, I concentrated. And

there, right in front of Ben, I murmured, "This I vow, open
now!"

Maybe it was the spell, or coincidence, but I heard the lock
turn—and Thea, who'd done the unlocking, managed to jump
out of the way of the door as I flung it open.

Magic works by natural means.

"Where's Eleni?" I demanded, while Thea pointed,
wide-eyed, toward my cousin's bedroom. I bolted across
the living room just ahead of Ben, into the bedroom—and
froze in the doorway.

There Eleni lay in her nightshirt, dead still, on the floor.

*And something horribly cold, horribly unnatural, lurked
in the shadowy corners.*

"English," I heard Ben insisting just behind me, as Thea
went on and on in Greek. Maybe his grasp of the language
wasn't so great after all. "Slower, Thea, or in English. Please!"

"She...she just started screaming!"

The scene in front of me shifted subtly. For a long moment,
the awful yellow wallpaper of Eleni's bedroom faded, taking
on the muted tones of Diana's and my living room.

"I wanted to go to her," Thea continued, "but...but I could
not!"

"Why not?" demanded Ben.

The fake-wood-patterned linoleum beneath Eleni's prone
form shifted into blood-soaked carpet before my eyes.

"Something..." Thea began to sob. "Something is still in
there!"

Eleni's tangle of black hair, so like mine, seemed to turn
dark blond. Memories threatened to devour me. But then she
moaned, the faintest, protesting moan.

She was alive.

And from the corner, feeding off our fear, the something

that had kept Thea out of the room seemed to stretch, to grow, to loom over us with a silent promise: *You're next.*

If it had had some kind of shape—a werewolf, a demon, *something*—maybe it wouldn't have been so frightening. Even if it were something real—a killer. Victor. But this thing stank of evil magic, and it was nothing that could be described, nothing that could be seen or touched…and everything that could be feared.

And I'd be damned if I'd lose someone else.

"Back," I growled, reaching ahead of me with my hand flat, projective. "Whatever you are, *begone.*"

The shadows seemed to twist, to coil—but that could have been the shadow of Ben pressing closer behind me. Natural means.

"What the hell," he muttered. He sensed it, too. "Katie, *wait!*"

But I was walking into the room, walking right up to my cousin's form. "You want to take me on?" I asked whatever it was.

Nothing responded except for shifting shadows, eddying drafts and a stench of evil. But hey, this was an unexpected bonus to being a bad guy.

It thought *it* was evil?

"You came looking for me?" I demanded, only recognizing as the words escaped me that this was exactly what had happened. Whatever it was hadn't initially wanted Eleni. It had only come after her because I wasn't there—or maybe because I'd been standing with Ben and the protective *matia.* Eleni shared my blood. She made a good second choice. "Here I am."

The fact that I wasn't scared of it seemed to help. It hovered, a chill of nothingness all around us. Veiled threat. Secret danger.

"One," I counted, slowly turning in a circle. I searched the corners, the shadows, despite the fact that every survival instinct I had was screaming at me to look away. That's what evil *wants* you to do, look away. If you stare at it long enough, it can't keep up the illusion of being more powerful than you. "Two."

Still nothing.

"Three," I finished, my voice cold with a calm I didn't feel inside. "Protected be. By all the power of three times three."

I hadn't noticed Ben entering behind me until he crouched at Eleni's side, felt for her pulse. She moaned again.

Did I hear a hiss of frustration, or just imagine it?

Of course! Ben, with the *matia,* was now touching Eleni.

"My power is spun," I continued more loudly, accessing memories I hadn't known I had, "my spell is done. By all the power of three—"

That was a definite hissing.

"Two," I continued, raising my voice, and the room seemed to grow lighter even as I said it. *"One."*

Something rushed out the window, so hard that the ends of the curtains fluttered out after it.

And suddenly, the room felt normal.

"So mote it be," whispered Thea, from the bedroom doorway.

Her eyes fluttering open, Eleni faintly echoed at the floor, "So mote it be."

And Ben asked, "What the hell was *that?*"

"I think," I said, my voice finally beginning to shake, "that it was some kind of curse."

Thea convinced the neighbors that Eleni had had a horrible nightmare. Nightmare, night terror, night hag—the difference wasn't so clear that it counted as lying. Ben took a stab at making tea. And Eleni pulled a blanket around herself and insisted I sit with her, cuddling close, on the sofa.

Me? I stared at the living room's wallpaper and tried to think. Thinking wasn't exactly my forte.

Luckily, it was Ben's.

"That was *incredible*," he insisted, moving awkwardly around the pink-cabinet-lined recess that made up Eleni and Thea's tiny kitchenette. "I've read about spells of diminishing, but never thought I'd actually see one."

"Diminishing?" Thea went to his side to help get out teacups.

"What Katie did. Where the magic user counts down instead of counting up. The theory is that as the number gets smaller, so does whatever you're focusing on, right, Katie?"

Thank heavens that when Ben starts playing with ideas, he doesn't always expect an answer, because I couldn't say for sure. It had just felt right.

"And the rhyming—are you doing that off the top of your head, or is this stuff you've already memorized? There are plenty of theories about why rhymes can be powerful, but it seems so simple when you do it."

Thea relieved him in the kitchen. He came and sank onto the coffee table in front of Eleni and me. "I'd guessed you were a witch even before tonight, Katie, but I figured you were like the usual modern Wiccan, heavier on the nature beliefs than the hardcore magic. I never guessed you were some kind of überwitch."

Go figure. After years of avoiding my family tradition, I ended up attracted to a man who *wanted* me to be magic?

Finally I formed my mouth around an appropriate word. "No."

"Now you're just being modest. So what the hell happened

in there? I would have guessed night terror, from the way Eleni screamed, the way her heart was racing. The psychological type of night terror, I mean—you know, the kind of phenomenon that usually hits during the first hour of sleep, before the REM stage has been reached? But I felt whatever was in there, too. Unless it was a form of mass hallucination."

Eleni shook her head. "My English…it is not so good."

"Mine either," I whispered to her.

She laughed shakily, then did her best to explain what had happened. "I awake, afraid. I open my eyes, and all is blackness. There is no light from the street. No light from the hallway. Then he is there…!"

"He?" Ben asked.

"Thing," she insisted. So she probably meant *it*. "He presses down upon me, so very cold. My chest feels…" She spread her hands on her chest.

"Crushed?" Ben suggested, and she nodded.

"He drinks the breath out of me. But I call for protection, here." She pointed to her forehead. "I am able to scream, but I think nobody listens! He swallows me! Then Katie is here. She banishes him."

I got another big hug, for that.

"But how? Katie, you said it was a curse, but whatever that was felt…sentient. And cold, which I'd connect to, say, ghosts. What makes you think curse?"

Oh, I *had* said that, hadn't I?

"What it felt like…" I struggled to put words to a knowing that felt way too far beyond them. "Okay, you know how you can recognize someone's presence, sometimes? Not just their voice, or what they look like, but even before that?"

"It could be by their smell," Ben said. "Our sense of smell is more acute and more closely connected to memory than most of us realize. Or it could be something very subtle, like the way they breathe."

"Or it could just be their *presence*. Diana used to call it a magical signature. Well, I felt that presence on that whatever-it-was, that hatred filling Eleni's room." I faced Ben. "It was Victor's."

He sat back. "It wasn't Victor. It wasn't even human."

"It *belonged* to him. It was *sent* by him. Victor's dabbling in black magic." And yeah, I was aware of how hypocritical that might sound, coming from me. Then again, I'd once had magic training, long before I started slinging my own curses around. And I'd lived with witches all my life. Victor, on the other hand…

Ben shook his head. "Victor doesn't believe in magic."

Cancel the damned curse, he'd said on the Acropolis. "Oh, I think he does now."

"He is after the Hekate Grail," Eleni reminded us. "It is magic."

Which was as good a time as any for Thea to arrive with a tray of teacups and a warm teapot. Ben stood to pace. But he still watched me with a dark gaze, as if arguing with me in his head.

Only after Eleni and I had taken swallows of warm tea, and Thea had sat on a folding chair, did he say, "So you're saying anyone who wants to do magic can just do it?"

We three witches exchanged uncertain glances. This was magic we were talking about, not algebra. There weren't always clear right and wrong answers.

"It's like this," I tried, since I was the one who'd brought Ben in the first place—and English was my first language. "Everything is magic, right? It's all around us, all the time. When someone says 'Have a nice day,' it's like a little magic spell."

"And when someone says 'Drop dead'?"

"Same thing. But the reason you won't always have a nice day—and especially why you won't drop dead—is because most people don't put a lot of power into their wishes. To harness real magical power, you need four ingredients. You need to know what you're doing. You need the will to make things change." What were the other two, again? To know, to will, to something and… "And to keep silent. A good magic user doesn't talk about her magic very much, because that leeches power out of it. To know, to will, to…"

"Dare," offered Eleni softly.

That was it. To know, to will, to dare and to keep silent. "Yes, to dare. The strongest magic uses all four aspects. But that doesn't mean someone with a whole lot of one of them—like the will to hurt someone—can't occasionally blast off something nasty."

"Or good," Thea reminded us.

"I get the idea Victor doesn't have trouble daring to do things." I didn't mean that to come out as sourly as it did. "And apparently he wanted to hurt us. So somehow, he figured out how to…"

A sick feeling came over me, and I closed my eyes. Golly, where might Victor have picked up some basics on cursing? Maybe from…me?

Not everything I'd done that night had been out loud, though.

"How much does Al know about curses?" I asked, opening my eyes.

"No," said Ben, stopping midpace. "I don't know what Al's doing with Victor, and I'm pretty sure he was lying to me, but *curses?* That's even less Al's style than Vic's. He rarely remembers the things we've talked about by the next show. You're wrong. It's not Al."

Maybe he was right. And maybe he wasn't. But I knew one thing for sure. "Then you find out, Ben. Carry the amulet with you. Be careful. But find out. I've had enough."

He squinted at me, as if I were speaking Greek…or, well, Spanish…anyway, some language he didn't understand. "What do you mean, you've had enough?"

"There are two good ways to deal with a magical attack. One of them is to cut off all ties with the person who attacked you. Don't speak their name. Don't go near them. That's what Eleni and I are going to do. We're going to go help out at some women's rally, in Turkey, and we're going to get on with our lives."

"Are you sure?" asked Eleni, still shaky.

"I wasn't going to find the damned cup for He Whose Name Shall Not Be Spoken anyway," I said firmly.

"Okay." Ben shoved a hand through his hair, looking concerned…maybe because by cutting off all ties with his brother, I was kind of cutting ties with him, too. But it had to be done. "I'll let you know if I find out anything."

"You're going?" Okay, so that's what his path toward the door indicated.

"Should we wait for the next attack?" But he did pause in the doorway to ask, "So what's the second way to deal with a magical attack?"

The realization that he should know that, what with being cursed, closed my throat. Luckily, Eleni was able to answer for me. "This is easy. You send the spell back at its source."

"And that's *easy?*"

"It is natural," agreed Thea.

"Karma," I muttered—and felt not all that safe myself. Especially not after Ben left.

* * *

On the edge of the Plaka, in the Hotel Zeus, Victor Fisher awoke to complete darkness. He couldn't see, not even the sheet of paper on which he'd written Kate Trillo's name in a watercolor made of her own blood. He couldn't breathe. Something cold and heavy filled his room to choke him, crush him, punish him. And he couldn't even scream.

Not for long, eternal, heart-pounding minutes. Maybe hours. Maybe…

Then, on the slow realization that he was still somehow alive—he screamed like a girl.

The witch had beaten him again.

But it wasn't close to over.

Chapter 14

Getting out of Athens was almost too easy.

So was getting away from all that magic. I might have enough abilities to be dangerous, but soul-deep, where it counted, I wasn't really a witch at all.

Not a witch by choice, anyway. By choice, I was a nurse.

I was thankful that Hekate had saved me from Ben's killer brother, whose name I was trying not to think, much less say. I would always be grateful for that. But still.

Wasn't my life my own?

The problem, I realized after only one night in a small hotel in Istanbul, was that I didn't exactly *have* a life anymore. Diana was gone. My parents were long gone. I didn't want to leave Eleni alone, what with you-know-who playing with black magic back in Greece. And until I got my hand out of this damned itchy cast, it wasn't like I could do my full-time job anyway.

And the first kiss I'd had in months, from a really smart, really good, quietly sexy guy, had been the result of a spell gone bad.

So this weekend, I decided, was the start of my *new* life. Or my new *old* life, working as a nurse. In Turkey, a country I wouldn't have been able to find on the map before now. *Especially* what with it spanning two continents—Europe and Asia—the way Kansas City spans two states.

This new beginning was mostly the doing of Dr. Gaye Serif, who was kind of a Turkish equivalent of Eleni. Both were doctors who rotated working at different women's clinics, a week at a time. And both were considered remarkably progressive around here, partly because they were unmarried women doctors, and partly because they were working together to offer a free clinic, despite being Turkish and Greek.

Apparently, with the exception of helping each other out after earthquakes, Turkey and Greece don't usually play well together. I'd been instructed not to mention a place called Cyprus, just to keep the peace.

Anyway, Gaye and Eleni had raised money to rent an empty shop several blocks off of Beyazit Square to hold a three-day free health clinic for women. It would run from Monday through Wednesday, Tuesday being International Women's Day. Now I was volunteering to help, too. If one-handed.

And you know? I felt kind of proud of myself.

I could help women just fine *without* finding the Hekate Cup, and this way nothing was at risk of being stolen.

Or murdered.

"This is good," I told my cousin as we finally got out of the clinic on Sunday afternoon, a day before opening, to hand out flyers and to eventually find something to eat at the Sunday-only flea market. "What you and Gaye are doing, I mean. Thanks for letting me help."

"*Letting* you help?" She laughed and swatted at my shoulder, which was padded by my coat. "It is good to have the help of a trained nurse."

"I'm looking forward to seeing patients who aren't dying," I admitted, and Eleni gave me an odd look.

"We are all dying." Something about how she said that seemed *so* Diana.

"I'm just glad I came. I like leaving the cloak-and-dagger stuff behind us for a while."

Who knew? Depending on how hard the psychic backlash was from that entity we'd faced in her apartment, maybe the darkness was behind us forever. Even Vic—I mean, He Whose Name Must Not Be Spoken—wouldn't be stupid enough to try it again, would he? Not if he'd gotten even a portion of what we'd faced.

If he'd gotten it three times as powerful? He might just be history. If only we could be that lucky.

"And you do not miss Ben?" Eleni teased, stopping to buy us some juice. A swarthy man in white, with a red vest, was walking around carrying a large silver urn on his back and wearing cups around his waist. He bent low to pour the juice from over his shoulder into the cups. Neat trick.

Ben? We'd barely talked since that night, that kiss. It seemed…safer, this way. Considering that any attraction he felt toward me was the magic, I mean.

Instead of answering, I looked around us at more than just the juice vendor. Now that I knew how close Greece was to Turkey, I was surprised by all the differences. The biggest, it turned out, was that while Greece is a Christian country, Turkey's mainly Moslem. *Moderate* Moslem, Eleni had insisted, when I expressed an embarrassing concern—she said the majority of Islam was as different from the extremists in the news as standard Christians are from people who bomb abortion clinics. Even among that moderation, Turkey was considered laid-back. People ran around in blue jeans and T-shirts, just like in Greece or the United States. And yet…

In Athens, there had been long-bearded priests in black stovepipe hats, not something you see every day in Chicago, and some of the prettiest buildings were round medieval churches. Here in Istanbul, a lot of women wore headscarves and the skyline was spiky with minarets. I'd already heard the call to prayer broadcast from up high several times since our arrival yesterday, from all across the city, the singers' voices warbling into a strange harmony that gave me chills.

In a good way. A nonmagic way. *Peaceful.*

This huge square with its trees and street vendors and rectangular gray flagstones beneath our feet was named after the ancient Beyazit Mosque, looming to the east of us. The other sides were flanked by Istanbul University, the Grand Bazaar and the Old Book Bazaar.

I wondered if Ben knew there was a whole section of the city for books, here in Istanbul. That seemed his kind of thing. But I was trying not to think about Ben, as hard as I was trying not to think about magic.

Luckily, there was plenty here to distract me.

Plenty of people were gathering for what promised to be one hell of a demonstration. Two days away from the rally, and already a couple hundred demonstrators were thronging the square, painting signs, calling encouragement to each other, making impromptu speeches. Some of them wore T-shirts over long sleeves or under jackets, not that I could read the Turkish slogans. Some of them chanted with vigor, maybe practicing for the rally, or argued with the many policemen patrolling the crowd. Some worked on banners, which they happily unfurled to show off to the rest of us.

I couldn't read those, either. But I understood the smiles of the people around me—hopeful, determined, willing to believe that they could make a difference through *positive* methods. As I watched Eleni hand out flyers about the clinic, I couldn't help but get caught up in the excitement.

"So why do Turkish women need women's rights?" I asked, and she gave me another long *look*. Like I really didn't get it. "What?"

"It is the International Women's Day rally," she reminded me. "There will be demonstrations in Kuwait City, in Bangladesh, in Fiji..." Maybe she realized she was naming more places I couldn't find on the map, because she added, "And New York. It is not just for Turkey."

"Okay, then—so why are we in Turkey instead of Greece?" Or Fiji, or New York? See, I *did* have a point.

"Turkey wishes to join the European Union. To do so means change. They abolish the death penalty, and they change many laws to help women. But to change beliefs— this comes more slowly. All the world watches them." She gestured toward the bazaar, and I saw a news crew slowly panning their camera across the gathering crowd. "This country, it is good for women in many ways. Almost a hundred years ago, they give education to women, allow divorce, give the right to vote. They outlaw the veil. Turkey has the first woman Supreme Court justice, when our grandmothers are young. It is time to continue such progress."

She passed more flyers to a group of older women who were passing us. I let myself enjoy it all—the blue sky, the crisp air, the spirit of working to make the world a brighter place.

These people were my sisters—and brothers, since a lot of the demonstrators were guys. There were women as old as my *nonna* and children in baby carriages, and one particularly cute, curly-headed girl dancing in a circle like a ballerina. When you get a lot of women together, they come with children, after all. There were strong young men, and fatherly types, and lanky teenagers.

"So what's wrong that still needs to be changed? Is it… is there too much violence against women?"

"Of course," Eleni said simply. "As there is everywhere. Despite new laws, Turkey still sees honor killings. The government does not outlaw virginity testing, though they try. This, too, must be changed."

"Virginity testing?"

Her look told me that was exactly what I thought it was. Ugh. No wonder Dr. Gaye wanted to make an extra effort to reassure patients about well-woman exams and birth control.

Those minarets were starting to look more foreign by the minute.

"Then there is the woman trafficking," Eleni sighed, barely audible over the chanting of a group of women ahead of us.

"What?"

"White slavery. It is illegal. But outsiders take advantage of Turkey's visa laws, take advantage of poor women, especially from the Ukraine. This also must be changed."

"So why hasn't it been?"

"Tradition is powerful," she insisted with a shrug, passing several more flyers to a cluster of apparent students in blue jeans and fleece jackets, their bright headscarves tied in different ways as if to reflect their personalities. "Change comes slowly. But this does not mean it cannot come."

A police officer shouted at the chanters. They changed their line to something else, also militant sounding, also in Turkish. He yelled some more, then shook his head and stalked off, leaving them victorious.

"So what are they saying?" I asked, since my cousin spoke Turkish.

"'We are not intimidated,'" she translated. "'We resist.'"

Good for them. "And before that? Before he challenged them?"

I assumed their original battle cry had been something about the honor killings, or the virginity testing, or, oh, the white slavery? I wasn't at all prepared for Eleni's mundane answer.

"Equal pay for equal work," she said.

Well, didn't I feel silly? "We've still got some of that problem in the States," I admitted. I'd learned that when you're overseas, you call the United States of America "the States." "Woman-y jobs like teaching and nursing don't pay as well."

Eleni said, "You have a violence-against-women problem in the States, too. Every place does."

Which made me think of the time for goddess grails. But I had a good reason for not pursuing those, damn it! I tried to hand a flyer to a couple that passed us. They seemed distracted, though, by shouting farther down the square, a shouting that added to the air of revolution.

"At least we don't have to wear headscarves."

"Many women like the headscarves. They can go out without doing their hair." But Eleni was distracted, too. The disturbance toward the side of the square was getting louder.

A lot louder. Not just one shout, either.

A lot of shouting.

Victor, I thought, despite my resolve not to. That right away told me he was still winning, if I assumed anything that went wrong must be his fault.

No, this was something else. Something bigger than us.

Eleni noticed, too, and immediately looked concerned. "We should go back."

Some of the demonstrators, from the direction we'd been heading, were already doing that. Others were picking up their signs and heading toward the disturbance. "Why?"

"Something is wrong."

The yelling kind of gave that away. Something was *very* wrong, just ahead of us. And I noticed something else.

"Crossroads," I whispered, realizing where we were. A square wasn't just a square, it was a meeting of different streets, different directions. Which meant, in a way, magic. Where there are crossroads, there are decisions. Go back. Go forward. Those were both decisions.

But so was standing and watching, wasn't it? Oh woe, I thought—and grinned.

People around us were running in different directions. Some people were standing on their toes, or even climbing onto chairs or vending carts, to better see what was happening.

What kind of decision did *I* want to make?

My own words surprised me. So did the way I started forward, half resigned, half determined. "We should see what's wrong."

"*What?* Katie, no! It could be dangerous."

Which was true. But people were screaming now—*screaming,* just up ahead! And unless we moved forward, faced whatever was happening, we couldn't possibly help. And we had to help…didn't we?

"Stay here, then." I handed Eleni my flyers. "I've got to find out."

And I took off running.

Diana's voice laughed through my head. "You can't even speak the language!"

No, *I agreed silently, grimly. I can't.*

"So what makes you think you can help?"

But damn it, we already knew that, didn't we?

I could help because I had abilities, and not just as a nurse. I had powers, whether I wanted them or not. It had been easy to use them when I was being threatened. It had been instinct to use them when Eleni was in danger.

And now, for complete strangers?

Hell…how could I *not* do whatever I could? Magic wasn't just about knowing and willing, but *daring*.

Still, as I reached the knot of running people, shouting, screaming, I almost turned back, stunned.

Policemen in riot gear can have that effect.

Faceless behind helmets or gas masks, dozens of men had converged on the demonstrators. Tall, translucent shields that read *Polis* were being used to push through people, sometimes to knock them over. Truncheons rose and fell above the heads of the crowd.

One officer, not far from me, swung his baton again and again, clubbing a young woman down to the ground. Then he kicked her. Another officer wrenched one of the male protestors' arms behind him, despite the man's cry of pain, dragging him off to who knew where. Another demonstrator held his arms over his bent head, running, while not one but two policemen followed, beating him with their sticks.

Everywhere civilians ran, sobbed, tried to hide and

screamed pleas in a language I didn't even speak. The cruelty staggered me.

And I'd thought I could *help?*

Not alone, I couldn't. Not even with magic.

Oh…hell. Who had I been kidding?

Taking a deep breath, trying not to wince when an older woman tripped and fell hard not five yards in front of me, I sank down to my knees, spread my hands against the gray paving stones, and tried to draw power from beneath the earth, into myself.

"I call on you, Hekate," I murmured—it's not like, even if I'd yelled it, anybody would hear over the shouts. "Goddess of the Crossroads. Queen of the Night. Help me lead innocents to safety, as you lead souls to the safety beyond."

But something else seemed necessary. So…

"You're right," I admitted quietly. *"I'm yours."*

And like that, I stopped being scared.

Someone who didn't believe in goddesses or magic could argue that my sudden calm, as I then stood to what height I had, was more psychological than divine. Okay.

Did it matter? Either way, it helped. I was going in.

Running steps took me to the older woman who still lay on her hands and knees, weeping and frightened, where she'd fallen. I helped her to her feet, turned her in the direction I'd come from, hoped for guidance—

And I saw Eleni. Thank heavens!

"There," I shouted, but the old woman looked at me with blank panic. Instead of saying more, I gave her a little push. Eleni beckoned, calling in Turkish. The woman broke into a run.

I turned back to the confusion, trying to dodge the frantic people ready to trample me in their attempt to escape the beatings. "This way!" I called futilely. "This way!"

Some of the students I'd seen earlier must have understood English. With no other guidance they rushed, desperate, toward me. One of them bled heavily from her mouth, and I could sympathize.

"Over there!" I instructed, and they, too, ran for Eleni, who seemed to be passing them farther back to safety. Between the two of us, we were going to get at least some of these people out of here, weren't we? I couldn't think about the alternatives. Flanks of police were closing in, closing off escape routes. Something horrible burned in my nose, burned at my throat. My eyes began to water. That would explain the masks. *Tear gas.*

Who did these cops think they were up against? Choking, I dug my winter scarf out of the pocket of my coat and wrapped it around my face, like against a blizzard. Then, eyes streaming, I waded farther into the chaos. An escaping woman bodychecked me in her panic, spinning me around, almost knocking me over. Someone else, running backward to call for a friend, nearly took me down. I wished I could take another deep breath, call again on the Goddess, but considering the tears pouring from my stinging eyes…

No wonder people were panicked. I could hardly remember what direction safety was myself!

Too many innocents lay on the ground, trying to push themselves back up with their hands, their knees. Too many were beaten back down, literally *beaten*, blood splattering from mouths or noses. And I noticed something horrible about the police.

They were all men. Every last one of them.

And some of them were enjoying themselves.

Now I was in the midst of things, too, grabbing people as they spun in blind, panicked circles, still sending them in the direction I'd remembered seeing Eleni. In the midst of the chaos, most of them seemed desperate for any direction and immediately went. A few of them hit me—once on the upper arm, once upside my face—before they recognized that I was trying to help. Even then, their stares were glassy, their faces white with shock. I got them out, too.

Me and Hekate. Because Hekate had always been a part of me. We shared the same name, didn't we? We shared more than that.

Choking, I knew I'd have to get fresh air soon. I was too close to wherever the gas had been released. But then I saw a child, wandering amongst the stampeding crowd, screaming, reaching out in the way little kids do for their mommy. It was the curly-headed ballerina girl! I pushed my way through the chaos, wrapped my arms around her, picked her up—she couldn't have been more than five. Somewhere out there, I knew, there was a mother in hell.

I've got her, I thought, hard, wishing she could hear me. *I'll get her to safety.*

But when I turned, my luck ran out.

A cop, his eyes behind his helmet glazed not with panic but with bloodlust, lashed downward with his truncheon.

Chapter 15

And I stopped him.

No rhyme. No prayer. No pause to reorient myself to which way was north, south, east or west.

I reached upward—not with my good hand, which was busy clutching the little girl to me. With my cast hand, I reached up to block the blow as I met the policeman's crazed, evil gaze with my own angry stare.

And in that moment, I was caught in memories *that weren't even mine.* Villages beset by Mongol hordes. Towns pillaged by Vikings. Wars. More wars. Husbands and fathers and sons marching away, ready to kill and to die—and often doing just that. Enemy warriors claiming other men's mothers, wives and children as war prizes, as slaves, as concubines....

We're so powerful, we can kill infants. We're so powerful,

*we can take your women. If you don't do as we wish, we can
kill you. Look at how powerful we are.*

It gave new meaning to the idea of objectifying someone.
And it wasn't just in ancient times. Maybe it wasn't happening
in Chicago. Hopefully it wasn't! But it was still happening.
Now.

But. Not. Here.

Power blasted through me, up through my feet from the
Mother Earth beneath me, from all the memories and scars
She carried. And since my projective hand was busy clutching the little girl, all that fury must have burned out at my
monster of an attacker through my eyes.

The truncheon froze in midswing.

The policeman blinked, confused, as his soul bled slowly
back into his gaze. Then—then he looked ashamed.

He *wasn't* a monster. But he'd sure fallen into a blood
spell, one that had nothing to do with witchcraft. They all
had, damn it.

What had Ben said? *Evil is something people do, not something they are.* Could he be right?

Assured that he wouldn't come after us, I turned and
carried the little girl back toward where I'd last seen Eleni.

I should describe more, but things got kind of…dreamlike,
after that. I was aware of the chaos around me—lunging
bodies, frantic cries. But it seemed distant, now. I no longer
felt part of it.

I didn't feel the ground under my feet, but I kept walking.
I couldn't feel the little girl in my arms, but I didn't drop her.
Bodies staggered by us, but none touched.

Eleni came and swept us farther away from this brutal
roundup. Then a woman was there, tearing the child from my

arms, weeping. With a cry of welcome, the child nearly strangled her mother in return.

The world began to tip. I found Eleni, and reached out. Even though I watched her grasp my hand, and saw her eyes widen and her mouth move, she seemed farther and farther away.

"Magic," I said, or tried to, forcing my mouth around the word as if it was foreign. Whether I found voice to accompany the words, who knew? "Too much...magic."

Then everything vanished.

In my dream, I'm searching for something.
Someone.
"Where are you?" I keep shouting.
Slowly, I become aware of a quiet answer. "I'm right here."
Mom? Diana? "Where?"
"Here. Open your eyes."
"I can't find you. Where are you?"
"Everywhere. I am life, and death, and the struggle between them. I am promise, and fulfillment, and betrayal. I am the alpha and the omega, and everything between. I am not only the path, but its destination and its desertion. But I did not kill them." Then She says, "And neither did you."

Then Ben was there, propped against the headboard beside me, reading a book. I watched him until he turned the page. Then I swallowed and tried words. One, anyway. "Hi."

"You're back!" He put the book down—which I suspected was a compliment—and extended a hand toward my face, brushed my hair back. My skin tingled where he'd touched me. He smiled his lopsided smile, studying me with a sweeping gaze. "How are you feeling?"

Good question. Was I even awake? Not likely, with him right there in bed with me. *On* bed, anyway. "I'm not sure."

"You don't have a fever." Oh. So *that's* why he'd touched my face. I studied his for a moment—the angle of his jaw, his bright, dark eyes—and hoped I wasn't awake yet.

"That's not how you do it," I corrected him.

His brows furrowed—probably he'd read umpteen zillion books on temperature taking along with everything else he knew—but before he could question it, I touched my forehead. "You're supposed to kiss me. Here."

He blinked. "Oh. I suppose…lips are very sensitive to heat."

I smiled. My smile seemed to manage what a point-blank invitation hadn't. With his own ghost of a smile, Ben bent over me and pressed his lips gently to my forehead. Mmm.

"Like this?" he asked, his voice extra scratchy, and drew only an inch or two back.

I really hoped I wasn't awake yet, because I liked this dream. "You tell me," I whispered, and wrinkled my nose at him. "Am I hot?"

I got a full smile from that. "Now there's a loaded question. You've been asleep for a while, Katie. You could be disoriented. Maybe you should—"

I slid a hand behind his neck, into his curly black hair, and drew him back to me, drew his lips to mine. "Shut up, Ben."

I really don't think I put any magical kick into the command. But he kissed me anyway, deep and fervent, as wholly focused on this as he was on everything. *Yes.* That was better.

One kiss led to two, then three, then countless. I caught the belt loop of Ben's jeans with my good hand and tugged until he slung one of his legs across me, so he wouldn't have to crane his neck to keep up the kissing. He slid his hands under my head, his thumbs stroking my cheeks, tipping my face one way while he tipped his face the other, pressing harder, tasting deeper....

Not all men were evil. I loved what a great reminder of that Ben was, and tried to tell him with my tongue, which made him breathe faster and made a smile stretch his lips for a few long, lingering kisses. I loved having him over me, surrounding me like this. If my legs hadn't been trapped under the covers, I would have wrapped them around his. As it was, I had to make do with sliding my hand down his long, lean back, down to his blue-jeaned ass, and encouraging him to come down on me a little more firmly.

"Oh, God," he breathed, sinking onto me just like I'd wanted. "Katie. I was so worried...."

More lazy, contented kissing took care of that.

Outside the window, the faint sound of Istanbul's call to prayer began to warble across the city. Through Ben's jeans, I felt something hard. Well maybe that, too—but *this* was something else, something in his *back* pocket. Something disk-shaped. Something...oh, hell.

Is that a matia *in your pocket, or are you just glad to see me?*

He had the *matia* because I'd given it to him. And I'd given it to him to protect him. *From me.*

I'd cursed him. This incredible connection we felt together, this sense that everything was more whole with him here, was a side effect of the magic.

Damn it! I wasn't asleep.

But it's a good side effect, I thought stubbornly, squirming happily under Ben's insistent weight. Eager blood heated places I'd almost forgotten I had. I liked the resulting ache between my legs, the delicious heaviness in my breasts. To judge by his breathing, Ben liked this, too.

Magic, schmagic. *What would he care, as long as he gets some?*

But that was a problem with Ben being so good. He would probably care a lot.

If not right away.

Bad girl or not, I couldn't take advantage of him that way. With a groan, I rolled him off of me. I think that, for a moment, he thought I just wanted to be on top. His smile faded into confusion when I rolled back to where I'd been, beside him, trying to catch my breath. But not for long.

He followed, kissed me again. Damn, his mouth tasted good, like…like fennel seeds. Not too dry. Not too wet. Just the right eagerness, without being at all clumsy about it. Yes….

No! Ducking my head, so that he kissed my forehead, I asked, "How long, exactly?"

"Huh?" He tried to kiss me again, but this time I turned my head so that he got a cheek.

"How long have I been asleep?" I clarified, smiling apologetically as his sex-glazed fog seemed to slowly clear. "You said it was a while."

Still breathing hard, Ben fell to his side beside me, his dark gaze still caressing my face. "I…ah…"

Interesting. He really wasn't talking. Why did I take that as a compliment, too?

"It couldn't have been hours," I noted, sitting up to brace my back against the headboard, the way he'd been doing when I woke up. "Because the sun's still up. And you're here. But it can't be Monday morning already, can it?"

Ben licked his lips and finally managed, "It's been three days, Katie."

Now I was completely awake. *"What?"*

* * *

As it turned out, he was right.

Ben had arrived Sunday night—"As soon as I heard about the attack," he explained—and when I hadn't woken up by the time the temporary clinic opened on Monday morning, he offered to keep watch on me while Eleni was gone.

"And Eleni just left me with you?"

"Dr. Serif really needed her." Ben stood now, to put a little distance between us. In all fairness to him, I noticed that our hotel room didn't have a chair he could have taken instead of the bed. "And you said yourself that she could trust me."

"When? *I was unconscious.*"

"Not all the time. You woke up long enough to insist she not take you to the hospital, and later to tell her to trust me, and a couple of times to drink some Gatorade—that's good for restoring potassium. Interesting that you don't remember, but I'm not surprised. Somniloquy, or sleep talking, is one of the more common parasomnias. Something like five percent of adults talk in their sleep, but— and this is interesting—fifty percent of children—"

"Ben," I interrupted him.

"Oh. Sorry. Anyway, the police attack on the demonstration made the international news. Three people were hospitalized, and around sixty people were arrested, half of them women. A lot of countries are using it as an argument that Turkey isn't ready for the E.U. yet."

"What day is it?"

"It's Wednesday," Ben admitted gently.

Well…hell. I slid my good hand down my face, willing the last of my exhaustion to slide away with it, and swung my bare feet out of bed. I wore my nightshirt. I hoped Eleni was the one who'd put me into it. "Can you take me to Eleni? Once I shower and change?"

"Yes, but what just happened?" Ben gestured toward the bed. "Are you sorry we—I mean, did you not mean for—"

So I stood up and kissed him again, thoroughly, just to reassure him that it wasn't anything he'd done. It seemed a little safer, standing up…but just as sexy. He had the body of a runner, sinewy and tight. Now I had a new reason for wishing my cast was off. I wanted to run two hands over him, instead of just one. Except—

"We'll talk," I gasped, drawing back later than I meant to. "After I see Eleni."

"I'll hold you to it," Ben warned, quietly pleased.

I hoped that wasn't the only thing he'd be holding me to.

Eleni was thrilled to see me at the clinic, and hugged me like three times before she went back to work. I offered to stay and help, glad to see the folding chairs of their temporary waiting room full with head-scarved women and dark-haired children, but both Eleni and Dr. Gaye refused. I needed to get something to eat, they said. And wow, they were right.

I mean, Gatorade only goes so far.

Ben took me to a *lokanta,* which was a small restaurant with the menu listed on a blackboard outside the front door. I asked him to order for me. Not only was I still a little disoriented after my Sleeping Beauty routine, not to mention that making-out-with-Ben detour. But everything had names like *bamya bastisi* and *firinda manti.*

You see my challenge.

For the first part of the meal, I just plain ate. Our food ended up being a lamb and tomato stew and something vaguely like ravioli, plus some bread, some artichoke hearts and a sort of bean salad. Everything was delicious, especially after a three-day fast. Only as I started slowing down, moving from ravenous to mildly hungry, did I think to ask Ben what he'd learned from his brother and Al, back in Athens.

"Nothing," he said—and, for maybe the first time all afternoon, he looked away from me. Huh.

I actually paused, halfway toward taking another sip of my yogurt drink. It was good. Salty, but in a surprisingly refreshing way. "Nothing at *all?* You left right after that thing came after Eleni. I thought…"

I'd thought he meant to take care of it.

"Vic wasn't answering his phone. To be honest, I thought about what you'd said—you know, about the karmic backlash of doing a spell? Not that I completely bought the idea that Vic *would* do a spell, but…I got the management at the Hotel Zeus to check on him for me. It's not like I had to work very hard to convince them we were brothers. For a moment, I thought Vic was just sleeping like the dead."

I resisted the urge to ask him not to keep saying his brother's name. There's a fine line between magic and superstition. Better that I just watch what *I* said, and leave Ben's delivery alone. "*Like* the dead?"

"I woke him up, to make sure. He told me to, er, bug off. But Katie…" Ben's dark, haunted gaze lifted to me again. "You were right. He'd written your name on a piece of paper, with some pink water that might've been… I think it had blood in it. He'd driven a nail through it, like the paper the police found at your house the night of the murder. And there was a candle, what was left of one anyway. Apparently he'd let it burn itself out."

Or he'd been knocked off his ass before he had the chance to snuff it.

"I took it," admitted Ben, scowling.

"The candle?"

"All of it. The candle, the paper, the water—well, I poured the water down the drain, but I took the glass. I brought it all for you. I thought you and your cousin would know how to, um…disarm it?"

I took a deep, steadying breath. Then I took another bite of stew. I'd already known his brother had cast that awful spell on Eleni and me, already sensed his presence in the darkness, so that part wasn't surprising. The idea of Ben skulking around his brother's room, though, at risk of all sorts of retaliation… "Thanks. We'll burn it. So… I don't suppose you thought to bring me some of his hair or something, while you were at it?"

His eyes widened. I guess he hadn't.

"We've got to stop him somehow," I reminded him grimly.

"Yeah, but…magically? I thought you'd had enough."

"So did I, but—" I couldn't help but focus on his mouth, remember his kisses, and I lost my nerve. "I'll come back to that. What about Al? What did you find out from him?"

Ben looked stubborn.

"I was right about him, too?"

"No! I mean, not about him helping Victor, and certainly not with anything magical. Not exactly." I must have really been giving him the evil eye by then, *matia* or not, because Ben hurried to explain. "Al says Vic *did* want magical advice from him. But like I said, Al doesn't know that much about magic. He came to Greece hoping for a story. What he got was Victor's suspicions that, well…"

Again he averted his eyes. "Ben!"

"Vic thinks you've enchanted me," he muttered.

Oh. Oh my. I slowly took a bite of a bread called *ekmek*, so that I couldn't say anything. It was very good bread.

"According to Al," Ben continued, still not looking at me, "Vic thinks there's no other reason I would be helping you. That's how sure he is that he's in the right about this."

If I'd needed more proof that the man was crazy, that was it. And yet, I *had* put a spell on Ben, not an enchantment but a curse. Everyone thought the name in blood at the crime scene had been written by Diana. So far, I hadn't bothered to correct them.

Could Ben have kissed me the way he had this afternoon, if he knew? "And what do you think?"

"I think Vic's paranoid," admitted Ben. "And sociopathic, which is a bad combination. I think he's been vulnerable to evil since our parents' deaths—as if their violence infected him somehow—and this Comitatus group is encouraging his worst qualities. I think he needs to be stopped, and I don't know how. I mean—Katie, I was right there, standing over him, and he was asleep, completely helpless, and God help me, for a split second I actually thought…"

His elbows went onto the table, his head into his hands, his fingers into his hair. But he didn't have to tell me. I'd never considered myself a violent person either. But presented with such a quick, easy solution to all our concerns about what Ben's brother might do to my cousin, or me, to any number of actual innocents in the future…the temptation would have been there. But…I wasn't related to him.

I reached across the table, stroked my hand across his hair. It curled and licked at my fingertips, so very soft. I wondered what it would feel like between my—

"I don't know if I could have done it, either," I said quickly, before I lost all nerve, "and I hate your brother more than I've ever hated anyone in my life. Maybe in all my lives."

With a hard breath, he tipped his head up, so that his hands only masked the bottom of his face now. His eyes smiled wanly at me, over his fingers. I was willing to bet his mind was already starting to produce facts and figures about reincarnation...and that info dumps like that might be as close to meditation as Ben ever got.

We had other matters to focus on, of course. But as I drew my hand back, Ben caught it, kissed my knuckles, then let go. Such soft lips. Such earnest affection. He watched me for a long moment and then, when I said nothing, ducked his head and watched me warily through his lashes. It was a great effect, all the more powerful from my suspicion that he didn't know how good that made him look. And damn it. Damn it, damn it, damn it. I really had to tell him.

Now I was the one taking a deep breath. "Ben, about me thinking I'd had enough of magic, before."

He waited, hanging on to my every word.

"I thought I had. Maybe I did, at the time. I already told you that I didn't practice the way my mother and sister did."

Ben folded his arms on the table, cocked his head. "If what I saw you doing in Athens was amateur stuff, I'm going to have to revamp my ideas about how low-key magic is."

"Well... I went back into training, with my grandmother, after Diana died." I liked him kissing me, the way he had earlier. I liked him looking at me as if he was imagining me without clothes. It made me forget...

But if it was the magic drawing him, then he still lacked free will. I needed to know he wanted *me,* not the effects of my curse. "But it felt like circumstances had forced me into it, and I resented that. I didn't like the person I was turning into, what I thought the magic was turning me into. When I came to Turkey, I really was hoping to leave the magic behind, maybe with the exception... Are you still carrying the *matia?*"

He reached into his jeans pocket and pulled out the blue glass disk.

"Good." Damn, this was going to be hard. "Something happened during the rally, when the police came after the demonstrators."

"You did magic to help get people out," Ben agreed. "Eleni told me about it. It must have been some kind of whammy, if the backlash of it knocked you out for three days."

"That was part of it, sure. Even real magic has its limits. For me to be able to protect not just myself against the police, but everyone Eleni and I helped get out of there…magic on the demonstrators, magic on the police, magic on me. That's pretty big mojo. On top of that, especially since I didn't ask anyone's permission, I had the recoil to deal with."

"Come on, Katie. Do you think any of the people you rescued would have refused permission if you'd offered first?" I loved that Ben accepted the magic part so easily, and was only debating the ethics part with me. He really was a good guy. With the brain of a computer. And really remarkable lips.

But… "Who can say what their karmic journey is about? And you can bet, a lot of the police wouldn't have wanted me interfering." Although, remembering the horror that ravaged that one man's face as he came aware of what he'd been doing, maybe some of them would. "The point is that I was able to do some pretty huge magic. And the only way I was able to do it was to recommit myself to Hekate. To realize that this isn't all about dark magic, and curses, and revenge. It's about women who are trying to change the world, needing an extra push of magic to protect them.

The Goddess is only as strong as her children.

"Maggi Stuart was right, Ben. Even your brother was right. The time has come. I need to find the Hekate Chalice."

Then, before Ben could express the approval I saw in his eyes, I quickly added, "But you may not want to help me."

"Why wouldn't I want to—" Ben began, but I interrupted. "I cursed you."

Chapter 16

Well—that shut him up pretty quick. The understanding, then betrayal on his expressive face, made my heart hurt.

"The name in blood at the crime scene," I continued, hurrying to make a full confession while I still had the backbone. "Diana didn't write that, I did. Your brother told me his name was Ben, and I believed him, and even though I hadn't done magic in years, it was the only thing I could think of to stop him." But that wasn't completely true. Something about Ben, about his sheer decency, forced me to be true. "Besides, I wanted to. He'd killed Diana. He deserved everything horrible that hell and Hekate and I could throw at him."

Ben continued to stare at me.

"It wasn't until the second lineup that I realized he wasn't you. Or…vice versa. And by then it was too late. You can't exactly *modify* a curse. That's why I started training with my *nonna* again. While I figured out what to do next, I needed to learn how to protect you."

"And you," guessed Ben. He knew about karmic blowback.

"Yes, and me. I'm not saying I'm the good guy here. I know I'm not. *You're* the good guy here. I'm just trying to get through all this."

"With curses?"

"Only the one."

"*'I don't suppose you thought to bring me some of his hair or something, while you're at it?'*" That was his voice, still, but my words. Word for freaking word, damn it.

"Okay, one? I was joking." Sort of. "And two? If anyone deserves to be cursed—"

"Who are you to decide who deserves to be cursed?"

"Your brother's a murderer!"

"And you still don't care why! You still don't know if he's a victim, too. So yeah, *stop him*. Don't *curse* him. You stopped a car in midair. You stopped some kind of nightmare entity. Hell, Kate, you stopped police in full riot gear! Or did you curse all of them, too?"

The worst part about it? He was right. If I'd been more practiced, if I'd thought more clearly, maybe I could have used magic to knock Victor unconscious. Or to paralyze him. Or to make sure he ran out the door and right into a police car. If I'd done any of that, he might be in prison right now... or, considering how fast the legal system moves, at least facing trial with a better chance of conviction.

Instead, my sister's killer was walking free. Eleni was in danger. Ben and I were still suffering side effects of the curse—the really enjoyable effects, like a few hours ago, and the more dangerous ones. And now, on top of cursing the poor guy, I'd also betrayed him. Way to go, Katie.

But hindsight is twenty-twenty, right? We were where we were.

"You need to know one more thing." Keeping my voice level was a challenge, but it wasn't the sort of thing I wanted to use magic to help. This was too real, too…*us.* "Because I did a spell on you, we're connected. So any attraction we've been feeling, it's…it's not real."

Then I waited.

Ben Fisher wasn't a sit-still kind of guy. He looked down, looked away, shifted in his chair, glared at me. Then he looked away again. Was he remembering how I'd woken up, too? Or was that just me? I didn't want to have to say it again.

"I said, what we've been feeling—"

"I heard," he snapped, and he was angry enough that I guess he really had. "Come on. I'll walk you back to your hotel."

And dropping some lira banknotes on the table, he stood.

I stood, too, but to protest. "You don't have to do that."

"No." He held up a flat hand, to cut whatever I meant to argue. "I do have to."

"You don't even *like* me right now."

"I don't know what to think about you right now! But Katie—" Scowling, he ducked closer to me, as if he had a secret. "Have you ever considered that the way you treat people should be more about who you are than who they are? *Think about it.*"

And that was the last I got out of Ben.

Damn it.

This wasn't the sort of man problem most women have. I told Eleni about it, when she got back to the hotel full of news about how successful their temporary clinic had been.

Not surprisingly, she wasn't sure what to say.

"Perhaps he sees that this is a mistake," she suggested, at last. We were lying on the bed we'd had to share, staring out the window at our view of the Beyazit Tower on this, our last evening in Turkey.

"The curse?" I asked gloomily, trying not to remember Ben on the bed with me. Kissing me... "Or him helping me at all?"

She punched me lightly in the arm. "The curse! Ben helps you to stop his brother, does he not? That is not a mistake."

"But the curse was."

Eleni turned, pillowing her head on her elbow, and watched my face, letting me answer my own question. It was exhausting, doing those protective rituals for me and Ben every night. It was disheartening being a bad guy. And now, losing Ben just as I'd begun to realize I wanted him....

Except that I'd never had him.

Right now, I seriously hated that curse.

So...*were* there other kinds of magic that could stop Victor Fisher? Immediately I thought of the Hekate Chalice.

"I'm supposed to make a pilgrimage to Hekate's source." *Only there can you truly commune with Her. Only then can you right your wrongs and fulfill your destiny.*

That's where I'd probably find the real cup, too. How convenient.

"Then we will return to Eleusis," decided Eleni, with a satisfied nod. "Or other temples. I must work tomorrow and Friday, but when weekend comes, we will start. We can visit Delphi and Argos. If you stay another week, we travel north to Thessaloniki and Samothrace."

That idea worked so well for her, she sat up and stretched, mission accomplished. "Are you hungry? Gaye has invited us for dinner. The Turks, they are very hospitable."

But I felt sick to my stomach, and not because of the big meal I'd eaten recently.

Besides, I'd already been to Eleusis. I'd gotten nothing more than a walk down bad-memory lane with my dead sister and a big dose of dog breath. Then again…what was it Ben had talked about back at the Acropolis? The goddess Hekate hadn't begun in Greece. She began in a place called… K-something. I couldn't remember the specifics, but…hadn't it been in Turkey?

And now I was in Turkey.

Coincidence, my ass.

"You go ahead," I assured my cousin. "I have to work through some stuff."

She scowled dramatically. "No, come! Celebrate with us! The clinic, it does well. We give many exams, we educate many women."

"Go ahead and enjoy yourself. I'll be here when you get back, really. I just need to…to think."

It took more arguing before she left, but finally I was alone.

Dusk was drawing across Istanbul, certainly the part just outside our hotel window. But staring out the window wasn't the kind of thinking I had to do.

Instead, I placed a long-distance call to the number on the card Maggi Stuart had given me.

Maggi's voice sounded gravelly when she answered and accepted the charges. "Katie? Are you all right?"

"I'm fine. I'm sorry about calling collect. My cell phone doesn't work in Europe. Or Asia." Which side of the Bosphorus were we on, again? "And the instructions here for how to pay for a call—"

"It's not a problem. I can cover a phone call, really. What are you doing in Istanbul?"

I gave her the short version, leaving out most of the magic. "Now Ben and I have had a sort of falling out—not his fault, but still, I can't ask him for more help. And he once said something about Hekate coming from an old country that starts with a *K,* around the time of Egypt, that's in Turkey now."

"Karia," she supplied easily. "Sometimes it's spelled with a *C,* too, like Hekate. Alphabets change. Do you think he meant from the time of the Egyptian Dynasties?"

She didn't say it, but I guess since there was still an Egypt, "the time of Egypt" hadn't been very smart phrasing. How had Ben kept me from feeling stupid all the time? "Oh."

"Which, sorry—" She yawned. "That's a roundabout way of saying yes, he's right. Hekate's roots are probably Karian."

"Since Eleusis was such a bust, and since I'm in Turkey anyway, I think I should find the oldest Hekate site I can. But I don't know where to look."

"Are you sure your mother or grandmothers never taught you a rhyme or song about Hekate? Something like, 'Here in Anatolia lies…' or 'With the Cup of Hekate'? Songs like that can make pretty good treasure maps."

She'd mentioned that once already. All I'd been able to think of was a song about fairies, and one about a bunny rabbit.

Hekate has connections to frogs, bats, big black dogs. Not bunnies.

"Nothing. Do you suppose that means I'm not a Grail Keeper after all?"

"Hardly. It just means the song got forgotten, just like so much else about the Goddess." But she really was a mythology expert. "Okay, so in Turkey, the biggest problem will be narrowing down the possibilities. The country's full of goddess sites. I'd love to visit sometime."

A man's voice, apparently very close to her, murmured something I couldn't make out. She whispered back, "I didn't say right now, Your Highness."

Oh, no. "What time is it there?"

"Don't worry about it. I'll get on the computer and see what I can find out. Give me the number there, and I'll call you right back. How's that?"

"All right. And Maggi, thank you."

"Me? *You're* the one who's taking up the quest while I'm out of circulation. I'm thrilled to do anything I can to help. I'll call within the hour."

She was as good as her word. Within an hour she'd called back not only with what she called a "likely candidate"—a place called Stratonikea—but with reservations for a sleeper car on a train leaving the next night for a town called Pamukkale and a reservation for a hotel once I got there. They were paid reservations.

I protested, but Maggi insisted that she had a fund especially for Grail Keeper business and that she desperately wanted to contribute.

"I put you down for a week's stay." She sounded a lot more awake this time. "If you don't find anything in Stratonikea, you might want to check out some other sites in the area before you move on. Hierapolis has the biggest necropolis in Anatolia, which, considering Hekate's connections to the dead, might be worth a look. Besides, it's practically next door to your hotel. There's Ephesus—that bunch was so into their goddess that St. Paul had to write a letter instead of giving a speech there—and then Aphrodisias, which of course is the sacred home of Aphrodite."

Of course. Damn, I missed Ben.

"They should all be day trips from Pamukkale," Maggi continued. "But if you need more time, just let me know. And hey, Artemis eventually replaced Cybele as patron goddess of Ephesus. You know what Artemis's name was in Latin, right?"

I hadn't thought about it until that moment, but I took a good guess. "Diana?"

"You got it. So…is there anything else I can help with? Really, I'm happy to. I feel so useless, not being there to help look." There were no low-voiced comments from the background, so I figured she must have changed rooms to call me back. "No, edit that. Not useless. Marginalized, maybe, but in other ways, I've never felt so important. So…to each our own quest, right?"

Not everything was about me, was it? "When are you due?"

"Two months, so it's not as if I'd fly to Boston, much less Turkey. You'll call me if you find anything, right?"

"I promise." And that should have been it. But… "Maggi?"

"Hmm?"

"Do you really call your husband 'Your Highness'?"

She laughed. "Sometimes. But I still outrank him. He calls me 'Goddess.'"

Now I laughed, too.

"Goddess bless," she wished me, before we hung up.

I couldn't help thinking, just then, that I'd need it.

But something interesting began to happen, very gradually, with my decision to travel south. It continued when I ran out early the next morning to buy something I'd seen in a street vendor's cart, for Eleni—he called the glass disks, hung on a string, *boncuk.* But as far as I was concerned, they were close enough to the Greek *matia*—just with a light blue eye instead of a golden one—that they had to serve the same purpose.

I got two of them, keeping one and making Eleni take the other before she caught her flight back to Athens. She didn't want to leave me alone in Turkey, but I insisted.

"Just be careful," I told her, hoping fervently that this was the right choice. And since her job needed her, she reluctantly left.

The change in me continued as I spent the day by myself in Istanbul before catching the 17:35 Pamukkale Ekspresi. I wasn't scared to be alone. I didn't feel awkward, the way I had when I first traveled to Athens. Despite my inability to speak the language, the Turkish people I met were wonderfully patient with me. I ended up taking a sightseeing tour on a double-decker bus, and saw more wonderful things—palaces, mosques and markets—than I could have imagined. Then I picked up my luggage at the hotel and hailed my own cab. I found my own way to the train station, to the express I needed and then to my private compartment.

Maggi Stuart didn't do things by halves. She'd reserved both berths in my sleeper car, so that I wouldn't have to share with a stranger. But by now, I felt pretty sure I could have shared without worries.

I slept deeply in my berth, lulled by the slight sway and clacking of the train.

So what was going on with me? Maybe I was growing up a little, but that's the sort of thing you think as a teenager, back when you believe some perfect moment will arrive—graduation, or a driver's license, or sex—and poof, you'll be an adult. Or maybe I was coming into my power, accepting my role as a witch. Or maybe I was resigned to this quest, finally, and to learning from Hekate, Herself, what she wanted from me.

Yeah. Probably that last one.

I woke the next morning, well rested, with plenty of time to have breakfast in the restaurant car before we reached Pamukkale.

And yeah, I seriously missed Ben. I would have liked to see his intense eyes and his dark, floppy curls. It was because I would have liked to see him smile at me again. But I'd pretty much taken care of the smiles, hadn't I?

My large hotel room had a view of hot springs that flowed down scallop-shaped terraces, formed from the deposits in the water. The whole cliffside was covered with them! People were wading in the water, especially couples….

I wanted to be a couple. But it's not like I deserved it.

No, I was on a hunt for Hekate. So after locking my belongings up, I asked for help from the concierge, then caught a minibus called a *dolmus* going in the right direction.

The driver couldn't speak a word of English, but he said the name "Stratonikea" and nodded, smiling. He also chatted pleasantly with me over the hour-plus drive through the Turkish hills, between stops to pick up and let off other passengers. Instead of making me uncomfortable, I found the incomprehensible conversation strangely comforting.

This was the right place. I could feel it.

Me and Hekate. Hekate and me.

Here in…

"Stratonikea," announced the bus driver, pulling over. I thanked him—in Turkish even, *teşekkür ederim*, like I'd heard on the train. He beamed at me as he said something that probably meant "you're welcome." It felt good to get out, to stretch my legs. Only once he drove away and I looked around did I have second thoughts.

Where the hell was this?

Chapter 17

Mr. Bourikas frowned, unimpressed by the corpse sprawled across Victor's bed. "We had hopes for you, Fisher," he said in perfect, if accented, English. Then he lifted a crisp handkerchief to his nose. "But your discretion leaves much to be desired."

As if the gypsy girl had been dead long enough to smell! They were against him, was all. Everyone was against him.

And still Victor would prevail.

"You don't understand," he insisted, pacing, running a hand through his hair. When was the last time he'd had a haircut? Not important. "You have no idea how powerful I've become, even without the cup!"

Bourikas's lip curled. "The Comitatus already has the power to kill women."

Idiot! If this was the power of the Comitatus, no wonder they were letting a handful of witches run circles around them. "This wasn't about killing her," explained Victor, very patiently. "It was about getting her to scry for me."

The last few days had been a blur—there had been the magic, then the horror. That part was a test, of course. Then he'd been *somewhere else* for what seemed like a very, very long time. But once he'd returned to himself and seen that the proof of his magic had vanished, he'd known what he had to do. He had the power, he knew that now. He just needed the technique.

Luckily, Athens had gypsies—and a lot of them still advertised as fortune-tellers.

Stupid Bourikas wasn't even curious enough to ask about scrying. But that had been the Comitatus's problem all along, hadn't it? They rejected magic. "I have to ask if you've left any written records about our society or our quest," the Greek said now. "I must urge you, for the sake of your loved ones and your legacy, to make any such documents available to us. I cannot stress enough the importance of our continued secrecy."

Vic slowed in his pacing, then grinned. And these were the kind of men who *were* accepted into the secret society? "Do you realize, that's almost word for word what you guys said to my parents before you gutted them?"

Bourikas lunged at him, then. But Victor had seen this before, long before....

"I'm going back!" he announced, six years old all over again.

"Mommy said to run." That was Benny, always so ready to do what he was told, even scared. "She said to get help!"

He had Vic's hand, pulling on him hard. But the sound of their father's scream from the room beyond, gargling to an abrupt stop, startled him so much that his grip loosened.

"Then you get help." Vic pulled free, hurried deeper into the house. "I'm gonna see."

"Mommy said to watch each other!"

Benny sounded like he was going to cry. But Vic didn't care. He had to see what was going on. He had to! He rounded the corner....

Anyway, he knew what was coming. It was almost too easy to catch the man's arm, to turn the serrated knife—

To drive it to the hilt, into Bourikas's chest. Right past the ribs and…yeah, deep. Like that. Just like the men in black had done to Mommy.

Even he didn't have the strength to easily pull the knife back out, so Vic let go, shaking his head in annoyance. "You really don't get it. Neither did Prescott, when I called him about this. There really is power in magic. Dark power. I've seen it. I've *felt* it."

Hell, he'd wielded it.

The Greek businessman, envoy for the local Comitatus, opened his mouth like a fish and gurgled. Blood welled up over his bottom lip as he dropped to his knees, stunned.

"That's why I had the bitch scry for me," Vic explained, flourishing his hand toward the corpse on his bed. "Prescott wouldn't help me. You wouldn't help me. But she did. Now I don't merely know where Kate Trillo *is*. I know where she's *going to be*. Let's see your precious warrior society top *that*."

Bourikas fell to his side, open eyes blind now, open mouth silent. What a freaking letdown.

Oh, well. Since he'd discovered magic, Vic had more important reasons for finding the Hekate Chalice than the Comitatus. Who needed some secret society that might deign to let him in at the bottom of their precious pyramid structure?

Screw that! Not when he liked to be on top.

Before he left, Vic made sure to tidy up. He collected Bourikas's blood on a tissue, for future use. He took the condom he'd worn earlier, and the towel he'd used to clean up afterward, so that he wouldn't have to face any more of that damned DNA evidence. Not that the gypsy girl had been worth the effort, but hell—without Katie around, her very presence drawing him, he'd thought it couldn't hurt, right?

He put plastic on Bourikas's chest before using his foot as leverage to yank the knife out. After wiping his prints off it, he folded the weapon into the gypsy girl's hand.

There. Nice and neat. Good enough to buy him time to leave the country, anyway.

"Thanks for the lesson in fortune-telling," he told the dead gypsy, with his most charming smile. The one women couldn't resist. And for the Comitatus? "And thanks for nothing."

Now. Time to claim the powers of hell for himself.

Stratonikea stood in the middle of absolute nowhere. From the highway, I'd thought there was a village just up the hill. But as I hiked higher up the gravel road, I saw differently. The cluster of charming houses, with their faded plaster walls and quaint, red-tiled roofs, was deserted and falling apart. A sulfur smell hung heavy across the whole area. As I topped the hill and saw what lay just beyond, I guessed I knew why.

Stratonikea was even worse off than Eleusis. What lingered of the ancient city sat atop grass and stony dirt, with some short, scrubby trees here and there. Ruins outnumbered the trees, though—the rubble of partial foundations, segments of crumbling wall and columns that only went halfway up, as if they'd been partly erased by the gray sky.

Around it stretched a modern wasteland. Mining of some kind.

"Hello, progress," I muttered darkly.

The city, which Maggi had said once held one of the earliest known temples to Hekate, was in pieces. The village I'd first spotted had apparently been built among the ruins. Now the village itself had been shut down by mining.

Damn, it was depressing.

And on top of everything, a rumble in the sky drew my attention to the horizon, where the sky darkened ominously.

Goody. Storm coming.

Still, it wasn't like another *dolmus* would come by right away, even if they did run regularly. This place was frequented often enough to have signs pointing toward it and a rock road leading up to it.

And I'd come here for a reason.

So I readjusted my backpack, heavy with the supplies I'd been able to collect, and hiked over the hillside. I might as well explore this place that had once, over two thousand years ago, worshipped my namesake. If Hekate's sacred cup had been hidden at her source, it hopefully would be here.

Somewhere.

The oddest thing about Stratonikea wasn't the smell from the surrounding mines. It wasn't the hauntingly empty houses. Some of those were very large and displayed ragged remains of beauty in their intricate trim or Arabic-style doors—where the plaster wasn't falling off and leaving gaping holes in the wall, anyway. It wasn't even the eerie effect of the ruins, where solid walls suddenly descended into piles of stone blocks, or ornate stone gateways arched upward into broken nothingness. The once-white rock displayed all shades of gray, streaked black with age. Some hardy vines grew over the arches. And still, that wasn't it.

No, the oddest part was not having a tour guide.

If only Ben were here, he could probably have told me what kinds of foundations had been temples. Maybe Eleni could have read what an inscription said, carved by the crumbled remains of some small, long-lost building.

Instead, it was all up to me. I had to figure things out for myself. So…I did.

The line of masonry that came and went, until it vanished behind mining equipment—that would have been the wall surrounding the city. Just down the hill from the first building, an arena or theater had been dug into the hillside. The steps, or maybe they were seats, had grass growing between some of them, but they remained all the same.

I shivered and started to hike. And the longer I looked, the more starkly beautiful it all became.

In one place, broken-off columns and the bottom half of an archway fronted steps down to a still pond, framed by more stone. Was that on purpose, or the effect of sinking rock and a wet winter? In another area, shattered lengths of column tumbled so closely with carved stone moldings that they could have been building blocks in a child's toy box. Some of the column drums were hollow, holding more water.

Unlike at the Acropolis, I could touch these souvenirs of the past. I could run my hands across the pleated fluting of the columns. I could brace my feet on their base and boost myself up, standing as high as I could to look into any hollow pieces I found.

Thunder rumbled more loudly, echoing back off the desolate hillside. The darkening clouds loomed slowly closer. And I kept on exploring. Because I wasn't here as a tourist, after all.

I had a curse to break…or at least edit. I had a grail to find. *But it wasn't here.*

I walked through gates that led nowhere—gateways and doorways are sacred to Hekate—but I found nothing. I pressed my hands, my cheek against a single whole, smooth column, but felt nothing. I walked down an ancient road that was in better shape than the gravel road leading here, and went nowhere in particular. Oh, I sensed the age of the place. I even sensed an ancient, powerful presence that reminded me of Hekate. But a cup?

No cup. No goddess.

When the storm hit, it hit hard. One minute I was climbing unevenly up to the top of a wall, to get a better view of the rest of the ruins. The next, I heard a rattling, like hard wind in trees—and saw a sheet of rain coming at me, masking the landscape behind it.

I jumped to the ground, scooped up my backpack and took off for the nearest of the village houses. My feet flew over the stony ground. But the rain outran me, soaked me in a cold instant. Even when I managed to jump through a gaping, glassless window into what had once been a manor home, it gave iffy shelter. Rain dripped through holes in the roof and blew in sideways through the blank, open windows.

With a crash, lightning lit the ruins outside. Damn!

Then everything vanished into the gray again. And it only got blacker.

After a few minutes, I peeled off my wet coat. I hunkered shivering into a corner to wait out the storm, and thought, *What the hell am I doing here?*

"You're living," said Diana, rolling her eyes. *"Don't complain."*

I was so glad to see her. "I'd trade places with you in a minute, you know. You had so much to give the world."

"That's why those kinds of decisions aren't left up to you, doofus." She sat, cross-legged, in front of me. *"Look at you, Miss World Traveler!"*

I didn't smile. "Why do I keep seeing you, Diana?"

"Duh! Hekate is the goddess who leads dead souls to the afterlife. If anyone can manage a ghost or two, it's Her."

Or two? But she'd vanished again. Standing, I found a stick amongst the rubble and I drew a large circle around myself, through the dirt and leaf litter that covered what might have once been marble floors.

I tried not to think about the people who had lived here, who must have loved this place...who were dead. It was too sad.

I didn't have torches, like the ones Eleni had brought to Eleusis, so instead I put a symbol of each element at each point of the circle... or as near as I could guess without a compass. I put a chunk of white-and-gray marble at the north point, for Earth. I lit two sticks of incense from my pack, sandalwood and cypress, to signify Air with its smoke for the East. I put the matches at the southernmost point for Fire. And for Water?

Okay, so there was so much water around here at the moment, I could barely escape it. Still, it would be nice to have something to put it in. Digging through my pack, I withdrew the one votive candle I'd carried. It sat in a small holder, about the size of a shot glass. That would do.

I took it out into the rain, to collect fresh water.

Chunks of marble from ancient walls or steps littered the ground mere feet from the ruined house. Rain splattered hard off long-fallen columns, the power of nature continuing long after man-made structures crumbled.

The least witchy person in the world feels the power of a

rainstorm, don't they? Not just the electrical charge of lightning, but the noise of the thunder, the force of the wind, the
cleansing of the water and that wonderful, sharp air… I suspected Ben could explain why air in a storm smelled so alive.
In magic terms, Water is the element of dreams and psychic
images. It's the element of the emotions. If I was going to *feel*
the Hekate Grail anywhere around here, Water was the element that would help me.

Sometime after rain had filled the votive holder, I returned,
drenched, to the partial shelter of the abandoned manor home.
The water went in the West, where it belonged. And I knelt
in the center of my circle and lit the little candle.

I'd been working on my rhyme since the train.

"Here I've come to seek the chalice,
Here I've come to gain the grail,
Help me, Hekate, to find it,
Clear my vision, lift the veil.
Let me see where I should seek it
If, indeed, it should be sought.
Lead me, Lady, to thy chalice.
By the power—"

With a crash, light shot through the open, glassless windows—and I let out a surprised scream.

Because the man standing in the shadowy corner of the
cobwebby room was either Ben or Victor Fisher.

And whoever he was, I hadn't seen him come in.

I tensed all over. Other than that, though, I sat very, very
still. Was he even real?

"You're so blind," he said, laughing with amusement.

So…not Ben? Or a Ben who was still really mad?

"Stratonikea was founded in the third century B.C.," he continued, as if it were perfectly normal for him to be standing here, lecturing about history. Darkness washed back across him again, but he kept talking, a voice from the void. "Named after a king's wife. And stepmother."

Another strobe of lightning showed him laughing at that, like it was some big scandal. Since it was a freaking *ancient* scandal, I wasn't exactly impressed.

"How'd you find me?" I demanded. My first instinct was to try to find a weapon. The room fell dark again, a darkness that the flickering of my tiny votive candle couldn't begin to fight. Then again, that was our best weapon, wasn't it? Victor's and mine both.

Darkness. Just of a different kind.

Slowly recovering my senses, if not my ability to, oh, *breathe,* I stopped looking for earthly protection.

I was in a circle. Earth, Air, Fire, Water. Managing a tiny inhale, I tried to draw the power of the rainstorm into me in preparation for a battle.

Assuming it even was Victor. How would Victor know all this stuff? But why would Ben be so smarmy?

"Over the first century—that would be later, Katie, the years count backward B.C.?—Stratonikea and its temple to Hekate were repeatedly sacked, wholly destroyed. Eventually a temple was built here to Sarapis, the god of dreams brought by the Greeks from Egypt. This became His city."

I felt increasingly confused. So was this a Victor who suddenly knew about old gods, or a Ben who'd turned mean? "Why are you here?"

Hey, it didn't seem as stupid a question as *Who are you?* And my voice barely shook. The mingling scent of cypress and sandalwood smoke tickled my nose.

"*His* city, Katie," he insisted, his rasp of a voice intensifying from the shadows. "It no longer belongs to your lost goddess. It belongs to Sarapis. *SARAPIS!*"

"Fine, it belongs to—" At the last minute, I remembered the power of names. "To some other god. So are we supposed to ask *him* where the Hekate Grail is hidden?"

Another crash of thunder shook the ground beneath my wet knees. Birds flew out of the rafters in a feathery panic. More light blasted through the windows—

And he wasn't there. Not Victor. Not Ben.

Adrenaline had me on my feet. Where was he? And where was his voice coming from? Magic wasn't supposed to manifest this dramatically!

"*Think,* Katie," the voice instructed, even as I spun in a circle, searched the shadows. "Even you can figure this one out. *They took it with them!*"

Even you…this *had* to be Victor. But even witches as experienced as my grandmothers couldn't vanish, that wasn't how magic worked. I couldn't see him anywhere. Not during the next lightning strike, or the next.

I was shaking now, a bone-deep trembling. The space between each pulse of lightning, as I listened for some sign of him over the rain outside, over the fluttering of the birds, seemed to last forever. And those stretches just got longer. A line of incense smoke stretched, pale, upward. Rain drummed on what was left of the roof, and on the ruins outside. Thunder grumbled, then faded.

No attack came.

Outside, the rain finally began to slow. The sky lightened, and gray began to dilute the shadows of the deserted manor home.

Nobody was there. *Had he been?*

And if he hadn't, what had?

He couldn't be that good a magic user. I kept telling myself that, in hope that repetition would make it true. He couldn't be that powerful. Not so quickly.

Eventually I knelt again, thanking and dismissing the elements of Earth, Air, Fire and Water for attending my magic—for whatever protection the circle might have afforded me. But my hand shook as I snuffed the candle. As the post-storm light returned, I went to the corner where Victor had stood…and nothing was disturbed on the floor. No dirt scuffed away to reveal the marble beneath. No leaf litter broken or shifted. A few dusty feathers lay atop the mess, along with old poop from the birds in the rafters.

That's when my head began to swim. He *hadn't* been here?

"Diana?" I called, and my voice broke. "Diana!"

Nothing. Stupid, unreliable ghost.

So had he been a vision, maybe a dream? Or had *he* been a ghost? And if so…had he really been Victor's?

Foreboding constricted my chest, rushed my pulse into a thundering drumbeat. I tossed my supplies haphazardly into my backpack, climbed out the manor home window into the now sunny, muddy Turkish countryside, and took off in the direction of the highway.

I had to catch the first *dolmus* heading back to Pamukkale.

I had to make sure Ben was all right!

It didn't help, when I finally got back to my hotel, that the concierge caught me in the lobby.

"Trillo *hanim*," he called, with an elegant mix of discretion and urgency. "A thousand pardons, *hanim effendi*. You have had three telephone calls from your cousin. She pleads that you ring her back straight away on a matter of emergency."

I'd woken up on a freaking train this morning. I'd been caught in a thunderstorm—I *so* needed a hot bath, and clean clothes, and to blow-dry my cast—and I'd come face-to-face with…what? A dream? A *ghost?*

Other than Diana's, I mean.

This wasn't good. "Could you please help me make a phone call?"

He did more than that, taking me into his private office and having hot Turkish coffee fetched as he made the call himself. It's amazing, the kind of service you get when people think you have money. Once the call connected, he left me, the phone and the coffee to ourselves.

Not that I could have taken a sip, the way my hand shook. "Eleni?"

"Katie? Thank heavens I find you!" She'd had my itinerary, but I guess those three phone calls had given her plenty of time to worry.

"What's wrong? What happened?"

Please, not Ben. Please, not Ben.

"There is a murder." Eleni's voice barely shook. Never had I wished more strongly that my cousin had a better grasp on verb tenses. Did she mean there would be a murder? Or that there had been…?

Oh, please, no. "Ben?" I whispered, as my world swooped around me.

And Eleni said, "Yes."

Chapter 18

Ben?

I couldn't breathe. I couldn't think anything but one stark thought. No, two thoughts.

One thought was just *no, no, no,* echoing through my head with my pounding pulse, louder and louder. Soon the word would tear from my throat—I knew it would, I'd been here too painfully and too recently, and there was nothing I'd be able to do about it. *No!*

But my other thought was even worse.

This was my fault.

I'd cursed him. I'd put him at risk. In my need for vengeance, I hadn't done everything possible to beg Hekate to cancel the spell. And now...

Ben.

I hadn't even known him, outside of magic.

"Katie? Are you all right? There is a murder!"

Somehow I managed to force out a single question. "Who?" Of course I meant, who did it? It had to be Victor, right? And yet, Ben had been so damned sure his twin brother wouldn't hurt him....

"A gypsy girl," said Eleni.

Which was when I started to suspect I'd missed something here. "A gypsy girl killed Ben?"

"No! Ben is arrested for killing a gypsy girl."

And click. Now I understood. My relief came out as fury. "*Damn it,* Eleni! How could you do that to me? I thought you meant Ben had been murdered. *I thought he was dead!*"

"I do not say he is dead," my cousin protested.

No, she'd just said...

Okay, this wasn't helping anybody. "I'm sorry. I misunderstood. Ben's under arrest? Where—Greece or Turkey?"

"He is in Athens." Why *would* he have stayed in Turkey after our fight? "The girl, she and a shipping merchant, they are found dead in his brother's hotel."

"The Hotel Zeus? Then why did they arrest...oh."

It's not like I couldn't figure that part out.

"I'll be there as soon as I can," I told Eleni, and hung up. Only then, as my inhale stuttered, and my exhale caught, did I start to cry. Hard.

I was exhausted from feeling guilty.

Especially feeling *justifiably* guilty.

This had to end.

In half the time it had taken me to get to Pamukkale, I'd gotten myself back to Athens—but instead of a train, this trip involved a bus ride to the Denizli airport and a stopover in Istanbul. What followed was a wild-goose chase with rolling luggage. From the airport, I tried to find Ben at the jail. They told me he'd been released to the consulate. By then it was night, but I finally found someone at the U.S. Embassy who admitted that Ben had gotten permission to leave the country—I guess the evidence against him for the Athens murders was even flimsier than what they'd had in Chicago.

Then again, I hadn't been there to "help," this time.

When I called his hostel, he'd already checked out. So I made a late-night rush back to the shiny new Athens airport. Only two flights to the United States remained to depart that night, both of them to New York, so I bought a damned ticket to New York just so I could get through the security check to look for him. I nearly screamed when my credit card didn't go through. I had to call them and give the company my mother's maiden name to reassure them that it really was me making all these overseas charges before I could get my ticket.

Yeah, it was a long shot. And maybe illegal, from an international-security standpoint. But I had to try. Ever since seeing that ghostly image in Stratonikea—Ben's or Victor's, I still wasn't positive—I had to try.

I suppose I could have tried a spell to speed up the process of finding him. But…magic was what had screwed things up between us in the first place.

I dragged my rolling suitcase to the first departing gate to New York. No Ben. So I hurried on to the only other departing flight, dodging travelers, breathing hard.

Luckily, all international flights left from the same "hall" of the main terminal, no matter the airline.

By now I was so stressed that I wasn't even wondering if I could get a refund for my ticket…or if they could force me to take the flight. It was one of those weird effects of travel, that I could only worry about the very next step, instead of several steps ahead. And the only step on my mind just then was that *I had to find*—

Al Barker?

My footsteps slowed. I rubbed my eyes with the fingertips of my cast hand—since my good hand still had a death grip on my rolling suitcase. But it was him, all right. As Ben and I had noticed just last week, the tall redhead stood out around here.

What to do, what to do?

Al might be a bad guy. He'd set me and Ben up, at the diner in Chicago. He'd gone to Victor's hotel room. Then again…

I was a bad guy, too.

So I intercepted him. "Where is he?"

His double take, as he recognized me, would have been funny if I'd had any sense of humor left. "Kate Trillo?"

"Where's Ben?"

Instead of answering, Al just lifted his gaze. Behind me, a familiar, raspy voice said, "Katie?"

I turned—and there Ben stood, alive and real and okay. Seeing him eased my soul in places I hadn't thought were alive, until that moment. He looked about as exhausted as I felt, with stubble on his angular jaw and dark smudges under his intensely dark, intensely wary eyes. His hair needed a comb.

A fast-food bag dangled, forgotten, from his hand.

And I'd cursed him. No wonder he'd been mad. And I hadn't even said…

"I'm sorry," I whispered.

He swallowed. Hard. "Okay."

So I threw myself at him. Literally. My suitcase went over with a loud *whack* sound as I knocked him back a surprised step. Ben said "Oof!" as my cast hit his shoulder blades when I flung my arms around him. But then the paper bag in his hand hit the shiny floor and his arms cinched hard around me, too. Then he was kissing me, and everything—at least for that moment—was absolutely good.

In fact...

Damn, the man really could kiss.

It occurred to me that this deep sense of connection, even of completion, was still part of the curse's backlash.

Then it occurred to me to just enjoy it, for once.

I buried my fingers into the loopy black curls behind Ben's ear, and I caressed his stubbly jaw with my thumb. He nuzzled my cheek, my nose. I arched into him and his kisses. And I felt happy. Happy...

And then I felt surprised, because it had been a month since I'd been happy. Because there were times I'd feared I'd never be happy ever again. And look at me.

But I wasn't surprised enough to stop kissing him. Not even when Ben's widening grin made his lips a little less flexible. I just focused on his lower lip, then.

"Uh...sorry to interrupt." That was Al. "They've started boarding our flight."

Oh, damn. Flight?

Ben cleared his throat, leaning back slightly from me. Very slightly, considering how firmly I'd locked my arm behind him. I liked the press of our bodies too much to give him much slack. "You're not going home, too, are you?"

"No. I mean—I bought a ticket. But that was to get in and find you. I'm hoping they'll credit me or something."

He laughed. "Couldn't you have tried a courtesy page?"

A...? *Damn.* I hated feeling stupid.

Then again, would a courtesy page have led to this kind of kissing? Even now that the kissing had stopped, I couldn't seem to stop caressing his warm cheek with my thumb. "I had to make sure you were okay. I heard about the arrest...."

"Eyewitnesses." He made a face. "Al got me a lawyer, as soon as it happened. Once he proved that we were twins, and the room was Victor's... I'm fine. Really. Don't worry."

But he seemed adorably pleased that I'd worried at all.

I had a curse to lift, didn't I? "I guess I'll stay here, then. Or go back to Turkey. I need to track where Hekate's priestesses would have gone after they fled Stratonikea."

You could practically see Ben's ears perk up. "Where's Stratonikea? What did you find out?"

"Ben," urged Al in that deep, dramatic voice of his.

Ben waved him off. "They're still boarding the first-class passengers. Come on, Katie. Talk to me."

He collected the things we'd dropped and drew me over to some plastic seats. But he didn't let go of my hand even as we sat. We bent close to each other, and not just because of our subject matter. Our jeaned knees pressed against each other, and that was good, too.

Comforting, even. Halfway around the world, but not alone.

While the gate agents called out the different groups of passengers to board—in a whole list of languages—I filled Ben in on the basics of my encounter in Stratonikea.

"Fascinating," he murmured, his intense gaze tracking the invisible progress in his head. "You know, it might not have been me *or* Victor who spoke to you. It could have been a vision or, considering your recent brush with parasomnia, even a waking dream. This figure spoke of Sarapis, right?"

"God of *dreams*." Okay. I got it now. "Are you saying that ancient gods and goddesses are having some kind of turf war over a deserted village?"

"I wouldn't begin to presume, but...things don't have to

be one or the other in dreams. Maybe the person you saw was both me *and* Victor. And neither of us, at the same time."

I stared at him, and he ducked his head, winced up toward me. "Too abstract?"

Yes. And it was damned sexy. "I just need to know where to go next. We've been so busy looking backward, it never occurred to me to track the cup forward, but my visitor had a point. If the women who worshipped Hekate took her cup somewhere else, where would it be? I mean, there's a whole lot of—"

Ben sat up. "Italy."

"Benny," said Al again. This time, he had a point. Few stragglers still stood in line with their boarding passes. The gate agent glanced meaningfully at us, to hurry us up.

"Where in Italy?" I asked, and Ben laughed again. Apparently, kissing had a good effect on him, too.

"I doubt I could come up with a location in just—no, wait. Rome! Or Naples. They're ancient. I bet it will be one or the other."

I blinked at him. Damn, he was smart. But… "Rome *or* Naples?"

"Oh…hell. Come on." And, *still* holding my hand, he shouldered his carry-on, snagged my rolling suitcase, and led me over to the desk by the gate. "We can't go to New York," he told the ticket agent, quietly but firmly. "We need to go to Naples."

"I'm sorry, sir, but once you've checked luggage, you're committed to boarding the plane."

"But I haven't checked luggage." He turned to me. "Did you check any luggage?"

"No. I've only got the one bag."

The ticket agent asked for our passes and started typing in information, probably accessing records to make sure we weren't lying. In the meantime, Al pulled Ben backward by the shoulder, forcing us to let go of each other's hands at last.

I strained to hear...but it didn't work.

"Sir?" interrupted the ticket agent. "Ma'am? Although we can give you credit toward future flights, we don't have service to Naples."

"What about other airlines?" I asked, like I was rolling in money. The ticket agent typed a little more.

"Another carrier has a flight out to Rome in half an hour. They would have to tell you if there are still seats."

At the same time, the gate agent got onto the loudspeaker. "Will a Mr. Alister Barker please report to Gate 13? Your flight has boarded. Alister Barker, please report to gate 13." She repeated herself in what I assumed was Greek.

Al quickly leaned close to me. "Just try to keep him away from his brother, okay?"

Turns out Al *had* checked baggage. It was time to either board, or give them a damned good reason to delay the flight and pull his suitcase.

Which is how Ben and I ended up spending the night alone together, in Rome.

True, it was after midnight when we checked into our double room at the hotel. And we'd talked so much on the plane, about my grail quest in Turkey and about his brush with the law in Athens. He insisted that Al had been in Athens only to pursue the story—"sell his mom for publicity, remember?"—and I wasn't convinced. By the time we got to our room, we were kind of talked out. Or shy. Or both.

Ben put his duffel bag and my suitcase down against the wall, leaving the choice of the two beds to me. "So..." he said, holding my gaze in a way that felt a lot like him holding my hand had. Meaningful, I mean. Solid.

My throat closed up with something that felt a lot like… panic? I'd been shattered when I thought he was dead, elated to know he lived. And it felt wonderful, traveling with him. Rome—the Eternal City, Ben had called it in the cab—was seriously romantic at night, its monuments and fountains lit with colored floodlights against a nearly full moon.

Then again, we didn't know each other that well. We were exhausted. And I'd only had two other lovers in my life—or four, depending on how you define sexual relations. With only mixed success. But my biggest hesitation?

Instead of calling dibs on one of the beds, I asked, "How much does it bother you? That what we're feeling might not be real, I mean. That it might only be the magic?"

"Not so much," he admitted, his voice hoarse with desire. "How about—?"

But by then, I'd crossed the few steps between us and tipped my face up for his kisses, which he right away gave— with the same intense focus Ben gave everything.

And I mean, *everything*.

Kissing upright became kissing on the bed became increasingly heavy petting—and don't forget, he had two good hands. The hotter it got, the more clothes we took off, and his dark gaze was a caress on my naked body, and his body…

He was tight, and lean, and wonderful.

The sensations of body against warm body, breath across hot breath, became everything. Our whole conversation consisted of me gasping, "My toiletry bag," which he got for me—I felt so horribly cold, during the few seconds he was gone—and, after I'd dug out a two-year-old condom, him holding my face long enough to ask, "Are you sure?"

I couldn't even answer with words, I was so dizzy with wanting him. *Sure?* On the one hand, of course not. We hadn't known each other long enough to be in love, had we? We were under a spell. My sister hadn't been dead for two months yet. His brother had murdered her.

On the other hand, we weren't dead. And this, *this* was as alive as we could get. So I nodded, and hoped that was enough.

Ben smiled a lopsided smile of sheer relief and began kissing me again, and touching me again, and finally filling me, hard and real and solid and right....

But no more words. For now, we didn't need them.

We moaned happily. We gasped for breath. I think I screamed a couple of times, spreading my arms out beneath him, somehow flying on the ecstasy of it even as Ben's hard rocking drove my body down, down into the bed, down under his, over and over....

Nope. No more talking. Which I really, really loved.

And his timing was as good as his focus.

Afterward, after the yells and the shudders and the sheer release of it all, after his strength and my softness and getting rid of the condom with a tissue, he pulled the side of the bedspread up over us. Then he wrapped his arms tight around me, as if he never wanted to let me go, and he rested his chin on my shoulder, and he went to sleep.

Magic. In the best and worst ways, it was magic.

I didn't want to sleep. I wanted to memorize the feeling of his body alongside mine, to memorize the sound of his breath, to save the moment so that I could come back to it in my thoughts, anytime I needed to.

Because this might be the only chance I got.

Because those other two-to-four lovers in my life had nothing on Ben Fisher.

But the day had already been way, way too long. It had to end sometime.

And I slept.

* * *

When I woke, it was to the sound of typing. Ben had set up his laptop on the desk, by the data port. Wearing nothing but boxer shorts, he seemed to be doing some major Web surfing. Sunlight peeked around the very edge of the drapes, but other than that, only his screen lit the room.

I rolled quietly over and scanned the floor, past the edge of the bed, for something to wear. I found my underpants, which I wiggled into under the covers, and his T-shirt from the night before. It was big on me, and soft, and smelled like him.

Then properly armed, I said, "Good morning."

"Hey! Good morning." He stopped typing to turn in his chair toward me, smiling with what looked like honest pleasure. Instead of disappointment or annoyance or any number of more negative reactions he might have had, in hindsight, after our magic-fueled sex. That was a relief, but by the time I realized that this was the perfect moment for one of us to kiss the other one hello, we'd both let the moment slip past. I saw it pass when Ben's smile faltered, then returned with extra cheer. "I think I've found it. Not just a selection of Hekate sites here in Italy, *the* Hekate site here in Italy. Have you read Virgil's *Aeneid?*"

"I...forget." Liar, liar, pants on fire. I didn't even know who Virgil was, so chances were pretty low I'd read anything by him.

"There's a famous chapter where Aeneas descends into the underworld, guided by a sibyl, to talk to his dead father. It's very similar to the part in the *Odyssey* where Odysseus ventures into Hades, but then that's no surprise. I mean, Homer, Virgil."

He even did a weighing gesture with his hands, like, who *wouldn't* expect Homer and Virgil to be tight?

"Uh-huh," I said, and felt seriously stupid. Now I was the one forcing the cheer. You'd think, with a clear view of his chest, it would be easier to feel cheerful.

"Anyway, legend has it that Aeneas's entrance to the underworld was in an area north of Naples called the Phlegraean Fields. The area has a lot of hot springs, sulfur deposits, steam, fumaroles…you get the picture. Hell-like. Anyway, there's an archeological park that was once ancient Cumae, which of course was one of the oldest Grecian colonies in Italy."

Of course. I smiled harder and began to feel panicked.

Thank heavens he'd liked the sex.

But that may have been Hekate's doing, more than mine.

"And *there*—" Ben was really starting to look excited now, leaning forward, spreading his arms. "There's an ancient cave, called the Sybil's Grotto. It was undoubtedly one of the three famous oracles of antiquity."

Undoubtedly. "That's great," I said weakly.

Ben started to look confused. "So…should I get us tickets to Naples? This is your quest, Katie. I'm just along for the ride—I mean, to make sure…you know."

He thought he could protect me from Victor. But if Victor had really taken up black magic, there might not be much Ben could do… except endanger himself.

Still, that was kind of his decision.

"Naples would be great," I said. "I'll get washed up."

I escaped to the bathroom…and leaned back against the door, feeling sick from the obviousness of just how unevenly Ben and I were matched. And not just intellectually, but ethically.

I remembered the touch of his hands on my body. Of his body *in* my body. I wondered if he'd be as attracted, once the curse…

Up until now, my only reason not to lift the curse was vengeance. Victor really did deserve everything Hekate could throw at him.

But who could have guessed how badly I'd want to leave the curse in place, just to keep a man?

Chapter 19

"It's here," I whispered.

Ben turned to me, eyes widening, in the backseat of the car sent by the bed and breakfast. "You can tell already?"

I nodded, almost as surprised as he was. I'd felt something even as our train approached the Napoli Centrale station about two hours after leaving the Roma Termini. But "something," that's a pretty vague feeling. Sure, it could have been something psychic. Or it could have been a boost in blood sugar from breakfast, you know?

Or it could have been the pleasure of Ben's company, heightened by the fear of losing that if I canceled the curse. No, *when*. Definitely *when* I canceled it.

Damn it.

Is everything okay? he'd asked me, when I got out of the bathroom. He'd pulled jeans on, and another maroon T-shirt.

I'm sorry. I don't do this that often, so I might have neglected
some kind of morning-after expression of, uh, gratitude or...

That was the Ben I couldn't take advantage of. That was
the Ben for whom I had to find the Hekate site.

Once we'd transferred onto the Napoli-Torregaveta
subway line out of town, I could finally name this strange hy-
perawareness. It was excitement. Anticipation, even.

Like the night before your birthday, when you're a kid.

The Villa Minerva's proprietor, Signor Vecchio, met us at
the station and transferred our luggage into the back of his
car. While he did, I looked at the green and brown hills around
us, and the bright blue sky with just a few cotton-ball clouds.
I breathed in the seaside air, and I was home.

As surely as if I heard my mother's voice calling to me,
from just over the next hill. *This was the place.*

The goddess grail was here.

We drove past the almost perfectly round Lake Averno below
us, which Signor Vecchio explained had formed from a volcanic
crater. "There is path, from villa to *lago*. Very nice. Very pretty."

"And the archeological park?" asked Ben, as we lost sight
of the lake behind some trees.

Driving us under a very old, narrow archway, Signor
Vecchio made another turn. "Perhaps one mile, perhaps two.
No farther. Easy walk, for healthy Americans like you."

Excellent.

Villa Minerva sat, elegant with its buff-stone walls and
black shutters, in the midst of a lush green lawn. The "double"
room Ben had reserved meant that it had only one full-size
or "double" bed in a truly gorgeous room. Everything was
muted shades of white and gold, with a slate tiled floor, a
stone niche framing the head of the bed, and white French
doors opening onto a sunny garden full of flowers.

"Beautiful," I assured them, when Ben looked uneasy with the one bed, as if he didn't want to seem pushy.

He didn't have to be pushy. Part of me wanted another night of incredible sex with him so much that thinking too hard about it distracted me from forming complete sentences.

Part of me, however, feared taking anything for granted. Because if, after I found the Hekate site and lifted the curse, we decided we'd made a mistake…

That thought hurt enough to stop all words completely.

But not enough, I hoped, to stop me from finishing the job.

As soon as we'd had lunch, in Villa Minerva's sun-dappled courtyard, Ben and I headed for the archeological park. Armed with a photocopied map, we followed the paved pathway that circled the rim of Lake Averno—"Lake Hell," Ben said that might mean—in the direction of ancient Cumae. If this was Hell, it got really bad press. Little bitty ducks hid under tufts of long grass at the edge of the water, just beyond a quaint wooden fence made of slim logs in long Xs. To the east sat the ruins of some big old Roman building—part of what must have been a round wall, uneven windows still copping to its man-made origins despite the grooves of erosion and the grass growing on top of it—but we headed west. The midday sky seemed huge, partly because "west" not only took us toward Averno's sister lake, Lake Lucrino, but toward the sea. The temperature was in the low sixties, mild and sunny.

Much nicer than Stratonikea, back in Turkey. Nicer than Eleusis, in Greece. This place, progress hadn't screwed with yet.

And then there was the sacred feeling all around me, like

a humming in my ears. It felt like my heart beat faster, like my breath came deeper, like the air around us vibrated. I could barely keep from fidgeting. This was definitely a magic place. And if I had to swallow my pride to understand why priestesses of Hekate might have hidden their sacred cup in some cave around here, then…so be it.

"So tell me," I said, as Ben and I strode along together, and I tried not to wince. "What exactly is a sibyl?"

He laughed, like I'd told a joke. Then he looked stricken as he realized I'd been serious. "But…*you're* a sibyl, Katie. Kind of."

I narrowed my eyes at him. "Go on."

"Sibyls were priestesses in ancient Greece. They told fortunes—usually in the form of riddles—at sacred sites called oracles. Well…the shrine was called an oracle, and so was the sibyl who prophesied at the shrine."

I nodded. So far, so good.

"Now if you do just a pass-through of ancient history, you'll read that the sibyls were priestesses of the sun god, Apollo. But that's because history's written by the winners. By Greece's golden age, sun gods were being elevated far above earth goddesses. So to speak."

The way he pointed upward toward the sun, then down toward the ground, made me laugh, which made him smile his lopsided smile.

"In fact, many scholars believe the sibyls were originally priestesses to an older chthonic goddess. One of the more ancient of those was Cybele. You can hear the similarity between the words."

"And chthonic means…?"

This time he didn't laugh. "Relating to the underworld."

And that's when I got it. I *got* it! "And Hekate's the goddess who guides souls to the underworld, just like the sibyl guides whatsisname to the underworld in that Virgil book!"

"Aeneas," agreed Ben, then staggered backward because I'd flung myself at him again. His kiss was only a little distracted by trying to keep his balance against my sneak attack. Otherwise, he seemed glad to comply, no questions asked.

I answered, all the same. Though not with, *I'm trying to stock up, just in case.*

"You're brilliant," I told him, my nose touching his.

"You're the one who figured out that we needed to go forward instead of backward to find the grail," he reminded me, after another kiss.

"No, you did that. Or your brother, or Sarapis. Whoever it was who appeared to me in Stratonikea. I haven't been big about going forward lately." Deflated, I turned to continue with him toward the archeological park. I almost didn't feel his fingers slide down my hair, one last time, before he let me go.

The path got steeper as we left the lake behind us. Soon the entrance to the park—a high stone wall with open, ironwork gates—came into view.

Beyond them, all thick trees and looming hillside, waited the end of our quest. It was enough to make me dizzy. Really.

Ben dug out money for our entrance fee. "Let me. This is tax deductible."

That last part was because I'd gotten my own wallet out. "How is this tax deductible?"

"We can do a segment on sibyls for the *Superrational Show.*"

Since I had no idea what euros exchanged to anyway, I let him get in line. I hung back, randomly studying the blue signs that identified Cumae in four different languages. Did I say I was dizzy? The buzzing in my head felt so loud now, I could hardly think through it. It wasn't a bad sensation. In fact it was kind of like being drunk, where things are swoopy and off balance.

That's how big the magic was, here.

So much bigger than me, it scared me.

"Come on." Ben caught my hand with that same old sense of completion to lead me at a fast pace into the park.

"This is the way to the Sibyl's Cave?"

Instead of answering, he broke into a run, towing me with him down one of several paths. And…something was wrong. Something *other* than the magical buzz.

By the time I'd processed that, and yanked my hand free to collect myself, we'd rounded a corner into the hilly woods. "What's the hurry?" I asked, wishing I could concentrate a little better around all this swooping dizziness. I mean…this *was Ben*, right? He was wearing the faded maroon T-shirt and jeans that had been his standard wardrobe since Athens. His hair was kind of long and loopy….

And he looked hurt by my suspicious studying of him.

Damn, I was paranoid.

He flashed his shy, ducking-his-head smile, and that was a little better. "Have I told you how great you look today, Katie?"

Which was nice to hear, so why did everything seem so… off-kilter? "No."

"You do. You're gorgeous. Your dark hair. That olive skin…"

"Ben, something's wrong," I admitted. "I'm really…dizzy."

I mean, seriously. Had the Villa Minerva drugged my food?

"C'mere." Concerned, he led me to a rock hewn bench, beyond which loomed a pathway—half dirt, half stone stairs—up to the ruins of some huge structure. Italian ruins, apparently, were golden brown instead of white. We both sat. "Tell me about it."

"I think it's the magic. Like I told you, I *know* this is the place, and I'm glad." Except for the fear of losing him, once the magic ended, but I wouldn't admit that part. "But it's like…like sensory overload."

"So maybe you need to concentrate on something else?" Ben suggested—and his mouth covered mine, searching, tasting. His arms encircled me, pulled me to him. The connection clicked between us, strong as ever. He really was a hell of a kisser. And I really did want to stock up. But something still seemed wrong.

"How's that?" he asked, throaty, between kisses.

Taking his advice, I tried to concentrate on just one thing. *Him.* And the way he was leaning me back across the bench, following me down with his hard body, running a hand up my ribs and across one of my breasts as he filled my mouth with his…

The dizziness overwhelmed me, all the same.

"God, you're so hot." He lowered his head to kiss across my breasts, his mouth open, his tongue hot, which distracted me right back.

Then he was tugging my shirt out of the waistband of my jeans "Ben." I managed to protest. "We're kind of…in public."

With a grin, he wrapped his arms around me and rolled us off the bench, into the grass on the side opposite the pathway. Since it was a big, blocky bench of solid rock, someone would have to walk right by us to see.

Coincidentally, he'd landed on top. "Problem solved," he said, and freed enough of my shirt to push it upward, following it with his hot, hot tongue in my belly button. "I'm—" his words were muffled now "—a problem solver."

Part of me was shocked. We were *still* in public, even more than the time Sal Milano and I were in the backseat of his Grand Prix in high school. But I've got to admit…the part of me that had taken up with the dark side lately was kind of turned-on by the risk of it.

Especially as Ben kissed upward from my belly button, up my sternum and unclipped the front of my bra. "Oh, God," he breathed again.

Then his hot mouth covered the tip of my breast. Dizziness and desire and danger merged in an overwhelming intoxication.

I threw my head back in the leaves and grass, arched under him like I had last night, wasted my one good hand by stuffing it in my mouth so that I wouldn't attract the attention of some field trip kids or something. Oh, yeah. This was my kind of wicked. Except…

"Something's wrong," I gasped. Even drunk on magic and arousal, I knew that much. It wasn't the way he'd moved to the other breast, his soft hair tickling the one he'd left wet. It wasn't the hardness I could feel through our jeans, pressing the seams against my own need for him….

His head stilled on me. He pushed himself far enough off me to squint down at me. "Wrong? Nothing's wrong."

Then he started to tell me, in a raspy whisper, exactly what he wanted to do to me, and how right it would feel. I wove my fingers into his hair…and just as I felt the scar on his scalp, I realized what was different.

Ben sure was talking a lot. In bed last night, he'd been practically wordless. I'd found that especially sexy, him not diluting what we did with commentary. But now…

He stripped off his maroon *Napoli* T-shirt, up and off his

beautiful chest and over his head, and tossed it aside—but I was the one who went cold. Sure, he had a great chest, tanned and ripped with just the right amount of hair trailing from over his pecs down the center of his six-pack and into his jeans. But—

A *Napoli* T-shirt? Not one from Chicago?

Oh-my-goddess-holy-hell, it was Victor!

Chapter 20

I went from hot to sickly cold in a split second.

My shirt was still bunched up under my arms, under my chin. My blood was still pounding. My breasts were still damp. And all from making out with *my sister's killer?*

"So sexy," murmured Vic, ducking back down to me. "I've needed to do this for so long—"

And I knocked him across the head with my cast.

"Hell!" If I'd had any lingering doubts, the way Victor Fisher reared up and backhanded me ended them. He drove my shoulders back into the dirt while my vision was still clearing, pinning me down. "Katie! What the fuck?"

"Get off me, *Victor!*"

His grin was a sneer. "But we're not done yet."

He loomed down for another kiss. When I strained my

head away, writhing helplessly under his weight, he stuck his hot tongue in my ear and said, "Mmm. *Yummy.*"

He was stronger, heavier. He had twice the working hands I did. And the son of a bitch was ruthless....

But I was a witch.

A witch so drunk on all the eddies and undertows of power around here—not to mention so desperate for his brother—that I'd fallen into his trap in the first place, sure.

But I wasn't exactly helpless.

I gathered energy like I might scoop water over myself, silently calling on the strength not only of Hekate, but any goddess worshippers who may have been here before me. That was a lot of strength. Then, with one desperate burst of power, I flung myself upward and slammed my forehead into his prominent nose.

I heard a crack on fleshy impact.

"Fuck!" He recoiled, just off balance enough for me to roll out from under him. Magic, or coincidence?

Did it freaking *matter?*

As dizzy from the head butt as the magic, I scrambled to get my feet under me.

His hand closed on my ankle, like a manacle, and he jerked me backward. I hit the dirt hard. An uneven rock sent a shriek of pain up my knee. But I kicked back at him, all the same. Again, I put every bit of magical power into it that I could. For every woman this place could remember being abused. For every woman this place could remember being attacked. For *every woman*—

My foot connected with a hard thud. My technique wasn't neat or graceful, but it worked; his grasp loosened on my ankle. I tried to pull free, almost had it. He grasped my shoe.

With a wrenching tug, I lost the shoe and ran, rocks poking hard through my sock on that foot.

Behind me, Vic loosed a mantra of swear words that could have been curses themselves. "You're the one who bewitched me, you bitch! You brought this on yourself!"

I fumbled my shirt back down as I fled.

Before I had reached the front gate, a guard intercepted me. He wore a white shirt, a white hat, dark pants and a look of increasing concern. "You are Signorina Trillo, *sì?*"

Apparently, he'd thought Ben was overreacting when he'd declared me missing—until he saw me.

Everything got crazy after that. In the modest office near the front gate I reported Victor's attack as just that, a simple attack. The guard got me an ice pack for my swollen cheek. The *polizia* were called in. Little police cars pulled up outside the gates, their foreign sirens screeching. At least six officers spread out to search the heavily wooded park. And after barely fifteen minutes, the kindly *poliziotto* who'd taken my abridged statement proudly announced that they'd captured my attacker.

This might be a goddess site, but could it be that easy?

The man they dragged back to the gate wore jeans and a maroon T-shirt, all right. He had curly black hair, too. The mingling of concern and frustration in his quick, dark eyes made him look more than a little maniacal.

But his shirt read University of Chicago. And when he saw me, he sagged with honest relief. "Katie!"

"Ben?" I surged forward—then slowed my step, hating this doubt his brother had planted. "Victor's here, and he's dressed almost exactly like you. Tell me something he wouldn't know."

Ben's brows angled with hurt, then furrowed into acceptance. For a moment I was very afraid he'd choose something like, *you close your eyes when I kiss you.* I'd already tucked in my shirt and combed most of the leaves out of my hair, and I was just as glad to take some of my encounter with Victor to my grave. The sexual nature of his attack was one part of the story I'd abridged, along with the magic.

Luckily, Ben's eyes followed some other invisible path of thought. He raised his gaze to me with taut decision. "You're possessive about the cutlery."

One of the first things he'd ever said to me.

I closed the gap between us and hugged him, then— incredibly glad. Incredibly guilty. How could I not have recognized the difference in their energies? Dizzy or not, why hadn't I noticed all the distracting words his brother had used?

Ben couldn't hug me back, what with the handcuffs, but he laid his cheek on my hair with a heavy sigh of relief. "Kate…."

The policemen started yelling.

Italian's a lot more familiar to me than Greek, but I've still never learned the language. My grandparents—Pop and Nonna—had always been big on making the family "act American." But I'd picked up enough to know that the cops thought I was lying.

It took us over an hour to set things straight—to get the original guard to identify Ben as the man who'd raised the alarm, to show them a picture from Ben's wallet of the two brothers together, to protest that we really hadn't filed a false report, despite the fact that I was now hanging off the man they'd thought was my attacker.

"You're sure you're okay?" Ben murmured, more than once, during the lulls when the *poliziotti* yelled at each other instead of at us.

"I'm fine. Really." I'd already put down the ice pack I'd

been given for my cheek. And one of the guards had found me a replacement shoe—an oversized brown loafer—from their lost-and-found box.

Ben's concern made me feel even worse for having mistaken his brother for him. I mean, the clues had been there all along. If Ben had rolled with me off a rock bench, I'd bet he would be sure to land first, to cushion my fall. Ben wouldn't have put me at risk of arrest by suggesting sex in public in the first place. Hell, he probably…

Let's face it. He probably wouldn't have suggested sex at all. He would have waited for me to suggest it.

Damn it.

If I needed more proof of how doing dark magic had helped corrupt me, this was it. Because, Hekate help me, for that brief interlude before I'd realized Victor was Victor…

Had I honestly found him even close to as hot as Ben?

I watched Ben rub his wrists, scowling, now that the police had uncuffed him. And I did the only thing I could. I made excuses to myself. Some women blame their choice of sex partners on having been drunk? Well, I'd been OD'ing on an ancient energy that had distracted me, disoriented me, made me…

Wait.

Why wasn't I dizzy anymore? I could still feel the energy of this place all around me and through me, like a sugar buzz. Just like when I'd gotten off the train, I knew beyond a doubt that the Hekate Chalice was here, so close it almost hurt not to be out finding it. But now that I was safe, now that it wouldn't have made as big a difference, I didn't feel drunk anymore. *Why not?*

Unfortunately, that question would have to wait for a little more privacy.

The last of the search party returned to the park offices,

and more yelling commenced. Ben leaned closer to me and translated, "They couldn't find him."

I'd kind of figured that much.

Clearly, to judge by the glares, the *poliziotti* were divided in their opinions of whether there had ever been a Victor. But the officer who'd first responded was polite enough to at least play along with our story.

"If he was in the park, he is not here now," the *poliziotto* told us. And, since by now they must have communicated with Athens, "We will continue to search for him beyond the park boundaries. For now, please allow me to drive you safely back to your lodgings."

Back to our lodgings? "But we haven't been to the cave," I protested. I was here to find a goddess cup!

For the good of women…and for the good of Ben.

The men exchanged incredulous looks and a few exclamations—I'd been attacked, as testified by my bruised cheek and still-missing shoe, and I wanted to sightsee?

The word "crazy"—*pazzesca*—got tossed around some. With a sharp glance in my direction, Ben joined the debate in careful Italian. He seemed to say something about how important this visit was to me. I heard the words *Antro della Sibilla.*

"Yes, the Sibyl's Cave," I agreed. "I came here to see the *Antro della Sibilla.* We can leave after that."

That caused more concern all around, including some gesturing at the clock—apparently the park would close in half an hour. But finally Ugo, the security guard who'd been so kind to me, agreed to give us a quick guided tour of the cave, just to be on the safe side.

On the one hand, if we actually found the Hekate Chalice, it would be hard to reclaim it around Ugo. No way would I be able to do any significant magic around him.

On the other hand…*security guard.* Psychotic killer wandering nearby. I really didn't mind having Ugo along.

Ben continued to scowl, even after we left the police, though that didn't keep him from taking my hand and keeping a tight hold on it. We headed down the wooded path and passed the steps toward the crumbling acropolis. That meant passing the bench where Victor and I had been….

Hello, guilt.

"Something really weird happened," I murmured to Ben, speaking quietly in case Ugo's English was better than I'd thought.

"Oh really?" Ben asked. Scowling. Okay, so he knew I'd been smacked upside the face. He'd been mistakenly held by police for the second time in two days, and the third time in just over a month. That *had* to be getting old. I reminded myself that this was Victor's fault this time, not mine.

"While I was waiting for you to get our tickets, and Victor tricked me away? It's like I couldn't think clearly." His dark gaze, when he slid it toward me, seemed dubious. "Really! It was like a buzzing in my head."

Ugo paused by a sign that read *Antro della Sibilla,* with an arrow, and waved us down the correct path.

Ben looked grudgingly intrigued. "Buzzing. An electric discharge, maybe? Like standing near a generator?"

"Yeah. I thought it might have to do with this place."

"There are a lot of theories about earth memory," he agreed, and I felt myself relaxing as Ben eased into explanation. Well…relaxing as much as I could, with the knowledge that Victor could be anywhere around us, watching us. "In fact, it's one of the more popular explanations for ghost sightings. The idea is that a location that's seen an event of overwhelming hatred, or pain, or despair gets imprinted with those emotions, the way clothing picks up the scent of ciga-rette smoke. Places like Gettysburg, for example, or Culloden in Scotland are believed to still radiate the horrors of what happened there. So it's no great leap to assume the same phenomenon for holy places. Notre Dame—"

"But it stopped," I interrupted quickly, since Ugo was now waiting for us by a rock wall at the foot of the hill. "I mean, I can feel *something* now, but it's not overwhelming me anymore."

Ben considered this, then leaned close to whisper, "Did you use magic to get away from Vic?"

His breath on my ear made me shiver. I nodded.

"That may have released the charge. For lack of a better analogy, I mean, I don't pretend to—"

"*Antro della Sibilla.*" With a flourish to hurry us along, Ugo indicated a rock stairway down into the earth. Greenery hung over the ledge. Moss smeared the gray stone. And a rec-tangular opening at the bottom beckoned darkly.

I could feel something call to me from within, all the same. More magical pressure, throbbing, pulsing, waiting for me to reach it.

"Watch the step," urged Ugo, gallantly taking the elbow of my cast arm as I slowly descended into the darkness. He was almost as old as my grandfather, but that didn't make him any less Italian.

Taking a deep breath, as if I was about to submerge myself in water, I entered the Cave of the Sibyl.

It was…magical. More stone steps, so old that they dipped in the middle, slanted downward until the bottom. There, they crumbled into one extra big step and made a hairpin turn. That's where the tunnel really got serious.

It was a lot more tunnel than it was cave.

"What's this shape?" I asked, after Ben let go of my hand so Ugo could help me over the large bottom step.

Ben jumped easily to the tunnel floor beside me and whistled through his teeth. "Hexagonal? Sort of."

A hexagon would be six sides, right? Flat on the bottom and top? Maybe if you took a hexagon and stretched the top half twice as high as the bottom half, maybe that would explain the methodical way these walls had been cut. Wooden poles stretched across the narrowing roof of the tunnel, maybe for support. Over them, like a natural skylight, a hole in the ground above us let in the sun. Farther down the tunnel, another doorway—also in the shape of a tall, skinny hexagon—beckoned deeper yet into the underground.

"*Facilis descensus Averno,*" said Ugo, in the same kind of spooky voice old men might use to tell ghost stories.

I paused. "That's not Italian."

"Latin," said Ben behind me, his voice echoing despite the openings above us. "It's a quote from the *Aeneid* about this place. 'The way to hell is easy.'"

Thanks a lot, Ugo.

Then again, if this really had been the way to hell—according to Virgil or Homer or whoever—it *was* easy. I'd been imagining the kind of caves that require climbing and ducking, not a path this straight. As we three continued on, the tunnel took on a dreamlike quality. At even intervals, more slits had been dug to the surface, so that the stone floor was intersected with stripes of natural light. It gave the impression of going on forever. The volcanic rock—*tufo,* Ugo called it—was soft beneath our feet. He showed us how easily it could be scraped off the wall, too, with his penknife.

Considering that we were now well under the hill between Cumae and Lake Averno, I hoped he wouldn't do that again.

"Apparently," said Ben, his voice hushed, "people would come to the sibyl for advice about everything from national wars to their love lives. Ancient writings speak of the priestess being surrounded by fumes…it's uncertain whether they meant steam, like from the volcanic activity in this area, or some form of narcotic incense. The word could even mean breath…or souls."

Souls, I thought firmly. I'm not sure how I knew, but I did. Maybe because Hekate seemed so connected to ghosts?

I also knew to stop where the passageway we were in intersected with two others, creating a vaulted room. Here the long, hard lines of the hexagonal tunnel rounded into more feminine curved arches. "Here," I announced. "This is where it would happen."

At the crossroads, of course.

Stone-slab benches had been constructed, long ago, against several walls—for the sibyl, or for her customers? Sheets of sunlight streamed into the chamber from the world above, partitioning the underground darkness. I knew this was the place….

And I knew that the actual magic happened even farther in. So I entered the next tunnel to the right and kept walking. Now I was going first, with both Ugo and Ben close behind me.

"There is little more," protested Ugo, as I headed down more worn steps —and he was right about this route, anyway. The soft rock had caved in, cutting off the passageway completely.

I shook my head. "No, there's more."

And I skirted past both surprised men, heading up the stairs for the main chamber and the third passageway.

"Once, this cave connects to Lago d'Averno," Ugo

agreed. "But this was long ago. The passageway, it no longer goes through."

And yet, as I headed down the stairs off this next tunnel, I knew it had to go a *little* farther. Because I could sense the magic of the grail, somewhere ahead of me, somewhere below me—

I stopped abruptly. The stairs vanished underwater.

"You see," announced Ugo, coming up behind me.

But I continued down the stairs, wading into the water. Damn, it was cold!

Ugo called, "Wait! This is not safe."

But safe or not, it also didn't go through. By the time I'd waded bust deep, I'd reached the far wall. The only way to keep going would be to dive…and who knew how long it would continue before the passageway resurfaced to air?

Besides, my arm was in this damned cast. I couldn't swim.

It couldn't end like this. *It couldn't!*

"Please, Signorina Trillo," pleaded Ugo. "Please, come to safety. You—"

He cut off abruptly, I think due to something Ben did, since Ben more quietly asked, "What are you sensing, Katie?"

I would have answered him, too.

But then came the laugh, echoing down from far above us through one of the rough-hewn skylights.

Victor's laugh.

Chapter 21

By the time we'd made our way back to the surface, Victor was long gone. Ugo got another guard to drive us back to the Villa Minerva—after laying towels down on the backseat, since I was still sloshing as I walked.

Even after a long shower, a change of clothes and a quick call to make sure Eleni was okay, I didn't feel any better. I just stood there, alone in our room, staring out the French doors into the garden, and felt defeated.

Why did this have to be so hard?

"You expected it to be easy?" teased Diana. But when I turned toward the spot where I'd imagined her voice, she wasn't there. Instead, Ben was opening the door with a cautious knock.

"Signor Vecchio knows of a department store that's still open in Pozzuoli," he said. "He's offered to drive us there to get you some new shoes."

I glanced back out the doors. The sun hadn't even set, and we were talking about stores "still open"? I suddenly wished I was back home in Chicago. "You go ahead."

The long silence, behind me, was thick enough to drown in. I turned and faced Ben. "What?"

He looked incredulous. "You want me to go shoe shopping for you?"

"No! I just meant—if you want to go to town, go ahead. I'm fine here."

"With these." He picked up my wet sneaker and the soggy, mismatched brown loafer, which I'd left by the bed.

"For now, yeah." I didn't like the stubborn furrow of his brow. "Look, I didn't ask you to set up a ride for us. I don't want to go out. All I've been doing for over a week is going, going, going, and what good has it done?"

"You said you sensed the chalice down there."

"Where I can't get at it!"

Ben shrugged and dropped the shoes with two squishy thuds. "You're a witch. Think of something."

It would have been a great exit line, except that he stopped before opening the door to look over his shoulder. "In case there's any confusion when I get back, Kate, the secret password is 'Relationship.'"

Then he left.

Before I could throw anything at him. Not that I wasn't tempted. Had he guessed at what had happened between me and Victor? Or was he just pissed that I'd mistaken Victor for him at all?

I flopped back on the room's one bed to sulk.

"When the moon is full and high," warbled Diana. She never was much of a singer.

"Shut up," I told her.

"You heard Ben. You want to find the chalice? Be a witch."

I rolled over with a groan, face first in the pillow. Now my words were muffled. "It's not that easy."

"It's what you are," she persisted, *from somewhere behind me. "What you were born to. Stop ignoring it."*

Rather than argue with a freaking *dead woman,* I rolled off the bed, stuffed my feet into my wet, mismatched shoes, and squished out into the garden. Turns out "garden" was another way of saying "yard." The Villa Minerva had a huge one, distantly framed with a neat, vine-covered wall of the same buff stone that made up the house.

Yeah. I was aware that a simple low wall wouldn't be enough to keep Victor away, if he knew where we were staying. But when the thought of going back in occurred to me, it just pissed me off. Was I supposed to stay inside, behind locked doors, for the rest of my life?

Italian sunlight fell gently across me and the lush lawn, shadows long with the day's lateness. Lemon and orange trees sent a wonderfully clear, clean fragrance across the yard—garden— whatever. Witches celebrate mid-March as a time of renewal and growth and the return of the light.

Until that moment, I hadn't fully realized just how much time I'd spent out at night lately…or underground. Now, wandering, I found myself appreciating the vines and flowers and butterflies and birds as if it had been years. Off to one side of the large yard, guarded by a tall hedge, a clear blue swimming pool beckoned. Back home, there might still be snow. Here in Italy, it was almost seventy degrees—certainly warm enough to swim…if I weren't wearing this stupid cast.

One more week, I reminded myself—that's when the nasty fiberglass tube was supposed to come off. I couldn't wait. It itched. It felt loose. And maybe worst of all…

I'd been wearing the damned thing since Diana's death.

My hand had been broken at the same time my old life ended.

Suddenly it felt as if my whole life was imprisoned in some hard, smelly, itchy confine…and I wanted it off. Now. *Desperately.*

To know, to will, to dare… I had some medical knowledge, though I'm sure my orthopedist would question that, if he knew what I was considering. I had the willpower. But did I dare…?

Damn right I did.

So I found Mrs. Vecchio and borrowed a pair of her garden shears. Then I went back to Ben's and my room, disinfected them—and I slowly, carefully, cut my cast off by myself.

Do not try this at home! This went against everything medical training advised. It's unwise to stick anything into a cast because your skin is so tender that it's easy to cause an infection. And, of course, it's not smart to remove a cast before your bones are completely healed. But I was only a week away from my doctor's predicted deadline. By now, the break would have pretty much knitted…it just needed a little extra protection, for a little while longer.

I could be careful. And if I couldn't? Too late now. With the first crunching cut of the shears, I was committed.

In a few minutes, I'd freed my hand, my arm. It looked terrible—the skin too pale and ashy, the hairs too dark. But when I washed my hands with warm water, carefully sudsing up to my elbows, and then rubbed some lotion on, it felt... *new.* Fragile, maybe, like a butterfly emerging from a cocoon. But full of possibility, too.

Before cleaning and returning Mrs. Vecchio's shears, I butchered the sleeves and neckline out of one of my older T-shirts, so that it fell off one shoulder. I turned one of my two pairs of jeans into cutoffs. Then I went swimming, damn it.

In Italy.

Surrounded by the butterflies and the flowers.

Stretched out on a deck chair to dry in the orange sunset, I closed my eyes with complete satisfaction. Maybe Victor *had* broken me.

But maybe I'd healed.

When the moon is full and high,
Do not seek me in the sky.
Look below, wear pads of light,
Fairy seekers from the night....

I opened my eyes, suspicious now. This was the second time today I'd thought of that—what Diana and I had called the "Fairy Seekers" song as children. It didn't have anything to do with goddess grails or Hekate. At least, I hadn't thought it did.

But...I sat up. Maybe I was still missing something.

Be a witch, Diana had said. And witches celebrate holidays other than the solstices, the equinoxes and the greater sabbats.

Witches celebrate the full moon.

* * *

By the time Ben got back to our room, carrying two shopping bags by their rope handles, I'd written the whole thing down.

"Look!" I exclaimed, handing him the page of Villa Minerva stationary.

"What happened to your cast?" he asked, looking at my hand instead of at the song.

"I ditched it."

"You can do that?"

Instead of answering, I gestured at the paper. Only then, as he began to read it, did I notice how good Ben looked in a pale green, button-down shirt. "Hey, nice threads."

"I decided not to be so predictable," he muttered, continuing to read, then slanted his gaze back to me. "Oh, yeah. The secret password—"

"Shut up, Ben." But I smiled when I said it, because even with the nice shirt he was so obviously Ben. And that was such a good thing.

He smiled back, one of his here-and-gone smiles. "What is this?"

"It's an old song Diana and I used to sing with our mom."

"I thought you didn't know any rhymes about goddess cups?"

"I didn't think it *was* about a goddess cup. It's about the full moon."

He squinted at it. "Are you sure this is supposed to be 'fairy,' like Tinkerbell, and not 'ferry,' like a boat?"

Of course I wasn't sure—we'd sung it, not spelled it out, and what kid thinks of boats when they can think of fairies? At my urging, Ben sat down with the song and marked places where he thought different words might fit... and damned if it didn't make more sense.

When the Moon is full and high
Do not seek Me in the sky
Look below, where paths of light
Ferry seekers from the night.

Only when the moon is round
Can those not damned go underground
And find what those, far in your past
Did set aside so I might last.

They who foretold the future knew
That someone wicked wise like you
Could claim my treasure, hid below
Where my cold moonbeams rarely go.

I was bouncing with impatience by the time Ben raised his dark gaze to me. "It's someplace that you can only see on the full moon?"

I nodded. "Like maybe the Cave of the Sibyl, with those openings to the surface."

"Except the cave was a dead end. Wasn't it?" He looked worried. "You aren't going to suggest we break into the park, sneak into the cave and try to swim under that one place where the water comes in, are you?"

I shook my head. "Remember what Ugo said? The Cave of the Sibyl once connected all the way to Lake Averno. So… isn't it possible that there's an entrance on this side, too?"

Ben began to smile. "And the full moon?"

I nodded. "Tonight."

Now he grinned. "Good thing I bought you new shoes."

* * *

Ben looked up the time of the moonrise on his laptop computer. Together we took the path Signor Vecchio had told us about, down to Lake Averno, with about fifteen minutes to spare.

Ben insisted on going first, but his step slowed as he reached the beach. "Did you do this? You know…" He wiggled his fingers, like doing magic.

"Do what?" I looked, and grinned. "Nope. But I should have." And hey, coincidences are a kind of magic, too.

Turns out, Villa Minerva owned a rowboat.

Ben rowed us toward the center of the lake, the oars making soft, splashy noises. For a while, I just watched him row. It showed off his shoulders, his arms, the way he gritted his teeth when he exerted himself. I'd noticed that one of the bags he brought back from Pozzuoli was a pharmacy bag, and somehow knew it held condoms…but I didn't know if we would ever get to use them, after tonight. But I was distracting myself.

Be a witch, Diana had said. So I spread my arms and stretched my whole being out around us, into the seemingly bottomless water, into the cloud-streaked night sky. From the center of the perfectly round crater, it was easy to see the rim of what had once been a volcano. It was harder to imagine a mountaintop where there was now air, or fiery lava where there was now water.

Earth, Air, Fire, Water. Nature changes, sometimes explosively. That was a kind of magic, too.

I could see the light, first a silver glow against the purple dusk over the rim of the crater—and I began to feel drunk again. Swoopy. Dizzy. *Damn it,* I started to think…

Then it occurred to me not to fight it. *I am the daughter*

of a witch, the granddaughter of a witch, the sister of a witch.

The moon crested over the hill, and *wham!*

The power blasted right through me. I was drowning… floating…lost….

I am named for the Goddess of Witchcraft.

The power rolled me, crushed me. Not fighting it may be the hardest thing I've ever done. Opening myself to that kind of energy felt suicidal. I could no sooner step off a high cliff, no sooner inhale deeply underwater, no sooner…

But I had to. And I had magical training to help.

Words, I remembered. *Words.* So I whispered, "I…am… Hekate."

Suddenly, instead of pounding over me, the power was rushing through me. I could feel it streaming out of my fingertips, beaming out of my eyes, flowing off the ends of my hair. And then…

And then, I just was. Me. Katie, strong and healthy and whole. I hadn't lost myself after all. Maybe I'd found myself.

And speaking of *finding…*

The moon cast a path of silver over the rim of the lake, across its mirrored surface and to a rocky area to the west.

I pointed. "That way."

My voice only shook a little.

Ben nodded and put his back into rowing, so casually accepting that I finally had to ask.

"Did you notice anything? A minute ago?" He'd been facing me.

He widened his eyes as he pulled on the oars. "Should I have?"

Didn't you see me glow? But instead of asking that, I just laughed. It didn't matter if he'd seen it or not. That was the importance of the fourth element of magic—not just knowing, willing and daring, but keeping silent. Sometimes, it's enough for the witch herself to understand what has happened.

"I'm glad you're enjoying yourself." Ben was breathing hard now, and no wonder. "But have you noticed—" he glanced over his shoulder, in the direction we were headed "—that we're on a crash course with some rocks?"

"Some rocks, and a cave entrance." No way would I have seen the cave, if the moonlight hadn't pointed the way. And to be honest, I still didn't "see" it—just the possibility of it. It looked like a ledge, with shadows underneath. It was barely high enough for the rowboat to fit under the shelf, much less us.

"Lie down," I suggested, sliding off my wooden seat into the foot well of the boat, onto my hands and knees, ready to crouch even lower.

He looked over his shoulder again. "I don't see a cave."

"It's there," I insisted.

Ben dragged the oars to slow us down, sending ripples away from us across the lake's dark surface. "And if it isn't?"

"Then we might break the boat and sink." But I laughed as I said that, too, full of sunshine and moonlight and magic and Ben's help...and new shoes. "Good thing I got rid of the cast."

The stony shelf loomed closer. We could hear the even lapping of lake water against nearby rocks, now.

Ben lifted the oars from the water—I think to start rowing backward, before we hit the rocks.

"Trust me," I said. "Me and Hekate."

"You and Hekate cursed me," he reminded me, clearly torn.

Good point. "We're sorry about that," I said.

Ben rolled his eyes. But he also slid off his seat at the prow of the rowboat, onto his knees, and bowed down into the space between us, his head beside mine. "You'd better be right," he whispered.

And with only a slight scraping of wood against rock, we drifted into the underworld.

Victor watched the rocks swallow the rowboat like a big dog would. *Gulp!*

Once upon a time, he wouldn't have wanted to be swallowed like that.

Goodbye. So long. Th-th-that's all, folks.

Cue watery grave.

He knew better, now. He could always sense Benny, even when he didn't want to. And Benny was still there.

With her.

It wasn't fair. *Not fair!*

He watched and watched. But the earth didn't spit the rowboat back out.

Victor broke into a run.

Chapter 22

I tried to sit up and bumped my head against overhanging stone. "Ow!"

"Stay down." Ben's fingers found the sore spot in the darkness. "We'll be able to hear if it opens up."

If? It was one thing to imagine swimming to safety when I'd imagined safety—in the form of the lake's surface—only a few feet from us. With each breath, safety floated farther and farther away. Instead, we got looming rock walls and crushing darkness.

The urge to laugh with the joy of the moonshine faded, the farther and more slowly we drifted.

I tried not to remember the place on the other end of the Sibyl's Cave, where the tunnel had caved in. But I remembered it anyway.

Should we turn back? I came really close to saying just

that, despite how strongly I could sense something sacred—the cup?—up ahead. And then—

Just as Ben had promised, I could hear when the ceiling lifted away from us. It sounded like water and echoes and space. And as the ceiling rose, so did the submerged tunnel floor, beneath us, until it was barely submerged at all.

With a slushy scrape, the boat lurched to a stop.

We sat up—well, I did. It *sounded* like Ben sat up, but the blackness around us was so thick, no way could I—

Oh. A small white beam reflected off the water, lighting several feet of tunnel and Ben, holding a tiny penlight.

"Wow," he said, sending the little beam across the angles of the ancient hewn roof. That didn't light everything as well as shining it off the water, though. When he turned it behind us, I could see how the tunnel must have once climbed just a little from its lake entrance. That's why it rose out of the water, what allowed Ben to stand now. "You were right."

"Don't tunnels usually go down?" I asked, eycing the water warily.

"Not if they emerge on a hillside." With a careful splash, Ben climbed out of the boat. I grasped the edge as it teetered, glad my center of gravity was still low. When he offered a hand, I gratefully took it to scramble to the stony floor.

Ben handed me the penlight so he could haul the rowboat more firmly out of the water.

Watching him almost distracted me from the call of the grail. Almost.

From what I could tell, the Sibyl's Cave on the Lake Averno side looked a whole lot like the Cumae side had. It had the same long, angular walls. Soft stone floors. The occasional blocky bench, made of rock slabs. But unlike the tunnel we'd explored earlier that day, there didn't seem to be any openings to the surface.

Or maybe…?

"Hold up," I whispered. This seemed too sacred a place to use my outside voice. I turned off the penlight—

And after a blink or two, I could see a silver glow somewhere ahead of us.

I groped beside me, found Ben's arm, and tugged. "Come on."

His fingers twined with mine as he did.

The sensation of walking through the blackness, having to just trust that there would be ground under my next step, then my next, unsettled me. But in a good way, like a roller coaster or…or a dare to jump from rooftop to rooftop.

I began to relax into it. My shuffling, careful baby steps became strides into the unknown. Ben's hand felt like the only solid thing here. The echoes sounded as if there were twenty of us, instead of just two. And then, as we rounded a curve in the tunnel—

I gasped.

Sheet after sheet of silver moonlight streamed down from above, about every seven feet, lighting the way forward.

"Wow," said Ben again.

I let go of him to spread my hands—both hands—ahead of me into the first wash of moonlight, watching silver slide across my palms and around my fingers. "Why wasn't there light until now, do you think?"

"Any number of factors. The ground up top may be overgrown, this close to the lake, covering any openings that might have once been there. Or the angle of illumination as the moon rises…"

Yes, that seemed right. I'd started walking again, and he

stopped talking to follow. Eventually, the tunnel opened into a rounded chamber, splitting off into two other tunnels. Slab benches lined each wall and moonlight sheeted in from three different openings above us, all converging in the now bare center of the room.

A crossroads. Paths of energy so powerful, the place fairly hummed with it.

For a brief moment, I envisioned women in togalike dresses, holding hands, moving in a slow circle. Then, like ghosts, the image faded.

"This is where they would hold rituals," I whispered, lifting my face to the light.

But I turned fast enough when a voice said, "Then this is where they would have hidden the grail, right, Katie?"

Even before I spun at the same time Ben did, to face his dripping wet brother in the tunnel behind us, I knew that hadn't been Ben.

Victor's Naples T-shirt stuck to his shoulders and chest. His water-shiny black hair really had grown out over the last month; it wasn't that surprising that he'd been able to imitate his brother so well, with a few of Ben's mannerisms thrown in.

I'd *known* I would lead him to the grail. Damn it to hell. That's why I hadn't wanted to look for it in the first place. And now—

And now, both his and Ben's eyes widened in absolute shock, fixed on some spot over my shoulder.

"Uh, Katie?" said Ben.

Victor, just past him, whispered a drawn-out "Fuuuck."

Slowly, my hair on end, I turned to look—and my shoulders sank in relief. It was just Diana. But she looked real this time. Not imagined. Not transparent. Not ghostly. She stood there, wearing a toga-style gown like the one I'd imagined the ancient goddess worshippers wearing, bathed in the silver moonlight. She smiled at me, the goofy, special kind of smile she'd reserved for birthdays and graduations. And *she was real.*

Real enough that the Fisher brothers could see her, too.

Tears burned my eyes. Tears of reunion. Tears of loss. "Di?"

But behind me, Victor growled, "You bitch. This was all your—"

I spun on him.

But not before Ben Fisher slammed his twin into the wall. *"Shut up!"*

That's when things really got weird. Magic? Sure. Hidden, underground caverns? Why not? And ghosts? Natch. But this was Ben the good, Ben the kind, Ben the gentle.

Beating the holy crap out of his brother.

I guess everyone has their breaking point.

Yeah, Victor was fighting back. But maybe he'd been as stunned as me, because Ben landed three good punches into Victor's gut before Vic even swung at him.

"Benny!" Vic protested, staggering back.

"The name—" Ben used his forearm as a wedge to drive Vic into the cave wall again. "Is *Ben.*"

Vic slammed a fist into Ben's jaw, knocking him sideways.

Real fights are quieter than you'd think. Even the impact of the punches seemed muffled. Most of the noise came from their gasped words—and the occasional grunt of pain.

"She bewitched you, Benny!" Victor caught Ben with an uppercut that spun Ben around.

Ben pushed off the wall that caught him and shoulder-checked Vic, driving a fist into his gut. Again. "And you killed her sister!"

Sister!

I spun back to where Diana waited, solid and real...and

amused. With three fast steps I'd reached her, spread my arms, thrown them around—

Except I stumbled right through her, solid or not.

The only real thing about her was the whisper of *I love you* that tickled through my head during that moment when our two souls mingled. No. *No!*

She shrugged, smiled sadly—and pointed at one of the benches.

I widened my eyes and looked over my shoulder at the brothers now rolling on the soft stone floor, kneeing each other, pounding on each other. Even as I watched, the one on the bottom—Ben—clasped a hand over his other fist and swung, two-handed, into the side of Vic's head. Vic fell off him. Ben followed the roll and hit him again, this time from on top. "How could you do that? How could you *be* something like that?"

"It's not my fault! You've always known that, bro. They attacked me. Mom said to keep an eye on me, but you didn't, and they *hurt* me!"

"Mom said for us to get help. You went back."

Damn, Vic could put on the innocence when he needed to. "I was a kid!"

But I guess if anyone could read him… "Not," growled Ben, "when you murdered Diana Trillo."

Victor's head lolled to one side. Blood ran from his mouth, and his eyes shone pure murder at Diana and me. "It's their fault—"

Ben's fist cracked against Victor's cheek. "Grow up!"

I looked quickly back at Diana. She extended her hands toward my face, as if to say how pretty I was—but she wasn't talking at all. For Diana, that seemed awfully strange. But for a ghost…

And she was a ghost. The truth of it hurt my heart. No matter how real she looked, my sister was only a ghost, now.

As her hands slid down and through my cheek, another whisper tickled through my head. *I'm real. So is Hekate. Trust Her.*

Then she drew back and pointed at the same bench, holding my gaze with the stern look she'd reserved for broken curfews and failing grades.

"But Victor…" I whispered.

She narrowed her eyes and, again, pointed downward.

So I knelt beside the bench, the humming in my head almost deafening me. When I laid my hands on the stone, it made my palms tingle. I tried to push the top slab off.

Nothing happened. Since it was as big as me, not surprising.

Diana knelt beside me, still so solid looking that only her silence and her odd dress convinced me she was a ghost— that, and the whole falling-through-her thing. She pushed upward, from below. She did *not* fall through the rock.

Following her illustration, I pushed the same way. Me and my sister, working to uncover—

When it happened, it was so easy that I gasped. Apparently there'd been some kind of slanted opening built behind the bench. When the slab that made the seat tipped upward and back, it slid into the hidden pocket in the cave wall. Gravity took care of the rest. With an echoing, deafening scrape, the slab sank backward—

And I was staring down into the now open bench, at something that wasn't a cup at all.

It was a buff-colored stone jug. The weirdest jug I'd ever seen. It was narrow at the bottom, but the rest of it was as round as a pregnant woman, seeming all the wider because of three faded red horizontal stripes around it. A flat ceramic handle arched over the top of it, and beside that a spout protruded upward, topped with a ceramic stopper.

"That's a grail?" I whispered—I guess to Diana. But I could already *feel* that it was the grail. It certainly felt more sacred than anything I'd ever been this near.

"It's…" Ben was there then, panting, over my shoulder. He dropped to his knees, either because he wanted a closer look…or because he couldn't stand anymore. His nose was bleeding, his face smeared with dirt and blood. His lip was swollen. His gaze cut from the jug to where Diana stood, a few feet from me, then back to the jug. "I think it's a Mycenaean stirrup cup. But Katie, we're really seeing a ghost!"

It was Ben, all right. I could sense that as surely as I knew the difference between day and night, and not just because of the green shirt. But I glanced over my shoulder, all the same.

Victor lay on the stone floor, apparently unconscious, his arms drawn behind him.

Diana walked silently, barefoot, to stand over him—and sadly shook her head.

Ben drew his raw-knuckled hand across his bleeding nose. "I tied him up with my shoelaces." He gulped more breath, as if he couldn't talk and breathe at the same time. "I've read a lot about knots. You really do see her, don't you?"

Maybe it's me being a bad guy or something, but damn, he looked sexy right then. Still—I had a grail in front of me!

"Yes, I see her." I reached for the jug.

"No!" Ben gently touched my wrist with his bloody hand, stilling my reach. "This looks like it could be two, even three thousand years old. Why didn't we bring a camera?"

Well, Hekate was a very ancient goddess, wasn't she?

Since I'd found this "grail" for a reason, I picked it up anyway, and something inside it sloshed. "It still has liquid in it!"

I didn't need to look over my shoulder at Diana's now smiling ghost to know what that meant. Victor had killed for this. She'd died for this. I'd come halfway around the world and explored three countries for this.

And I was a daughter of Hekate.

With a quick wrench, before Ben's *"Don't!"* could make a difference, I'd pulled the ceramic stopper free. Ben looked horrified, but his horror wasn't so intense that he couldn't examine the stopper.

"Paraffin wax," he murmured. "I've heard of this kind of thing being recovered from ancient shipwrecks, but— never mind."

I sniffed the spout, and whatever was in there smelled... watery. And a little like bay leaf.

Diana, standing silently in a sheet of moonlight between Ben and Victor, nodded her encouragement.

I glanced once more at Ben.

"Hail, Hekate," I whispered, like on a dare—and drank.

"You—" he began to protest.

It *was* water, faintly stale, wonderfully cool, with a faint bay flavor familiar from a lifetime of spaghetti sauce. And... that was *all?* I felt betrayed by the normalcy of it.

What a freaking anticlimax!

Except that, when I turned to Ben to say just that, he wasn't moving. At all. It wasn't like he'd gone still, so much as if I'd gone somewhere, some*time* else. What the...?

"Hail, Hekate," said Diana, turning toward one of the tunnels and bending low from the waist.

Now she spoke?

My breath fell shallow. I saw the torchlight first, approaching from one of the tunnels leading to this juncture. Mist rolled out toward us, knee-high, and shadows seemed to bend and warp across us. So did time. Two large black dogs loped out of the tunnel then, of a breed I couldn't begin to name. They sat, one by each entrance. And then…?

Then She came.

Somehow I managed to put the stirrup cup down before I could drop it. I didn't even try to stand. Leaving a very still Ben and maybe reality behind, I just crawled over to where my sister still bowed. I probably should have bent my head, too, but I couldn't help peeking. I grasped for Diana's hand, the way I used to as a child when something was too scary. Her hand closed around mine, just the same.

Solid. *Real.*

The same Sibyl's Cave surrounded us. I wore the same clothes. Ben and Vic remained motionless and silent, like a video on pause. But this was a reality—or vision, or hallucination— where I could hold my sister's hand, and that was enough for me to accept it with all my heart.

"Hail, Hekate Light Bringer," whispered Diana. "Hail, Hekate of the Earth."

Except what I heard was *Hekate Phosphoros* and *Hekate Cthonia.* I just understood what they meant, here.

The Goddess emerged very slowly from the tunnel, cloaked completely in black, a flickering torch burning in each withered hand. Her form was that of a stooped old woman, but Her presence filled the chamber—hell, filled the rock around us, filled the lake beyond us, filled the world.

"Hail, Hekate of the Night," said Diana. "Hail, Hekate the Messenger." *Hekate Nykterian. Hekate Angelos.*

The old Goddess wore a rope belt with a scythe-shaped

knife hanging from it, and a ring of keys, and an equal-armed cross like the kind I'd seen in Greece. Without having to be told, I understood that the knife was a sign of midwifery. The keys were to unlock the doors to the underworld. The cross represented crossroads. Choices....

She stopped before She'd come close enough for me to see under Her hooded cloak and glimpse Her face, even kneeling like I was.

"Welcome, Katie Trillo," She said. "I am old. I am forgotten. Why dost thou seek Me now?" At one point, She sounded like a teenager. Suddenly, Her voice was that of an old woman. Then when She spoke my name, She sounded like my mother.

And Her powerful presence wasn't at all like someone who felt old—not in any decrepit way—*or* forgotten.

"Hekate of the Three Ways," whispered Diana. *Hekate Trevia.*

"But...you aren't forgotten," I told her. "There are women seeking goddess grails, to help reawaken you."

"Why dost thou seek Me?" Her voice reverberated off the tunnel walls. Okay. Rule one? Don't contradict a goddess. *"What dost thou wish?"*

"Hekate Queen," whispered Diana. *Hekate Basileia.*

I meant to ask Her to lift the curse. Really I did. I'd only had two real goals on this quest to find Her, all along—locate the grail and lift the curse. But instead, I found myself standing—and not bowed, either. I found myself straightening my back, squaring my shoulders, lifting my chin and glaring at my matron Goddess.

And what I said was, *"Give. Them. Back."*

The silence around us seemed to echo the force of my demand. Hekate only stood, ageless, faceless, unmoving.

So I stepped closer, shaking with fury. "I said, *give them back!* Diana. Mom. Dad. Ben's parents. It's not fair that they're gone. It's not!"

The Dark Goddess, torchlight playing across Her cloak, quietly said, "No."

"You took them!" And I guess I really was a bad guy, because I ran at Her, and I pushed Her. *Hard.* If She'd really been an old lady, She probably would have fallen just as hard. She could have maybe broken a hip or an arm in the impact.

Instead, it was like pushing rock.

So I started to hit her. Stupid, girly hits, sure, but blows all the same, pounding against her shoulders and arms, at one point punching her in the withered breast. "You're the one who took them! You can give them back to me. *I want them back!*"

"No," she repeated, placing Her torches into sconces at either side of the tunnel. Then Her arms encircled me despite my blows, like a mother gently holding an enraged toddler. Her cloak wrapped me like a blanket. "No, it is not fair."

I sank to my knees, my arms around her old waist. I wept into her blackness, and she held me, and I finally, finally let go. After not just weeks but years, I let go. At least a little.

"Loss will always hurt," she promised me in my mother's voice. When I craned my neck up I could see under her cowl, and she wore my mommy's face, too, and I missed her more than ever. "Loss of a parent. A sibling. A lover. A child. A pet. That pain, my darling, is the shadow side of love."

"But you can change that!"

She shook her head, and at some point in the movement her face became my old YaYa's. "There is no birth without death, no love without pain."

She stroked my hair, and now she looked like Diana. Maiden, Mother and Crone. *Hekate Triformus.*

"I am life, and death, and the struggle between them," Hekate said. "I am promise, and fulfillment, and betrayal. I am the alpha and the omega, and everything between. I am not only the path, but its destination and its desertion. But *I did not kill them,* my darling."

Her withered hand found my chin and tipped my face upward toward Hers—and now She was an old woman my eyes didn't recognize, but my heart knew instantly. *She was Goddess.* "And neither did you."

I gasped, not so much in shock as in acknowledgment. How long had I carried this darkness with me, this fear? It was a fear as old as my childish curse of a second-grade rival, as old as the loss of my parents. Even now, despite an almost physical yearning to believe Her, I couldn't just accept Her reassurance.

"But if I'm really a witch, I should have been able to save them." I couldn't have just been…helpless.

Better to be guilty, to be wicked, than to be helpless.

"There has to be something I could have done and didn't do, or something I did that I shouldn't have, or—"

Hekate shook Her head, Her wisdom as irrefutable as the earth's power echoing through me. "You take too much on yourself, Katie. You expect too much of yourself. You are not evil. You are not negligent. And you are not helpless. You are human. Mend what you can—and be done with it."

And what I could mend…

That's when I knew what I had to do—and this time, on a soul-deep level. She waited, expectant.

So I spread my arms, leaned back from her, and said, "I free you, Ben and Victor Fisher, of my curse."

A rush of strength straightened my spine and squared my shoulders, far stronger than rage had. My whole body shuddered with power.

"I no longer wish you agony or despair—let anything that comes to you be of your own making. I no longer call death to you, because death needs no incentive. Your suffering is your own, and your peace is your own. Your happiness is your own, and your misery is your own."

I took a deep, deep breath.

My Lady nodded Her encouragement.

"I call upon Hekate, the Dark Goddess, to release you from any downfall that I wished upon you, Ben and Victor Fisher. In the name of the Queen of the Night, I free you. In the name of the Goddess of the Crossroads, I free you. In the name of Her, my own namesake, I lift my curse and remove my will over your destinies.

"So mote it be!"

Hekate swept a cloaked arm outward, and I swear that thunder shook the earth around us. Mist and shadow swirled around me, faster and faster. As if from a distance, I saw Hekate turn and make Her slow way down the tunnel, Her dogs loping ahead—and Diana holding Her elbow.

My sister looked over her shoulder, one last time, with an encouraging smile. I almost called out to her, but I stopped myself. It was past time for her to go, wasn't it?

And it wasn't like she'd ever be completely gone.

A final reminder floated back toward me from the darkness. "I am only as strong as my children," the Goddess chided. "I need your strength...."

And then I was kneeling beside Ben and the stone bench, the jug still in my hands.

"—don't even know what's in there!" he exclaimed, as if I'd

only just drunk from the grail. "It could be a ritual poison, for all you know, or something that's turned toxic over the centuries."

"It's water," I reassured him, warmed by his concern. "Don't—"

But maybe he had reason to worry.

"Ben!" I screamed.

Just as Victor emerged from the shadows and drove a knife, two-handed, into Ben's back.

Chapter 23

An ungodly cry ripped from Ben's throat as he arched impossibly back, pinned on his brother's blade—the same kind of knife that had killed their parents.

So much for shoelaces.

"Thanks for lifting the curse," said Victor, grinning, with a freakish giggle. How he could know I had was the least of my concerns.

I jumped to my feet beside him, my right hand—my projective hand—thrust into the space between me, Ben and Victor. The power of this place, of the grail, of the ages and of Hekate Herself ripped through me—and out of me, straight at him.

"I bind you, Victor Fisher!"

His glee faltered as he realized that there were other kinds of magic than curses—and that binding spells don't carry anywhere near the karmic backlash.

Ben had slumped sideways, seeming to fight the hurt that moaned from his throat. His dark eyes, glazed with pain, held me, but he didn't protest.

He'd chosen, hadn't he? Me over his brother.

But at what cost?

"Harm no one else," I continued, grasping at the repetition, the desperation that had made my curse such a doozy. "I bind you, Victor Fisher! Work no more evil!"

He shook his head. *"No!"*

Ben was dragging himself slowly up the rock wall to his feet, despite the knife still protruding from his back. Victor had to be stopped. So I spread my fingers, lifted my face and shouted:

"In the name of Hekate, the Dark Goddess, and in the memory of my dead sister, *I! Bind! You!*"

The magic shuddered through me, rippled through the cave, popped my ears. And then, with a cutting look to show Victor just how helpless he was now, I turned to Ben.

That Ben was conscious was a good sign, though lying down would be safer. Minimal blood stained his dirty, pale shirt, so if the knife had pierced anything vital, it was putting pressure on the laceration. That was why we should leave it in him, despite the ick factor, until we got him to a hospital.

True, Victor stood between us and the way out. But that wouldn't last long.

Ben's breathing sounded shaky from pain, but not labored. The hand he stretched outward in protest when Victor lunged at us trembled uselessly.

I didn't move an inch, like in a game of chicken. "You can't hurt us."

I believed it.

But instead of us, Victor grabbed the ceramic jar at my feet. *The Hekate Grail.*

For a moment, my certainty faltered. Hadn't the spell worked, even in this sacred cave? After all this, *would Victor destroy the goddess grail?*

But instead of harming it, he lifted it over his head, tipped it back—and put its spout to his lips.

"No!" I screamed, horrified by his blasphemy.

Then I remembered what Diana had told me. *Trust Her….*

So instead of trying to wrestle the jar away from Victor, I spread my hands and took a step back.

Let anything that comes to you be of your own making. There is a serious, serious difference, karma-wise, between hurting someone—and simply watching while they hurt themselves.

"Vic," gasped Ben, his teeth clenched, his neck strained in agony. He stood hunched from a pain he couldn't escape, his eyes bottomless with fury and betrayal. *"No…."*

At first, Victor's expression was one of complete bliss. He closed his eyes. I could practically *see* the power sliding through him with each gulp. It flushed his skin, straightened his spine. He made me think of a patient after a morphine shot.

Was that how I'd looked?

Then Victor's eyes opened wide—and he began to tremble.

It started subtly, like the chills of mild hypothermia, but graduated into full-body shudders. In moments, he was convulsing. His complexion took on a bluish, waxy look. His lips and eyes began to swell. His breath began to wheeze in his throat, in his chest.

Anaphylactic shock, maybe. Or maybe just the power of one pissed-off Goddess.

Then Victor's screams started—insane, unbalanced screams. Pissed-off goddess, it is.

"Can you…" moaned Ben, under Victor's wails. He didn't finish the request, but I knew what he wanted. Despite the fact that his brother had murdered Diana and literally stabbed him in the back, Ben wanted me to *help* the bastard?

I guess that's what made Ben one of the good guys.

And, honestly, what made me *not*.

Because when Victor dropped the grail, I dove for *that*, not for him. The round jar plummeted for the stone floor. I dropped with it, slid across the rock, stretched both hands in front of me—

And I caught it.

I caught it, and I cradled it in my arms, while Victor—still screaming—took off for the entrance to the cave.

Ben staggered after him.

"Ben!" Now I ran after him, grail in hand. "Stop!"

I caught up to him fast enough. But when I tried to slow him, with a hand to his arm, Ben wrenched free of my touch— and cried out from the movement. The knife, protruding from the back of his shoulder, was its own kind of blasphemy.

"He's dangerous," I protested. "And you're hurt!"

Ben stumbled on. His second guess earlier, that the moon had to reach a certain height in the sky, must have been the right one. Sheets of silver moonlight, filtered with the shadow of leaves, lit our way back toward the boat.

"He's…dying," Ben gasped. I didn't bother to ask how he could know that. *Twins.*

Instead, I got in front of him to argue. "He did it to himself!"

Bent almost double now, Ben glared, then tried to go around me. He didn't have the balance to make it. He stopped, panting through what had to be excruciating pain, and strained his face upward to meet my gaze with his own.

"He's my brother, and *he needs help*. Oh, God."

He said that last part because ahead, the screaming stopped in an echoing splash.

Ben staggered in that direction, bumping into me as he went, moaning when he did, and kept going. I knew he would go in after Victor. It didn't matter that Ben wasn't moving one arm, that he would probably drown, himself.

The watery tunnel that had brought us in from the lake must have been a dangerous enough swim for someone who was sane. Or at least sane-ish.

No way could Victor make it back out like this.

Damn, damn, damn! "You stay here," I ordered him, running past. "And for heaven's sake, sit down! Watch the grail. I'll get him."

I put down the precious Hekate jar. And, my steps turning into strides, then a full-out run, I passed the rowboat we'd pulled from the lake water—and I dove into the basin of the submerged tunnel.

The echo vanished under the surface of the cold water. I pushed water behind me with both hands, glad I no longer wore the cast, and kicked my feet And I squinted through the murkiness, trying to see something, anything, in the dark.

Half spells rhymed through my head. *By the power of the night, help me save a life tonight.*

And, *I will find him, I will save him, from the madness Goddess gave him.*

I had to surface then, gasping for breath, walled in by narrowing cave walls and sheets of moonlight. "Victor!" I called, treading water.

My voice, and the splish of water, echoed back at me. No screams. No struggles. Nothing.

I reached upward and hit my hand against the ceiling. Again, I had the illusion of the rock closing in on me.

"Ben!" I called. But would I really tell him I'd failed?

Still nothing.

Damn!

I dove again, deeper this time—but I stopped with the rhymes. For magic to work takes knowing, and daring, and silence. But it also takes will.

No way was my heart in this enough to accomplish it with a spell.

For Ben, I had to do it the old-fashioned way. By flailing through the water.

I surfaced, gasped more air. "Ben! I can't find him!"

Nothing. For all I knew, Ben had gone into shock—or worse. He needed medical intervention. I was wasting time on my sister's murderer.

But I'd promised. So damn it to hell, I dove again.

And again.

Until my hand hit a warm, limp body.

Thank goodness the water was no more than eight feet deep, here. Victor's body was heavy, unwieldy. I had to push hard off of the submerged tunnel floor to get us both to the surface, scissoring my legs with all my strength. We emerged into a patch of darkness under the heavy rock overhang, his curly, wet head slumped forward in the water, deathly still.

And for a second, just a microsecond, I thought—*I could leave him.*

Diana had always said, better to smack someone across the face than to work a spell against them. By that logic, better to leave a psychopathic killer to drown than to magic him to death—with my magic, anyway. Hekate's vengeance was her own.

I thought it, and for that microsecond, I was tempted. So maybe I'd never be a good guy.

But I knew I couldn't be a bad guy anymore, either.

As a nurse, I knew mouth-to-mouth and CPR. And after Red Cross lifesaving courses, I knew how to breathe for someone while swimming them to safety. So I wrestled his face out of the water, despite continuously sinking myself, despite swallowing water. I turned him so that he would float on his back—

And the knife hilt in his shoulder bumped my arm.

Ben!

Idiot. *Idiot!* He'd gone in after his brother anyway.

The collision of possible realities nearly deafened me, sickened me, panicked me. I'd almost let him die. If I'd chosen the dark path at this crossroads, *I would have let Ben die!*

But there was no time to dwell on that, because I still had no guarantee he'd live. So I snapped into my lifesaving training. I tipped his head back while treading water. I took a deep, deep breath, then covered his lips and breathed into his mouth. Twice.

Then I swam for shore like all the hounds of hell were after me. It seemed to take so long, too horribly long….

Then I remembered that I wasn't exactly helpless.

"By the power of the night," I whispered weakly, between gasps for air. "Let me save a life tonight."

And this time, I willed it with everything I had. Here in the Sibyl's Cave, that was a whole freaking lot of power.

Ben began to choke on lake water, alive, alive, alive.

Ben had breathed so much lake that coughs racked him. He vomited water, despite his need to hold still against the knife. I tore his new shirt into strips to stabilize the weapon, then somehow managed to half drag him into the rowboat.

"Wait…" he moaned.

"Shut up," I said, and this time I meant it. Then I realized that I had to push the boat—now weighed down with him—back into the water. Oh, hell. I met his dark told-you-so gaze, then simply did it. With a lot of pushing, a lot of straining, a lot of scraping and a whole lot of praying.

Lady, help me. Help me. Help me….

Finally, the boat floated. I climbed in. But we were facing the wrong direction, and I couldn't make the oars work right.

"You need to…" Ben, who was half lying and half sitting on the bottom, propping himself with the elbow of his good arm on the seat, tried to extend the hand on his hurt side to point out the oarlock thingie—and passed out, just like that.

This time, need meant *need*.

Somehow, I got the oars in place. Somehow, with much splashing and cursing and bumping against the tunnel walls, I got the damned boat turned around—but at least I knew why the oarlocks were there, because twice I fumbled an oar, and they kept it from falling into the water. I'd barely managed any speed before the tunnel ceiling descended onto us, so I had to pull us along, finding crevices and handholds in the rock ceiling. I'd done so much magic in the last hour, even that seemed to fail me. So it fell to the prayer. *Help me. Help me….*

Every straining inch of the way. Afraid that at any moment, Victor would rear out of the water and finish his job.

Afraid Ben would die…and it would be my fault for bringing him here in the first place.

What seemed like forever later, sweating and exhausted, I heard the sound of waves lapping against rock. I managed to pull us free of the overhang and sit up. I rowed us farther into the water, just in case Victor lurked out there to leap on top of us—I would believe he'd drowned when I saw the body—but then I stopped to check Ben's vitals. "Ben, please!"

"Still here," he muttered. His pulse wasn't great, but I didn't expect more. If he was talking, he was breathing. So I gave his cheek a teary kiss, sank back onto my seat in the prow of the boat and put my back into rowing us to the closest shore.

It still took me too damned long, especially compared to how easy he'd made it look. I could barely row a straight line. My strokes were shorter. My back ached, and my arms trembled from exhaustion. I looked up at the moon. Without the breath to speak, I thought, *If you let him die…*

But She was only as strong as Her children.

So somehow, I gathered the last threads of energy I could, siphoning them out of the lake, stealing them out of the moon. "By the power," I gasped, still rowing. "Of the night. Help me…save this life—"

The searchlight hit us then. A man's voice blared at us through a megaphone, commanding something, but he spoke Italian. *"Poliziotti,"* he said. I only stopped rowing long enough to scream, "Someone's hurt! He needs help! *Aiutilo!"*

Then I started rowing again, or whatever you'd call my poor excuse for it, aiming roughly for the shore. There were more shouts in that direction, and then—

Then, with a splash, a figure reared out of the water!

If I could have gotten the oar out of its lock, I would have clubbed him. Luckily, I couldn't. Not just yet.

"Sit tight," advised an unusually deep, pretentious voice. Then he began to swim, pushing the boat toward the shore. "And don't," he gasped, "hit me."

"Hi, Al," Ben managed.

"I left my equipment...on shore," Al complained. "If someone...steals it..."

Ben's excuse for a smile was even more lopsided than ever. "Good heart," he whispered, before his eyes closed. Even if his partner would sell his own mother for publicity.

I was happy to let Ben be right about this one. Especially if Al could help me hide the grail without stealing it. He slipped it into his oversized camera bag when we got ashore—which meant leaving the cameras under a bush— muttering about the chance of rain.

The next hour became a blur of police and ambulances— and yelling, frustrated Italians. While we waited for word of Ben outside the emergency room, Al explained that he'd changed planes in London—when he could get his luggage— and headed back to Rome, both to keep an eye on his partner and in hopes of getting more of a story. That Ben had been using their corporate credit card the whole time made him pretty easy to track. Al saw Victor go into the cave after us, so he called the police.

I stopped pacing. "Why didn't you come after us?"

Al stopped pacing, too. "Because Victor's a psychotic killer? Was, anyway."

I hoped he was right. The doctors managed to remove the knife and repair most of the damage that it had caused, and that's what really mattered. Ben was going to be okay.

But nobody found Victor.

Not that day. Not the next.

"I think he's dead," said Ben, finally.

I'd come up behind him where he sat on a bench by the lakeshore, watching the *polizia* dredge Lago d'Averno. I wasn't even sure he knew I was there, until he said that. He'd just gotten out of the hospital that morning. His arm was in a sling, to help keep him from pulling the stitches in his shoulder. He was on painkillers.

And he wasn't magically bound to me anymore.

At least I'd had the distraction of Maggi Stuart's long-distance help, arranging for me to carry the Hekate Grail to a place in England called Glastonbury. I was supposed to leave later this afternoon, but I hated to leave Ben, even with Al, until he had his answers. Or before I had mine.

Yeah, I'd won...more or less. And I definitely felt stronger now. But I didn't feel triumphant. Diana was still dead. My world was still permanently changed.

And Ben had lost, too. In so many ways.

Without that subtle bond of the curse, I felt awkward around him. In a way, we were still strangers. Everything between us, up until now, had been colored by either magic or murder.

But I couldn't just leave.

"What do you mean, you *think?*" I settled onto the grass by his feet so that I could lean on the bench, beside his thigh. That way I could comfortably watch him while he watched the lake. "I thought twins were psychically connected."

Ben didn't even go into a long explanation about that, which seemed especially sad. He just said, "The person I knew as Victor is definitely gone."

"Are you sure you ever really knew him?"

Ben nodded, his dark eyes still focused on the boat. I wondered if he was hoping they would find a body—or hoping they wouldn't. "Yeah, I really knew him. I knew a part of him I think was lost even to himself. He didn't use the knife at first. Did you notice?"

I looked up, in time for Ben's gaze to drop to mine, and he looked…stronger. More tired. More balanced.

Still Ben, of course. There was no chance that this might be Victor in disguise. But I couldn't help thinking that Ben had found a little more of his power over the last few days, too.

"When we were fighting," he clarified. "In the cave. Victor must have had the knife on him, but he didn't use it on me."

I reached up and touched his sling. "He used it on you."

"Only after he saw the grail. That's—" He swallowed, hard. "That's when I really lost him. The sense of him, I mean."

Oh, hell. More guilt. "Because of Hekate?"

To my relief, Ben shook his head. "Because of his need for power. I still think he was a victim, in his own way. He was injured when our parents died. Did you know that the majority of serial killers suffered frontal-lobe injuries as children?"

I shook my head. I hadn't known that last part. But I wasn't surprised that Ben did.

"Sure, he should have come with me, gone for help like we'd been told, instead of heading back into trouble…but he was only six. I could have tried harder to protect him."

"You were only six, too."

"Still, in the things he had some say over…he chose power over everything else. That's what destroyed him."

"And you. It almost destroyed you."

Ben shrugged, then winced, probably from whatever pangs were caused by his injury. "That's how it works. We're brothers."

And for the first time since Vic's disappearance, it occurred to me just what that meant—what I'd been asking Ben to give up all along. Sociopath or not, Victor had been part of his life. They'd suffered the loss of their parents together, and even if Victor hadn't reacted the same way, his presence had probably helped "Benny" not feel so alone. They'd had birthdays together for decades, a routine that Ben had now lost. If Victor really was dead, Ben had lost his brother at holiday dinners, had lost the chance of nieces and nephews, had lost all hope that maybe, just maybe, something could have saved the murderer who, all the same, shared his DNA and his history.

In comparison, I was lucky. Diana had left me with mostly happy memories.

I slid up onto the bench beside him, on his uninjured side. "We've both lost the last of our immediate family, haven't we?"

Ben's dark gaze sliced quickly over to me, suspicious, like maybe he expected me to gloat. Like I thought we were even now. I hadn't meant it that way, though I guess I could understand....

"I just mean... I'm here for you. If you need me."

He studied my face, then asked, uneven, "Like a sibling?"

It's not like I'm the sort of woman really smart men seek out. On the other hand... I didn't scare as easy as I used to. "Not like a sibling. Unless that's what you want, I mean. If—"

"Shut up, Katie." But Ben said that very softly, with a sad, lopsided smile. Then he kissed me....

And damned if I didn't feel our immediate connection, curse or not. It was every bit as good, as slow, as tender as when we'd been linked by magical energies.

When Ben drew back, I almost slumped onto him, for wanting to not let him move away.

"Vic was right, wasn't he?" he asked. "In the cave. You removed the curse before he ever drank from the grail?"

Before he ever went crazy and drowned himself? I nodded, relieved.

So Ben kissed me again—not shy, not tentative, and not at all bewitched. "I guess you were right," he whispered. "Everything *is* magic."

So what we'd had together…was *real?*

Ben looked back out at the lake, at the dying hope that he'd ever know what had happened to his brother. And I tried to make peace with what he'd just said, despite me having said it first. *Everything…?*

Since my vision of Hekate, on the night of the full moon, that truth was becoming undeniable. Even sitting here, I could feel magic in the warmth of the Italian sun on my face, in the coolness of the lake water at the shore, in the scent of new spring grass under our feet. There was stabilizing magic in the earth, beneath us, and expansive magic in the sky, above us. There was the magic of beginnings, off to the east—*Greece,* I thought, *and Turkey*—and the magic of endings off to the west, where England waited, then home. If I reached out, with my fingers spread, I imagined that the magic would ripple around me, like when you trail fingers through water from a boat, or spread a hand out a car window to comb the wind.

Hekate was only as strong as her children. She needed my strength. That meant my happiness as well as my magic. And…daring.

"You're going after the Comitatus, aren't you?" I asked, after a while. I suppose I could have found that out with tarot cards or a scrying bowl, but truth is, it just made sense.

"To expose them, if nothing else."

"Do you want help? From a witch, I mean?"

Ben asked, "Do *you* want help going after more goddess cups?"

I nodded. And Ben nodded. And that was that.

My gaze memorized the angle of his jaw, and the dark quickness of his deep-set eyes, and the way his hair fell in those wonderfully floppy black curls across his forehead, over his ears, along his collar. Then I followed his gaze to the lake. He hadn't asked me for help in locating Victor's body….

Taking slow, deep breaths, I tried to extend my awareness outward, seeking Victor. And I found…absolutely nothing.

The same nothingness that had greeted me when I tried to find Diana, the last few days—except when I thought to look inside myself.

It had to be enough.

And with the strength of Hekate inside me, and Ben beside me, you know what? It was.

More than enough, in fact. Because we two were alive, and together. In more ways than one.

And I guessed that might be the best magic there is.

I should know, after all.

I'm a witch.

* * * * *

Don't miss Evelyn Vaughn's next book!
LOST CALLING, first of the MADONNA KEY stories,
will be available in July 2006
wherever Silhouette series books are sold.

*There's more coming your way
from Silhouette Bombshell!
Turn the page for a sneak peek at
one of next month's releases*

*NEVER LOOK BACK
by Sheri WhiteFeather*

Chapter 1

Lord, the angel in her painting was gorgeous. But he wasn't your ordinary garden-variety angel. She'd given him a long, muscular body with enormous black wings. His hair, as dark and shiny as his wings, flowed long and free, and he had piercing brown eyes. He was rough and primitive.

"If only you would come alive," Allie Whirlwind said.

Without warning, the wind howled, pushing against the window screen, popping the device from its hinges. It landed at Allie's feet, where the hem of her dress billowed, mimicking Marilyn Monroe's fanning garment in *The Seven Year Itch*.

Talk about feeling sexy.

Foolish as it was, she was waiting for her angel, her heart thumping in anticipation.

Only it was a big black bird that flew into the loft and circled the studio, its wings whooshing past her.

Allie blinked. A raven?

So much for getting laid.

She looked up, watching the raven perch on a rafter, one of the highest spots in the studio. The raven stood about two feet tall, with an impressive wingspan.

Allie tried to shoo the stupid raven back out the window. But it flew straight at her instead. Startled, she smacked it with her flailing hands, sending the wild creature to the floor, where it landed on the linoleum with a thud.

She gasped, stunned by the force with which she'd hit it. "I didn't mean to." Guilty, Allie knelt over the fallen raven. Whispering an apology, she stroked the bird, and it opened its eyes.

It was stunned, not dead.

Oddly enough, the raven simply stared at her, as though it understood her apology. Then it cawed. Lord Almighty. It sounded like the messenger of death.

A strange chill crept up Allie's spine. And then she recalled that in some forms of folklore, ravens *were* omens of death.

Shit.

She warned herself to stay calm, to think clearly. Wasn't Raven the creator of the world to some of the Northwest Indians? Wasn't he highly revered?

Of course Allie wasn't from a Northwest tribe. Anxious, she scrambled to remember what ravens represented in her culture. She was half Chiricahua Apache and half Oglala Lakota Sioux, and sometimes their traditions didn't mesh.

To the Apache, the appearance of a crow was a good sign. But did that go for ravens, too? Allie didn't know. As for the Lakota, she couldn't remember what ravens meant to them. Or maybe she never knew to begin with.

But then, before her eyes, the raven was shifting, transforming…into a man.

No, not a man.

Her angel. Her protector. As big as life, as glorious as her watercolor, with his clothes clinging to his body and his hair dripping with rain.

She gulped, and his wings swooshed, making a powerful sound. Beneath his work boots were crushed berries. He stood in the center of her studio.

Allie didn't know what to do, what to say. His eyes, the same pitch brown eyes she'd painted, were staring straight at her.

She fought to stay conscious, to touch him, to talk to him, but she couldn't hold on. She drifted into oblivion.

USA TODAY
BESTSELLING AUTHOR

Shirl HENKE

BRINGS YOU

SNEAK AND RESCUE
March 2006

Rescuing a brainwashed rich kid
from the Space Quest TV show
convention should have been a cinch
for retrieval specialist Sam Ballanger.
But when gun-toting thugs gave chase,
Sam found herself on the run with a truly
motley crew, including the spaced-out
teen, her flustered husband and one
very suspicious Elvis impersonator....

Signature Select™

From the author of the bestselling COLBY AGENCY miniseries

DEBRA WEBB

VOWS of SILENCE

A gripping new novel of romantic suspense.

A secret pact made long ago between best friends Lacy, Melinda, Cassidy and Kira resurfaces when a ten-year-old murder is uncovered. Chief Rick Summers knows they're hiding something, but isn't sure he can be objective...especially if his old flame Lacy is guilty of murder.

"Debra Webb's fast-paced thriller will make you shiver in passion and fear."
—*Romantic Times*

***Vows of Silence*...coming in March 2006.**

If you enjoyed what you just read,
then we've got an offer you can't resist!

Take 2 bestselling
love stories FREE!
Plus get a FREE surprise gift!

COMING NEXT MONTH

#81 SNEAK AND RESCUE by Shirl Henke

Samantha Ballanger had the golden touch when it came to extracting people from dangerous places; she'd even married one of her rescued clients. But retrieving a brainwashed fan from the *Space Quest* TV show convention was a stretch. Even in her sexy sci-fi disguise, Sam couldn't coax the wealthy teenaged boy back to reality—not when she was up against one *very* suspicious Elvis impersonator keen on keeping the kid spaced-out….

#82 HELL ON HEELS by Carla Cassidy

Heiress turned bounty hunter Chantal Worthington was on her home turf when she went after a fellow blue blood who'd skipped bail on a rape charge—and years ago had raped her own best friend. But Chantal wasn't the only one on his trail. Instead of butting heads, spitfire Chantal teamed up with bad boy Luke Coleman on the case…and soon, from Kansas City to Mexico, even if the leads got cold, their passion stayed red-hot!

#83 THE DIAMOND SECRET by Ruth Wind

Good girl and wild woman by turns, multifaceted gemologist Sylvie Montague had a knack for trouble. So when a bag switcheroo at a Scottish airport left her in possession of a stolen medieval diamond, she had to escape being the fall guy—fast. As she scoured Paris and Bucharest for the jewel's rightful owner, could Sylvie protect herself from another grand larceny—the theft of her heart by the wealthy Frenchman behind the heist?

#84 NEVER LOOK BACK by Sheri WhiteFeather

Painter Allie Whirlwind preferred the quiet life. But mysticism was in her blood, and she stirred up a tempest when her painting of Native American spirit warrior Raven literally came to life. Now, with a handsome activist's help, Allie sought the talisman that would release Raven from her great-grandmother's hundred-year-old shape-shifting curse. In the face of evil, Allie could never look back…until she righted her troubled family's wrongs.